ZANE PRESENTS

SIN IN SOUL'S KITCHEN

A NOVEL

Dear Reader:

I am delighted to present to you *Sin in Soul's Kitchen* by Andrew Oyé, who makes a memorable debut with Strebor Books.

Andrew's motto is, "If you can't stand the heat, stay out of soul's kitchen."

This erotic psychological thriller is sure to allure readers with its creative cast of characters set in the New York arts scene.

The novel shows how relationships can turn from sweet to sour and how those involved can cook up plans to do evil to each other. Find out what happens when an affluent Thaddeus clashes with his girlfriend Chelsea in a power struggle; he wants to maintain a lifestyle that she opposes. It's a recipe for disaster.

Sin in Soul's Kitchen includes all the ingredients for a provocative read and tantalizes with its artistic flair. I read the novel within twenty-four hours and found it thought-provoking from the first page. The author, a fitness guru who resides in Hollywood, takes us on a neo-soul voyage with elements of music and the arts.

After digesting this novel's riveting ending, check out Andrew's reader's guide which is sure to intrigue your mind further.

Thank you for supporting Andrew Oyé's efforts and thank you for supporting one of the dozens of authors published under my imprint, Strebor Books. I try my best to bring you cutting-edge works of literature that will keep your attention and make you think long after you turn the last page.

Now sit back in your favorite chair or, better yet, chill in the bed, and be prepared to be entertained by yet another great read.

Peace and Many Blessings,

Zane

Zane
Publisher
Strebor Books
www.simonandschuster.com/streborbooks

ZANE PRESENTS

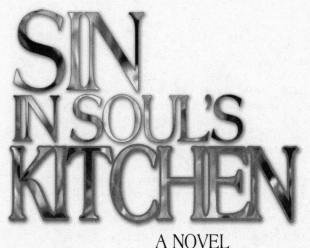

SIN IN SOUL'S KITCHEN

A NOVEL

ANDREW OYÉ

SBI

STREBOR BOOKS

NEW YORK LONDON TORONTO SYDNEY

Strebor Books
P.O. Box 6505
Largo, MD 20792
http://www.streborbooks.com

This book is a work of fiction. Names, characters, places and incidents are
products of the author's imagination or are used fictitiously. Any resemblance
to actual events or locales or persons, living or dead, is entirely coincidental.

ISBN 978-1-59309-255-9
LCCN 2009924324

First Strebor Books trade paperback edition July 2009

Cover design: www.mariondesigns.com
Cover photograph: © Keith Saunders/Marion Designs

10 9 8 7 6 5 4 3 2 1

Manufactured in the United States of America

For information regarding special discounts for bulk purchases,
please contact Simon & Schuster Special Sales at 1-866-506-1949
or business@simonandschuster.com

The Simon & Schuster Speakers Bureau can bring authors to your live event.
For more information or to book an event, contact the Simon & Schuster Speakers
Bureau at 1-866-248-3049 or visit our website at www.simonspeakers.com.

If you can't stand the heat,
stay out of soul's kitchen.

DEDICATION

To the mature, artistic, open-minded, rebellious, reflective, creative, and inquisitive among us.

Not intended as scholarly commentary on the state of religion or sex in American culture, *Sin in Soul's Kitchen* is seductively provocative fiction—the pious and prudish beware.

ACKNOWLEDGMENTS

Praise to the Creator...
> for blessing me with a creativity too abundant to remain contained, a voice too loud to be stifled, and a persistence to share both

Praise to my parents, Dominic and Theresa...
> for giving me a life filled with gifts (especially to my mom, who so boldly assumed the role of two when my father passed over to the other side)

Peace to my brothers & sisters...
> Tina, Charles, Anthonia, and Greg—my "blood" network that has my back (and I have yours) even though our paths seem so different

Props to my true people...
> friends, teachers and colleagues who knew it was only a matter of time before you held this book in your hands

Power to the poets, producers, & performers...
> who continue to create art in an age where technology can do it for us, but could never replace us

STARTING OVER AND OVERT SEDUCTION

Blood was everywhere.

It was splattered across the bedroom of the posh penthouse. A psychedelic pattern streaked the white bedspread and soaked into the white carpet. Crimson beads stained the surface of the armoire, and red specks dotted the butterfly-shaped mirror. Half of a snow-white wall was blackened by a fire that, now, was as dead as the lifeless man on the floor.

Kayla Harmon covered her mouth in horror, smearing her lipstick. She stumbled backward and bumped into a large, rigid presence behind her. She whirled around.

"You're not allowed in here!" The reprimand was a stern whisper.

"I'm sorry," she tried to say through the fear clogging her throat.

"We're setting up the last shot. Go wait outside at the news van, Kayla," Adolfo Alvarez said. The suited anchorman took the pretty intern by her trembling shoulders and led her down the arching hallway, past a weeping woman with blood-stained hands. a team of cops, and a behemoth camera prepared to broadcast the tragedy into thousands of homes. "You'll get your chance to do this soon enough."

The shining sun above bathed a finely dressed sea of friends and families gathered below to celebrate, while the operatic sound of "Pomp and Circumstance" lingered in the ears of the crowd assembled at Columbia University.

"Thaddeus Coleman Carmichael, Jr.," announced the decrepit dean of the business school with his customary smug air. Turning in Thad's direction, the old man peered over the glasses on the tip of his red nose and dangled a folio in his hand.

The knot of anticipation in Thad's stomach tightened. Returning the dean's glare, he crossed the imposing stage steeped in tradition, adorned with a rainbow of flowers in full bloom and a collage of prestigious pennants and whatnot. He confidently snatched his diploma and shook the hand of a man who had doubted that he would make it to graduation day. Thad left the stage, leaving behind his less-than-favorable memories with it. And, instantly, it was over. Life's pressure cooker was shut off, and he had been tossed out. But the handsome young man, often praised for his astuteness, didn't feel fully cooked or ready for the world waiting to eat him up, so he shot an empty smile at his other skeptic. His father, totally oblivious to other graduates getting their diplomas, had rushed the stage to film the moment.

Thaddeus Senior, a mammoth man in an expensive tan suit, handed the camera to his seventeen-year-old daughter, Cynthia, and vigorously shook his son's hand. "Junior, how does it feel to be a Columbia grad like your old man? Now, aren't you glad you listened to me? Three long years, but we did it. That diploma is proof. Anyway, we're going to do wonderful things together with the family business." He put an arm around his son and released an agonizing sigh. "Thought I wouldn't see this day. Guess I can rest easy now, huh?"

Thad tensed his body to avoid whopping his father with his fist. "Yeah, relax. *Your* work is done, Dad." Thad smirked, waving sheepishly at the lens that Cynthia pointed close to his nose.

Thad detested being on camera. He perspired under his black graduation gown, while the camera recorded his every uncomfortable reaction for posterity, to be laughed at later by those who took pleasure in watching moments he could never take back. With the weight of his father's arm across his shoulders, Thad longed to be in Brooklyn with his buddies.

"We're so proud of you, Junior," rejoiced Thad's mother. The slim woman in a chic beige summer dress gave her son a congratulatory kiss.

"Mr. Carmichael, Sr., and Mr. Carmichael, Jr.," a creepy voice suddenly greeted.

Turning around, Thad met familiar eyes of steel in a wrinkled face framed by thin silver hair. Thad gave the bearer half a handshake. "Dr. Hausbruck."

"As the long-standing dean of Columbia's Business School, I've seen many young minds come and go," Hausbruck commended Thaddeus Senior in a stale German accent. "Yet none quite as enthusiastic as your young Mr. Carmichael."

"Thank you. I'm just glad we can add another Columbia grad to the collection. I guess the MBA doesn't fall far from the tree." Thaddeus Senior beamed, patting his son on the back while sharing a hearty laugh with the old dean.

"He'll do well." Hausbruck forced a smile at Thad. "He certainly gave the administration a run for our money. He's a shrewd businessman. A real fighter."

"Well, if anyone here knows that I'm a real fighter, it's Dr. H." Thad chuckled. "Our dicey history has schooled each of us on the stubbornness of the other."

"Indeed." Hausbruck stepped close to Thad. "Good luck, Mr. Carmichael."

Bullets of different shades, their eyes locked. Instantly a new awareness hit Thad, who rested a hand on the shoulder of the short man with the tall ego. "Dr. H., don't forget my vow. It was a promise, not a threat." He flashed a smile that had the effect of a middle finger, as Hausbruck yanked his shoulder away and headed back to the stage.

"We're going to the chancellor's reception," Thaddeus Senior announced. "Some of my old classmates should be there."

"I'll pass," Thad replied. "I have a lunch date with Chelsea, and then the guys are having a party for me tonight."

A teary Mrs. Carmichael frowned. "Junior, don't you want to spend time with your family? You're cutting this special occasion short for us."

"Mom, the family's been here all week. I'm sure you've had enough of me."

"But, Thad, honey, this is the big day, the reason we traveled to New York." Mrs. Carmichael sighed, wiping lipstick from her son's cheek. "Okay, I won't pester you. We'll be at the Waldorf, and then we leave for Norfolk tomorrow. Call us with your plans, Junior."

"Hey, good job, Thad." Cynthia handed the camcorder to Thaddeus Senior to film her embrace with her older brother. "I'm proud of you."

"Thanks for flying in from the South to support me, Birdie," Thad whispered.

"Don't bring up my childhood nickname. This situation is corny enough." Cynthia slapped Thad's arm and looked shyly at the hem of her pink dress.

"Okay, well, I'm taking off. The professor who showed me the ropes here is leaving, and I just got schmoozed by the dean who wanted to lynch me with those ropes, so the energy in this space isn't tasting like celebration champagne."

"Junior, I told you I don't like you saying such things."

Thad ignored his father, removing his mortarboard and placing it on Cynthia's head. "Take care of that for me, Birdie." He handed his gown to his mother, which she folded over her arm with sad pride in her eyes.

"I'll take *that*!" Thaddeus Senior grabbed the diploma and tucked it tightly under his arm. "Good work, son. We'll talk about plans for the company later. Have a good time tonight. Let's go, Barbara. Cynthia," he said, walking off without them.

"Dad's anxious to stake claim to *his* latest accomplishment."

Mrs. Carmichael released a conflicted breath. "No, Dad's enthusiasm just gets misdirected sometimes."

"Toward loving selfishness?" Thad suggested, while Cynthia rolled her eyes, assuring him she understood his irritation. But as his mother and sister disappeared into the mingling mass of pressed and pretty people, Thad wondered if she truly did.

On One Hundred Thirteenth Street, the smell from Thad's favorite hotdog vendor called his name. He instinctively reached into his pocket for change before realizing he was en route to meet Chelsea Fuller for lunch at the eatery a couple of blocks down. Deep in thoughts that made the walk seem shorter than usual, he crossed over to Fifth Avenue. Striding past the last of the chichi dress shops, Thad entered Primrose Café and spotted Chelsea at their usual window table giggling into her cellular phone. Her hair was styled in perfect fluffy waves, and she was dressed in a preppy peach pantsuit and tasteful platinum accessories.

The tiny, quaint café was busy with its usual lively, chattering clique of young corporate America—old minds in young bodies; expensive ties on inexperienced necks; and hands that held tickets to filthy rich futures playing with the cute, desert rose napkins on the tables.

"Hi, Thaddeus." Chelsea stood to kiss him. "Congratulations, honey."

"Thank you, baby." Thad sat, squeezing her slender hand.

"Oh—my—God! I was just talking to Kayla. She's all broken up. I'm stuck in an office doing research, and she's up in the ritzy part of the Bronx on location at a crime scene with Adolfo Alvarez. Anyway…" Chelsea continued to speak, while Thad dove deep into her hazel eyes, trying to recall why he had not sprung for the chili cheese footlong with extra ketchup. "…Channel Two's running the broadcast all weekend. But enough about my drama," Chelsea insisted, petting his wrist. "So, my man got his MBA. Our future is looking oh so bright. I'm proud of you, Thaddeus."

"I'm just glad to be away from all those philistines and phony intellectuals. Damn, you should have seen them—all in a hurry to staple their new validations on their foreheads. As if that Columbia diploma means a damn thing in the real world."

"Hello! I still attend that school you're insulting."

"Sorry," Thad whispered. "Really, I simply wanted to get away from my father."

"Thaddeus, your father merely wants the best for you."

"Yeah, but it's hard to look at him as anything other than a well-intentioned bully. I wanted to be happier than I actually felt. In fact, in a corny kind of way, I'd hoped my graduation day would feel more like one of those UNCF ads."

"A UNCF ad?"

"Yeah, you know." Thad drifted off dreamily. "The universe was supposed to move in slow motion as a gospel choir harmonized an inspirational hymn. Mommy, Daddy, and baby sister were supposed to bawl like big babies as I proudly displayed a black man's greatest passport to the good life—my kente-cloth-covered diploma."

"Oh, for the love, Thaddeus. Please, stop with the *Roots* soap opera."

"But the pedigree on that lawn made reality set in. I felt leagues apart from the whole scene. You should've seen Cynthia."

"She's such a doll. Doesn't she have *my* effervescence?"

"She had that wistful look in her eyes that always makes me feel like she's about to ask me something deep—that baby-sister look that melts all the macho out of a big brother. She needs to get out of Norfolk in the worst way."

"Thaddeus, she's not trapped in some cage under your parents' roof."

"If you only knew. Cynthia's got a passion to do so much more than Dad lets her."

"Don't worry. In no time, she'll leave home for college, and she'll blossom like I did. I know what it's like to be Daddy's little girl."

"Chelsea, on my way here, my graduation hit me like an avalanche of hard reality rocks. Today is the beginning and the end of many milestones for me. I'm through trying to be a carbon copy of my father and battling the forces of Hausbruck's type of thinking. They both made my last three years a living hell."

"Are you still paranoid that the dean's after you?"

"Listen to me, Chelsea. Hausbruck's lackadaisical la-di-da-ism no longer fazes me. For so long, pressure from all sides determined my direction at any given moment. From here on out, I'm cutting loose ends and fulfilling the promises I've made to myself."

"That's beautiful, Thaddeus. Honey, I'm so sorry I missed the graduation," Chelsea cooed. "The people at the station have me running like crazy with the local political scandal and now this murder up in the Bronx. It's a wonder they let me have my full lunch hour, but I told them I *will* be with my man today."

"That's okay, baby."

"I ordered a chicken salad for you," Chelsea stated matter-of-factly.

"I'm in the mood for something other than the chicken salad today, Chelsea."

"Thaddeus, honey, don't be silly. Remember our pact to follow the menu in *Health for Now, Forever*. You will have the chicken salad." The victorious Chelsea sat up tall in her chair. "Besides, it's your favorite and here comes the waitress."

The waitress set a big, leafy pile of roughage in front of Thad. Suddenly, he felt it coming on, the spontaneous disorientation and the chaotic slideshow that plays in his mind when things became too much to bear. All at once, frightening images flashed in his brain: *Chelsea in a wedding gown; behind a news desk; with a screaming baby girl; with a leash around his neck…*

He snapped out of his temporary coma. "We need to talk."

"Why are you so tense? Jesus!" Chelsea dug into her salad. "Anyway, just think, in another year I'll have my journalism degree and a job with Channel Two. You'll be in the family business, then we'll get a cute place in—""

"Chelsea, you never listen to me. Did you hear me say we need to talk?"

"Thaddeus, relax, work on that salad, and let's have a nice lunch."

"Why don't you just call me Thad?"

"What do you mean? Why the sudden interest in my habits?"

"People close to me just call me Thad or Junior. As long as we've been together, why are you the only one who can't call me that?"

"First of all, I would never refer to you as 'Junior.'"

"You make it sound so juvenile and unsophisticated."

"Your mother named you Thaddeus, did she not? Now, you can't be serious. This is what you're jumping out of your chair to talk to me about? Thaddeus, please."

"See! Things that are important to me are so damn insignificant to you. Your way is always a step above, huh?" Thad set down his iced tea, and the force rattled the cubes in the glass. "Look at me!"

Chelsea looked up from her plate. She paused for effect, stroking his cheek. "Honey, it's your graduation day. That's important. I mean, let's face it. Columbia is one of the top schools in the nation and you conquered it. You ought to be proud."

He picked at his salad, his fire within dying down. "Thanks, sweetheart."

"Especially considering where you got your undergraduate degree from, you should be thankful that—"

"Damn it, Chelsea!" His flame was re-ignited. Thad slammed both hands on the table and shot up like hot toast from a toaster.

"Excuse me. Is there something else I can get for you?" The timid waitress slowly approached to calm the storm.

"Thaddeus, sit down!" Chelsea's whisper was tight. "People are staring!"

"As usual, you're concerned with saving face, with your glossy appearances!"

"Here we go again with your highly flammable nerves."

"This isn't my idea of a celebration—you throwing cheap shots from your ivory tower! My friends will support me, as usual, so save your cheap cheer for those tight-asses in your newsroom! Go chase more dirt with your stupid news camera."

"Thaddeus! Your family's in town. You'd rather spend tonight with those low-class rats of yours?!" Chelsea caught herself and lowered her voice. "What about me? What about lunch?"

"This lunch is over. You—I'm not so sure about." Thad tossed a twenty on the table and stormed out of the café, holding pride in his gut like indigestion.

Thad wandered aimlessly along Broadway, where faceless New Yorkers rushed to work, to dental appointments, to the gym, to the immigration office. Some rushed to do what they wanted but did not need to do, others to do what they needed but did not want to do. The rest didn't know why they rushed, didn't know what the heck they needed or wanted.

Brick and stucco loomed over them all. The colossal buildings jutting up to the far reaches of the sky could have collapsed onto the river of activity between them at any moment. Thad pondered what prevented that awesome inevitability—given all the wheeling and dealing conducted behind their walls and the hysteria lurking behind the scowls of the intense people swarming about.

Mediterranean diamond smugglers use that unassuming office building for their underhanded transactions, and that tough-looking kid in the baggy jacket is not a thug; he's going to visit his sick grandfather uptown, Thad thought. *That limping old lady has a pistol in her purse and she's heading to midtown to take out her insurance adjuster for screwing with her health benefits.* This bizarre people-watching, secret-guessing game kept Thad busy whenever he traveled the city streets. He found it an easy game to play because he assumed that everything and everyone hid behind barriers, shields of veiled insecurity, masks hiding what lived underneath the surface.

Taxicabs and commuters inhabited every square inch of Manhattan's avenues, while tourists packed Times Square. Bored with the bright lights and commercialism, Thad escaped to Central Park in search of a nonexistent solitude. He walked along the park's winding paths and grassy knolls until he found a bench near a spot where children played.

The sun's remnants spoke waning warmth through the trees. Thad sat, quietly entranced by the youthful activity nearby. In time, the children's laughter crept into his mind as he watched their sneakers skip about. Long ago, Chelsea had introduced him to the habit of noticing cute dogs, adorable kids, and other precious slices of life, but Thad knew that his Brooklyn-based buddies would kill him if they caught him thinking cotton-candy thoughts of cribs and crayons. Instinctively, his thoughts scampered back in the opposite direction.

Unable to think of anything but the typical American Dream, Thad's mind became occupied with the idea of the packaged deal—kids, a wife, conditional liberty, and the pursuit of shrinkwrapped happiness. Time was irrelevant. Eventually, the evening sky crept up on the residue of the afternoon, and Thad took twilight easing over Manhattan as a hint to hop a subway train to Brooklyn.

His friends' brownstone wasn't far from the subway station on Eighth Avenue, but Thad couldn't get there quick enough. His craving for relaxation directed him as he bounded up the dingy front steps and charged into the apartment. Once his feet hit the creaky wood floor, he was greeted by the usual easygoing ether of his friends' parlor pad—the frat-house energy, the rhythmic music, the soulful vibe. It all fit like an oven-warmed glove over fingers reaching back to Thad's college days at Howard University, where he met Rushon McKinney. A young Duke Ellington in appearance, Rush was a former sociology major and a philosophical thinker capable of imparting deep insight on any situation.

"Thad, you're early, man." Rush set a platter of cheese and pepperoni slices on the dining room table. "We just got in from work. Sorry we couldn't make it uptown to watch you walk that ceremonial walk."

Rush's roommate, Saadiq Abdul, was in the corner, shuffling through a stack of CDs. Music was the only thing that moved the tall, creative guy with dreadlocks dangling past his broad shoulders. If it wasn't funky or jazzy, Saadiq didn't want to hear it. He threw up a peace sign without missing a beat. "Congrats, Thad. Columbia gave you the paper. Now, we'll give you the party," Saadiq said, slipping on an acid jazz tune, closing his eyes, and slow-grooving with himself.

"Thanks, fellas. I always feel reconnected when I hit Brooklyn." Thad inhaled the place dressed in rootsy character—the Aaron Douglas print on the wall; the antique green velvet couch; the giant potted palm near the hand-carved Ivory Coast mask. The usual musk oil scent mingled with wafts of salsa and pina colada mix.

Thad plopped down onto the couch next to Virgil, who yapped to his current woman, Rozalyn, on the phone. A stocky and cocky dark-skinned man built like an NFL player, Virgil Davies broke from his conversation long enough to flash a smile at Thad and quip, "What's up, Mr. Executive?"

"Madness. It's been one of those days."

"Who was it this time? Daddy Dearest or Miss Evening News?" Rush, Thad's personal unlicensed psychologist for the last seven years, knew the routine.

"What am I going to do with her?" Thad sighed. "It's like, she's proud of my graduation, but she's such a selfish aspirant—always lumping our successes and futures together. And I told you how she's always living life according to some damn book. It's either her Cinderella fantasies, a crazy self-help book, or some new-age health guide, and I'm only along for the bumpy ride."

"Yeah, blah, blah, blah. But you 'love' her, right?"

"Yes, I do. I do."

"But it's always a pressure beat with Chelsea, Thad. I mean, your relationship's a time bomb, between her mood swings and your stress. You're moving in different directions, man," Rush observed for the zillionth time. "You've got us and NRK, and…"

"She's got *herself*," Saadiq piped in.

Rush resumed his thought. "The couple of times you've brought her here, she's never seemed comfortable."

"I've had it with the wicked head games and the whole prima donna act. I'm twenty-five, almost twenty-six, and I feel so childish for letting Chelsea's antics get to me. I want to stabilize my plans, before I consider bringing Chelsea or anyone else in to share them. As bad as I want to, I still haven't told her about NRK."

"You haven't told her yet?" Saadiq exclaimed. "Look, Thad, Chelsea was spoon-fed all that buppie-yuppie crap from her parents. She looks down on anyone who isn't up to par with her, and that includes *us*. You need to tell her what we're doing and why you won't be at the country club with her this summer!"

"Thad, she's got you sprung, dig? True, Chelsea's gorgeous. She's a fox, but is that the only reason you're with her?" Rush asked.

"You've never seen her in a lace thong." Thad smirked. "But, I mean, of course she's more than a pretty thrill to me. Chelsea's a great girl. She's bright. The station she's interning for is bound to take her on full-time."

"When you met Chelsea at that student mixer a year ago, that's what you were thinking? She's bright? Spare me." Saadiq sucked his teeth, limping coolly to the stereo. He gestured, mocking a game show host's voice. "Miss Chelsea Fuller is an A-plus, journalism co-ed with perfect hair, a pageant smile, and impeccable speech. Let's hear it for contestant number three, the *super-bright*—"

"Saadiq, don't clown me," Thad shot back, leaning far back into the couch. "Actually, it *is* easier to list things about Chelsea that work my nerves."

"Like the fact that she's from a bourgeois family and talks big about the future. Oh, wait a minute. I just described *you*, Thad."

Thad was devoid of patience. "Saadiq!"

"Thad, you do talk large about the future. But which future?" Rush asked rhetorically. "Chelsea's fantasy is you and her as cookie cut-outs of her parents."

"Yeah, but Chelsea's more like a female version of *my* father."

"*Hmm*, interesting," Saadiq noted. "But you can't stand to be alone with *him*, and you can't stop sexing *her*."

"Thad, we've got big plans, and we, or at least *I*, respect what you have with Chelsea. But how much longer can you hide our grand scheme from the woman in your life? I'm not asking you to choose, but—"

Thad stopped Rush with a raised index finger.

"For godsake, man. Don't you see the changes she puts you through?" Saadiq persisted. "Is it worth it? She's always interfering and trying to break up our cipher. Nip it in the bud, man! There's no stopping us. *You* said that, remember?"

Before Thad could profess his loyalty to their Revolution, the doorbell rang.

Virgil sprang up from the couch and opened the door. A few of Thad's Columbia classmates filtered in, followed by Kahlil Mousawi and Benny Broom, who arrived with the upstairs neighbor, Arianna Killborne, and her friend, Nenna Reid.

The Ivy League world Thad had left some hours before was suddenly a universe away as bass-heavy music, balmy incense, and hip chatter filled the apartment. The groove hovered, and Thad was lost in it, bobbing his head, digging the scene. With a brew in hand, he squeezed out a spot for himself on the couch between José Escobar and Caesar Ramirez, who had brought kung fu flicks on videotape. With the TV's volume muted, the crew performed their ritual of cheering fight scenes set to hip hop music. *Shaolin Showdown* was in the VCR; the reigning East Coast rap star was on the stereo.

Thad's groove lasted until Rush pulled out the rolling paper for the crew's other ritual. "Damn!" With a frown, Thad retreated to the window, as Benny whipped out the paper's filler.

Virgil torpedoed next to Thad, nearly spilling his beer. "What's up? It's over. You just got your freedom papers. You're supposed to be celebrating."

"I don't get down with that." Thad pointed toward the smoking cipher. He shook his head and rested against the windowsill. "For all intents and purposes, Rush is the most clear-headed guy I know, but he gets on that weed like it's his woman. That stuff irritates me."

"Ah, lighten up, man." The beer seeped into Virgil's speech. "You've seen ganja heads light up before."

"That doesn't mean I agree with it," Thad spat. "Rush says the lifestyle calls for it, that pot 'feeds the creativity,' but I don't buy that nonsense. Not with the money in *my* pocket."

"Man, did those hoity-toity college folks steal your soul? Relax, you're not running for the Republican drug control task force. Take a hit of that joint and get over yourself, *brotha*." Virgil limped away, rubbing his smooth head.

An hour into the party, Thad tired of watching his breath fog up the windowpane. Reaching for a bottle of cognac, he glanced at the front door and was surprised to see Tyler McDermott, the sole white guy he considered a real friend at Columbia, and his girlfriend, Nikki. Through the chronic cloud in the air, Thad watched the couple scan the room and stroll over to him.

"Thought we'd never find this place." Tyler lightly punched Thad's arm. "We did it, man! I saw your dad jump the stage with his camera. It was hilarious."

"I'm still laughing," Thad said without a smile. "What brings you two here?"

"Rush invited me. He thought it would trip you out."

"I *am* tripping. The ever-preppy Tyler in the middle of this raging Brooklyn scene? Hey, let me introduce you to some people," Thad said over a soul singer's vocals fluttering from the speakers. He escorted the latest guests to the area where his crew lounged. "Hey, guys, this is Tyler and Nikki. This man helped me through advanced accounting." Thad nudged Tyler. "We used to study together and debate racial politics for hours, swapping perspectives. Remember those discussions, Ty?"

"Of course. I'm not done schooling you, either."

"And you definitely haven't heard everything I have to say. Anyway, you met Rush when he visited me on campus. This is Nenna. That's Felicia, Caesar, and José. And this is Saadiq and Virgil, they're members of Rush's group, Subconscious Soul."

Nikki discreetly fanned smoke from her face. "What style of music do you play?"

"Actually, we go beyond music," Saadiq piped in with authority. "It's a mixed experience. We combine a montage of elements. Our performances are a fusion of soul and jazz, drumming, and spoken word poetry. I play African talking drums, and don't let Virgil's stature fool you—he plays a mean wooden flute with the grace of a little girl."

"Shut up, man. I play my piece like Bumpy Johnson on a Juilliard scholarship," Virgil snapped, ignoring Tyler's offer of a handshake.

"Virgil's fighting an identity crisis. The muscles and the music don't mix for him," Rush teased, beginning to soar as a joint dangled from his lips. "I'm the voice," he bellowed with syrupy richness. "And I hold the maraca."

"Over there, that's Kahlil and Benny." Thad pointed toward the kitchen. "They're the newest and youngest members of the group."

"We've been tweaking Subconscious Soul's tonal blend, and it's finally complete with Kahlil's djembe drum and Benny's sax."

"Cool." Tyler's face lit up. "I'd love to check you guys out some time."

Arianna interrupted them, tugging Thad's elbow. "Come to the door."

"Why? What's going on?"

"Some chick is in the hallway, said she's looking for 'Thaddeus." Arianna imitated a haughty tone and tossed her long braids like a prep-school cheerleader. "I invited her in, but she got real salty with me and insisted on waiting in the vestibule."

Thad trudged reluctantly to the front door and found Chelsea standing, arms crossed, in the hallway. Sitting on the stairs, legs crossed, even more removed from the scene was Chelsea's best friend. "What's *she* doing here?" Thad pointed to Kayla as the girl in the canary-colored, cutting-edge dress rolled her eyes at him.

"Don't worry about her, Thaddeus. You left me humiliated at the Primrose, and I don't appreciate that!"

"Oh, now you're ready to talk? So you just barge in on me and my friends, and we do it your way, right?"

"Thaddeus, you're being unreasonable. The slightest thing sets you off these days. Forever and a day, you've hinted that you want to tell me something, but you never get around to it. Instead, you get all hot in the pants whenever I suggest we look seriously at our future."

"That's what I'm trying to deal with—*my* future!" Thad clapped his hands. "I'm doing things I can't even confide in you about!"

Chelsea's eyes doubled in size, as Saadiq poked his head through the doorway, bringing the bumping beats of hip-hop music with him.

"Thad, what's keeping you—" Saadiq stopped when his eyes met Chelsea's.

"Saadiq, I'll join you guys in a minute," Thad said, breaking the tense spell between them.

Saadiq disappeared behind the slamming door.

Chelsea's mood suddenly softened. "Thaddeus, don't be like this," she purred, tickling his cheek. "Let's go back to my place, and we'll talk. There's a cab waiting outside for us. What do you say, hmm? *J'adore toi. Tu es un joli garçon.*"

"Ugh. I should've never taught you to speak French," Kayla grumbled.

"Chelsea, my friends are…" Thad struggled to express himself as the dim light of the hallway cast playful shadows on Chelsea's honey-dipped face.

Inches away from him, Chelsea brushed herself against Thad's rising sensitivity. "We'll go back to my place…" She lightly kissed his chin. "We'll talk…" She swept her lips across his cheek. "And we'll make up," she whispered, slowly biting his earlobe.

Feeling adored in all languages, Thad's nose was open wider than bell-bottoms. He went into the apartment and bid farewell to his friends.

When the taxi pulled in front of Chelsea and Kayla's apartment building on Manhattan's Upper West Side, Kayla grabbed an overnight bag from the trunk and walked a block to the condo of their friend Shola. Meanwhile, Chelsea grabbed Thad by the hand and commandingly led him upstairs and through her dark apartment to her bedroom.

"Whoa."

"What?" Chelsea asked, unbuttoning his ivory dress shirt.

"Uh, well…" Thad stuttered, watching her work quickly. "Your bedroom's already prepped in seduction mode? I mean, you've got the aromatic candles lit, silk sheets turned down, condom on the vanity. I thought you were supposed to work late at the station. You knew my parents were in town, and after the argument at lunch, I assumed…never mind, my mind's already on making up."

"So's mine," Chelsea whispered huskily, flipping on a Sade album for a ménage à trois via the CD player. She pushed Thad onto the comforter with force. She continued undressing him, stripping his limbs of their covering, pinning down his eager hands. Restraining Thad with one foot, Chelsea slithered out of her clothes and threw her naked body against his. They locked mouths. Chelsea slid the condom to Thad.

"Baby, I like you to put it on for me," Thad grunted, licking her face.

He shoved it back in her hand, and Chelsea sprang up and straddled him.

"Oh, don't worry, big boy. I'm gonna put it on you," she growled, as her eyes became narrow slits. She reached for a red silk scarf on the nightstand and dangled it over his face like bait on a sharp hook. "But first, I'm gonna put this on you."

"Ooh, kinky. We've never done this before." Thad sat up and allowed Chelsea to take control.

She slowly wrapped the scarf over his eyes, blindfolding him. She tied a knot tightly behind his skull with an angry desire, causing him to flinch in pain. Placing her palm against his forehead, she pushed him back to a flat, vulnerable position.

"Have mercy." Thad was breathless. "Damn. Hurry, baby, put it on."

Chelsea leaned over and blew out both candles, enveloping the room in blackness. She grabbed Thad tightly, massaging between his legs. She ripped the plastic square with her teeth, tugging viciously at the packaging. Slipping the condom onto his solid

sword, she rolled it down slowly, driving Thad mad with anticipation. She slid herself on top of him and kissed his mouth
greedily. ·

In a quick motion, Thad flipped Chelsea on her back and positioned himself for good leverage. Ignoring Sade's soothing plea
from the stereo, Thad thrust wildly, as Chelsea screamed and
clawed his lower back. He went deeper and deeper, digging as if
he'd lost something inside of her and desperately wanted it back.
Thad rammed himself against her, and, with each forceful pump,
the day's worries propelled from his body.

The blindfold helped him to avoid seeing the torture he
pounded onto her tiny body—intimate torment she welcomed,
wished for, wanted.

Chelsea wailed, accepting Thad's venting. She reached up,
slapped the sweat on his neck, and pulled him toward her, licking and biting his ear. Then she suddenly pushed him off of her
and onto his back. She grabbed him tightly, squeezing his man-
hood in her hands until he let out a deep guttural scream.

"What the hell are you doing, baby?" Thad barked. The piercing
pain down below shot straight up to his brain. He felt one last
violent tug before Chelsea clasped him in the grip of her thighs.
Swallowed in hot moistness, Thad tore into the sheets as the
sensation he felt quadrupled. "Mmm. Damn, that's good!"

Whimpering and hissing, Chelsea relentlessly rocked back and
forth to Sade's musical breakdown. She leaned over, licked Thad's
face, and bit his chest. Again, she rocked herself on top of him,
back and forth, gripping, clutching him inside. Harder, faster,
with animalistic hunger, until she felt his entire body tense up
into human steel.

Thad's torso and pelvis jerked forcefully, and he squeezed
Chelsea's breasts, growling like a grizzly bear. Sade hit her high

note, and Thad released everything he had as, for a moment, his mind was in a dark new world other than the real one.

Chelsea collapsed next to Thad on the soaked satin sheets, both of them panting, dripping. She leaned over and pulled off the blindfold.

"I still can't see you." He tried to chuckle but was too weak. "That was beautiful music."

"It's okay. I can see you," she said, as if she possessed powers unavailable to mere humans. She planted soft kisses all over his face and chest, massaging the good pain away. "And you'll hear the music we made forevermore, because I love you, Thaddeus."

"And I love you."

"Say forevermore."

"What?"

"Say you love me forevermore."

"Oh, of course…forevermore."

She pulled his arm around her and cuddled close to him, as the two drifted, breath by breath, into a deep sleep.

2

THE SAGE AND THE SORCERESS

Sunshine penetrated the curtains hanging from every window of Chelsea's apartment the next morning. Thad felt like he was in a different place and time, as though the calendar had turned itself over several times during the night. He did not say much to Chelsea, who constantly smiled as she prepared breakfast while draped in a slinky red nighty. Full of newfound guts, Thad finally dialed the Waldorf Astoria. "Hi, Mom."

"Hi, Junior. It's good to hear your voice."

"Hi, Mrs. Carmichael," Chelsea sang like an angel over the running water of the kitchen sink.

"Chelsea says hi," Thad said, focusing on his reason for calling.

"How was the party last night, honey?"

"It was fine, Mom. Is Dad there? I need to talk to him."

"Is everything all right?"

"Sure," Thad replied, as Chelsea took a seat across from him at the table.

"Junior, what's up?" his father's deep, gravelly voice boomed.

"Dad, I've thought long and hard about this, and I've decided to move in with Rushon and Saadiq in Brooklyn."

Chelsea froze, dropped her fork, and looked up from her French omelet. There was silence on the other end of the phone, and Thad sipped his hazelnut coffee casually, waiting for his father's response.

"Junior, what's this about?" Thaddeus Senior's voice was drier than sandpaper. "Your uncle just found a condo for you in Long Island!"

"This is best for me right now. Part-timing at the brokerage firm is only good for so much. If I move out of the grad school dormitory and into the brownstone, I'll have a support system around me while I put away more money."

"You took that job for the experience—you don't *need* to put away money. Junior, I don't like the sound of this! What do I tell your uncle?"

"I've made up my mind. It's final." Thad looked at a stunned Chelsea.

"Pardon me? Junior, how is living with those guys, who are doing nothing for themselves, supposed to be conducive to starting up the New York location of my company? Thad, this was not part of our agreement! What the hell—"

"It's settled," Thad interrupted resolutely. "Accept my decision for once!"

He heard his father huffing through the telephone wires. "Talk to your mother," Thaddeus Senior said through clenched teeth, slamming the receiver against a table.

"Junior, you're moving in with Rushon?" Mrs. Carmichael asked, strains of concern in her voice.

"Mom, it's what I want." Thad reached for Chelsea, who charged away from the table.

"I wish you would've given us a chance to discuss it first, but you seem sure about this. If it's what you want…"

"It is."

"Then do what you must, Junior."

"Thanks. I knew I could count on you. Understanding is your greatest gift."

"You know I'm here for you."

"Thanks for your unconditional support, *unlike some people*."

"We'll talk about it later. We leave for Virginia today. Give your father some time to simmer down, then call us at home."

"Tell Birdie I haven't forgotten about her."

"She knows that, honey."

"Tell her again. She'll know what I mean. Love you, Mom." Thad put down the phone, smiling broadly. With a swift glide to the window, Thad parted the curtains to inhale the raw perfume of the city. Following a mini celebration, he walked into the living room, rejuvenated.

"Is that what you've been wanting to tell me?"

"That's part of it." Thad sat next to Chelsea on her big pink sofa.

"What happened to the Long Island condo? I could never come see you at that other place. Your friends hate me, and I don't want to deal with that!"

"No, baby, you're more than welcome there." Thad rubbed Chelsea's thigh to stop her tightly crossed legs from bouncing up and down.

"That's not true, Thaddeus. I tried to reach out to them in the beginning, but they just wouldn't give me a chance. They make me nervous, especially that Saadiq." Chelsea put a finger directly between Thad's eyes. "You didn't even consult me about this!"

Thad stood coolly and walked to the bathroom, while Chelsea followed him, chanting, "Don't walk away from me!"

Thad tossed a towel on the swan-shaped hook and hopped into the shower.

Chelsea stood at the sink, yelling at the shower curtain. "Thaddeus, what are you saying to me?"

"I don't 'consult' you. I *informed* you of my decision," Thad answered, soaping up.

"Oh, yeah, apparently you can't confide in me, because you sure as hell haven't been *informing* me of much."

"Wow! *Now* you want to hear me out?" Thad poked his head through the curtain, feigning surprise. "All right, baby. I'll confide in you." Thad disappeared behind the curtain. "I'm going into business with those 'low-class rats' of mine."

With catlike quickness, Chelsea jumped into the tub. Glaring at Thad's naked body from behind a mask of wet hair, she seethed, "What did you say?"

"Damn, you're sexy," Thad replied, looking at Chelsea through the wall of steam between them. Her red teddy clung to her body, revealing the contours of her figure. His eyes traveled up, meeting hers. "But sometimes I don't know what to make of the fire in your eyes." He rinsed the soap from his chest and arms before answering her question. "Chelsea, I'm moving in with my friends, who are also my new business partners." He turned off the water. "Now, can you be my confidante and support me?" Thad flung the curtain open and snatched his towel.

Chelsea chased him to the bedroom. "Thaddeus, what are you planning with your friends?" Chelsea's voice was painfully hollow. "Your father laid the good life in your lap, with the new condo and Perennial. You had it made." She stood dripping over him as he dressed. "And, damn it, Thaddeus, what about *our* plans?"

Thad brushed past Chelsea and stood before the mirror to check himself. "*You* had plans for me, and *Daddy* had plans for me, but neither of you cared to hear from *me* in all this talk about 'we.' My dad's a six-foot-four-inch tank pushing his kids with a psychological bulldozer. When any semblance of success is in sight, he wants the world to watch as he soaks up the glory for *his* contribution. I have dreams and aspirations that may not measure up to the uppity rubric that you and Daddy used to feel good about yourselves, but they're mine just the same!" He spun around to face her. "Don't *ever* tell me what to be grateful for, you understand?"

"Thaddeus, don't do this. I love you."

"Do you, Chelsea? Do you love me or your fantasy?"

"We'll see how far you get with those lowlifes!" Chelsea shook violently, trembling as her inner rage took command of the nerves of her lips, arms and legs. "You're different, Thaddeus. You belong here!"

"You know where I'll be."

"Yeah, but can they give you what I gave you last night?"

Back in Brooklyn, the streets sizzled with the sounds that soothed Thad's soul. Two dogs fought over Chinese take-out Styrofoam in an alley, their territorial snarls mingling with the garish laughter of a throng of teen girls hanging by the arcade. Such ear candy crisscrossed with the occasional hip-hop concerts bumping from the stereos of passing cars. Thad walked up to the brownstone that would be his new home. The stoop was still dingy, but he climbed the stairs anyway, trying to hide his trepidation. Bursting through the door, he shouted, "I'm moving in!"

Rush set aside his poet's lyric notebook. "How'd your dad take the news?"

"Put it this way, Rush." Thad sighed, sinking down onto the couch, finally noticing just how green and old it was. "He's dealing with it."

"Ain't no stopping us now," Saadiq sang, dancing into the kitchen with an empty Jamaican gin bottle from the previous night's festivities.

"Hold it. Daddy's right-wing expectations and Thad's grassroots values are a deadly pyrotechnic combination. You told Thaddeus Senior about our business and he's just 'dealing with it'? I thought for sure he'd blow up like an A-bomb!"

"Not exactly, Rush. Dad doesn't know about NRK yet. I have to drop one bomb at a time. I mean, I'm giving up a world of limos and charge cards for one of thrift store couches and scraping for change in the cushions."

"Quit living a double life and hiding our plans from your folks. This is serious." Rush was in professor mode. "While everyone in our class at Howard dreamed about a good job and their own cubicle in corporate America's Grand Idiot Office, we conceived NRK like a combat mission. Remember? The time is now."

Saadiq reentered and sat on the couch. "Thad, we waited for you so we could do this together. We want you to be with us one hundred percent."

"I'm here. The MBA thing was for my father, but what we've built is for *us*."

"Don't ever say that." Rush pointed a stiff finger at Thad. "Going to Columbia was for *you*. We encouraged you because you're smart and we need your business expertise. I dropped out of Howard because the draw of New York's stages was too great. Every waking minute, I wish I didn't give up so damn close to the finish line. A part of me is still incomplete. But you—you're not supposed to be confused as to what you want most. No broken family, no run-ins with the law, no economic insecurity! Earth should look like heaven to you right now, Thad!"

Thad's expression hardened. "My family album is full of unfinished poems. Our string of unfulfilled dreams is long enough to knit sweaters for all the Rockefellers. My dad didn't parlay his experience as a Navy cook into a culinary career, and my mom didn't do more with her painting skill. And Brandon just—"

A nerve-shattering picture show flashed in Thad's brain: *Ghastly images of Brandon's misfortune, Thaddeus Senior wielding a wooden cooking spoon, his mother toting a protest poster, Birdie waiting with eager eyes…*

Thad diverted his gaze to his shoes, staring at his feet until the room disappeared. When nothing but his soul and his soles existed, the recollections came—the value of shoes during his childhood. Shoes were once tickets to a boy's freedom. Running was flying. That was until Thad saw an after-school TV special about a kid who blocked out bossy grown-ups with a game of mental escape, flashing pictures in his imagination of the fun places where he'd rather be. When a young, curious Thad ate Popsicles and wore sneakers, the game worked.

But the game had turned against a grown-up Thad who wore loafers and wondered how he'd eat while holding an MBA and dissing Daddy's handout. He no longer controlled it. It controlled him, and instead of images of fun, far-off places, as an adult Thad only got pictures of stress, pain, uncertainty, and horror at times when he could least tolerate them—like at that moment, when the greenness of the couch and the blackness of his shoes and the thoughts of finishing poems or just escaping scraped violently against the jagged edges of one another…

Thad's eyes welled with tears. The room's sudden hush was threatened only by the hum of the refrigerator leaking in from the kitchen. Thad's emotional release rendered Saadiq and Rush speechless.

"I can't believe I'm crying in front of my blood brothers." Thad laughed shakily, wiping his eyes. "You guys looked to me as a rock in our operation. I'm sorry."

"We're all going through a lot. Trina ended our relationship because she didn't support my artistic aspirations. Virgil's grandmother is still sick. But we've got each other's backs." Rush extended his hand to Saadiq, who laid his hand atop Rush's.

Thad reached a palm to the pile and cupped his friends' hands in brotherhood.

"Finish that poem, man. Remember, it's far better to be a passionate romantic, lauded for commitment to a cause that makes you happy, than a rooted pacifist, cheered for diligent caution in aims that make you miserable," Rush professed. "Don't commit the cardinal sin of turning your back on your passion, because when it comes to promises, those broken to the self are often the biggest sinkholes of shame."

Thad took a moment to absorb his counselor's words. "Thanks, Rush." Newly composed, he reached for the remote control. "By the way, did you guys take care of Tyler for me last night?"

"He was one of the last ones to leave the party." Saadiq laughed.

"How tight are he and his girl? Nikki looked ready to get out of here, because Ty left her alone in the corner and he was hanging tough with us," Rush recalled. "Before the night was over, Ty was banging on Saadiq's drums and dirty-dancing with Felicia. I don't think Virgil vibed with Ty, though."

"Tyler flips it like that sometimes, but you know how Virgil feels about our fair-feathered brethren. Rush, the smoking didn't turn into something else when I left, did it?" Thad said, surfing TV channels with the remote, while Rush gave him a signal to back off.

Adolfo Alvarez appeared on the TV screen behind the Channel Two Eyewitness News logo, and a woman's picture floated to the right side of his perfectly stiff hair. "Carolina Ann Smithey was taken into custody yesterday as the prime suspect in the murder of wealthy New York business tycoon Michael Wayne Smithey. Mr. Smithey was found among the ashes of their penthouse in the affluent Riverdale section of the Bronx, following an arson attempt. In what sources close to the Smitheys tell Channel Two was a crime of passion, thirty-six-year-old Mrs. Smithey also allegedly attacked another woman from the Soundview Housing Projects. The female victim was suspected to be having an affair with the slain forty-year-old owner of Lanier Financial, Incorporated. Police are withholding the second victim's name until further investigation yields more evidence."

"Your girl dragged you out of here quick last night."

"*Shhh*," Thad hushed Saadiq. "This guy, Smithey, did business with the company I work for. Damn. I can't believe it. I can't believe he's dead."

"Yeah, you could end up just like him if you keep letting your woman control you. What's up with Chelsea's headlock on you, Thad? I hope there won't be too much of her whip-cracking when we get our business up and running." Saadiq casually lit a bidi. "Damn, is her wet-stuff *that good*?"

Thad came out of the stupor into which the news story had thrown him. "Why are you always testing me? Want to find out how good Chelsea is for yourself?"

"Don't flatter yourself." Saadiq coolly blew smoke rings into the air.

"In fact, she was exceptionally wild last night, Saadiq. Want the details?" Thad bragged, slipping on an armor of macho bravado. Then a memory of last night's untamed tryst came to mind. Confusion poisoned his blood. Something about the sex did not feel right to him.

Rush noticed Thad's mood shift.

"Watch out, playboy. I've seen this fatal attraction shit before." Saadiq puffed on his bidi. "Chelsea hides behind her façade of the sweet little socialite and sorority girl, but it's obvious that she's a greedy and needy psycho completely obsessed with possessing you." He shook his head. "Something about that chick vexes me. As Hitchcock as it sounds, it's in her freaking eyes."

"Saadiq, you sound like the only mental case around here," Thad quipped.

"Don't sleep on this warning. There's a thin line between love and hate, and an even thinner line between devotion and obsession. Mark my words."

It was a windy Monday morning, but Thad wore a smile as he strolled into the lobby of the fifty-story Exchange Building on Wall Street.

"Hey, college boy," Reggie sang, swinging his ring of keys. "You're showin' extra teeth today. Usually you walk in here lookin' more sour than a lemon peel."

"Good morning, Reggie." Thad approached the beer-bellied security guard's counter. "This is my last week at Freeman-Webber, Inc. After two arduous years, I don't have to put up with my boss, Campbell's, crap anymore."

"Oh yeah, you told me. And here I was thinkin' you were giddy 'cause your fine lil' woman is upstairs waitin' for you. I forgot my college boy is gonna leave old Reggie." Reggie pretended to break down in tears, though his underlying sadness was real. The weathered man, forever wearing his cap off-center and chewing on a toothpick, had always told Thad he was proud of him, because he "spoke proper and wore all them spiffy suits, lookin' just like a young, civil rights activist."

"Chelsea's here?"

"Yep, and she's lookin' mighty pretty." Reggie removed his toothpick and placed it into the spit-filled crease on the left side of his lips. "You look shook, boy."

"We had a major fight this past weekend."

"What are you two arguin' 'bout? You need to go on and marry her and stop havin' her chase you 'round here every day. She's gonna turn on ya at that rate."

"Yeah, well, Saadiq may see to that first. Of all my friends, he's the most vocal about his distaste for Chelsea. He has a personal vendetta against her."

"Wait a minute. Saadiq don't like that sweet lil' thang?"

"He bashes Chelsea so much I think he's plotting to destroy my relationship with her, for the good of my friendship with my blood brothers and our big plans."

"I'm so proud you're startin' a business with your partners. I wish Marcus had the head to do some stuff like that, make his old man proud. 'Stead he's just hangin' 'round the house, claimin' he got a bad back at *twenty-four*! Can you believe that, Thad?" Reggie asked seriously, rubbing his salt-and-pepper beard.

"It's not easy. I drafted our business plan back when I was at Howard. Then, Rush and Saadiq scoped out a cool spot in Park Slope about five and a half months ago, but we've been putting away money for the past seven years or so. Rush and Saadiq pull in mad hours at the Brooklyn Academy of Music's programming department, and Virgil works his construction gigs."

"And you've been bustin' your tail at this brokerage firm above old Reggie, eh?" He reached across his counter to poke Thad's arm. "So young and smart."

Thad patted Reggie's shoulder. He checked his watch and walked to the elevator. "Time to face the good old boys," Thad yelled through the closing doors.

The doors shut out Reggie's sad, sincere laughter in his world of package deliveries and desk duty in his polyester uniform, while the elevator carried Thad to his world of power meetings with brokers in tailored suits. The elevator numbers flickered, while Thad took deep breaths in preparation to face the corporate wolves. By the time he reached the eleventh floor, he hid behind the mask he wore to survive the workweeks, until the weekends when he traveled back down to the real world, de-masked and felt free.

When the elevator doors reopened, Thad saw Chelsea through Freeman-Webber's glass wall. Wearing a sexy red skirt-suit, she sat in the waiting area with her nose in *The New York Post*. Thad entered the office, walked over to her chair, and stood swinging his briefcase until she finally looked up from the newspaper.

"Thaddeus." Chelsea folded the paper under her arm. "I'm reading about Carolina Smithey, the lady from the Bronx. Channel Two is doing a big story—"

"Follow me," Thad interrupted flatly, walking toward the back of the office.

Chelsea skipped behind Thad past rows of his co-workers screaming into big switchboard phones on fancy lacquer desks paired with post-modern, high-back chairs. In the employee lounge, Chelsea turned Thad around by the shoulders and straightened his tie with motherly concentration. "You look so handsome."

"I hate wearing this damn thing. Can't wait until I don't have to do this suit-and-tie routine anymore." Thad took a hold of her hands and placed them at her side. "Chelsea, are you here to make small talk or to apologize?"

"Thaddeus, how did you expect me to react when you've been planning things behind my back? And for this long? Hello? Trust issues?"

"The way I told you was not the best way, but—" Thad hushed as his supervisor, Pat Campbell, in slicked-back hair and a three-hundred-dollar dress shirt, walked over to the counter nearby and drained the contents of the coffeepot into his big Princeton mug.

"Good morning, Chelsea," Campbell said, with an ink pen in his mouth.

"Pat." Chelsea beamed, pulling wisps of her hair behind her ear.

"Pretty fucked up what happened to Smithey, eh, Carmichael?" Campbell removed the pen and took a swig from his mug.

"Yeah, I saw it on the news this weekend. It's tragic."

"That goddamn, no-good woman of his!" Campbell huffed. "No offense, Chelsea. Horrible. Anyway, the bosses are in meltdown over this. Listen, we've got a mess of calls to make, and those real estate contracts were drawn up totally half-assedly— they aren't worth shit. So the bosses are pissed about that, too." He slapped Thad's shoulder and turned to exit. "I'm leaving them for you to sort out. I'll be on a plane to Australia in, like, four hours."

"Chelsea, we can't do this now." Thad squirmed. "I just stopped by the office for a few minutes to pick up some papers and then—"

"Yo, Thad, the secretary sent me back to find you. Ready to go?"

Chelsea turned toward Saadiq's voice at the entrance of the employee lounge. Irritated, she spun to face Thad again. "Thaddeus, take an early lunch. Let's talk somewhere else," she grumbled, grabbing his hand tightly.

"Chelsea, I know we need to talk, but I already had plans to meet with Saadiq. I'll call you later, okay, baby? Don't be upset." Thad tried to kiss her, and Chelsea turned her lips, only allowing him to graze her cheek. "Saadiq, let me scoop up some papers from Campbell. I'll be right back."

"What the hell are you looking at?" Chelsea spat, straightening her skirt and flipping her hair, as Saadiq slowly approached her in the otherwise empty room.

"Just window shopping."

"Please! You *wish* you could afford this."

"We've never really talked before, Chelsea."

"Maybe there's a reason for that."

"Let's change that. I want to get to know you better. So, you're into books?"

"What do you want from me?"

"Ever read *Soul on Ice*?" Saadiq twisted the shell clip on the end of one of his locks. "Eldridge Cleaver?"

"I know who wrote it, and, no, I haven't read it!" Chelsea crossed her arms and backed away. "What's it to you, Malcolm X?"

"Read anything that expands your mind beyond *Cosmo* magazine?"

"I'm sorry I live in the present. No, on second thought, I don't apologize for leaving the Revolution in the Sixties, before you were even born. Listen, you don't need to remind me of my heritage or my history, okay?"

"Revolution has a new face, my sister. Maybe that just sounds like ghetto romance to you, but it's plenty real to me, baby," Saadiq whispered, standing closer to Chelsea than a set of breasts. He stared into the cleavage of hers spilling from her starched, fitted blouse.

Hiding outside the lounge's window, Thad watched Saadiq move close enough to kiss Chelsea.

"News flash—the shackles are off, we have civil rights now," Chelsea sneered, putting a finger in Saadiq's chest hair that peeked through his half-open shirt. She pushed him away from her face. "Why are you and your friends always looking for a movement to join?"

"Because people like *you* forget—people who live life with their fingers on the fast-forward button, who try to forget the past by running from it."

"Is CNN not part of your cable TV package? Did you miss the historical election? Obama made it to the White House. What else do you want?"

"That's a start. It's not the end."

"This is the end of this conversation. Go save the planet by yourself, but leave Thaddeus out of your spacey, bohemian revolt! Otherwise, you'll end up like the rest of your dead revolutionaries. Mark my words."

"I've been waiting to call this meeting to order," Thad announced that evening at the brownstone, shuffling documents on the table in front of him. "I'm losing my patience. Rush, the Revolution won't be televised."

Rush kept his eyes on the TV. "Part of the Revolution was televised. Obama gave CNN its highest ratings ever."

"Get over here, so we can review these agreement papers."

"The Knicks are down by three with eleven seconds left in the final quarter," Rush boohooed, as he joined Thad and Saadiq at the dining room table.

"Virgil, put down that phone before your ear falls off," Thad snapped.

Virgil sat next to Thad. "Don't distract me when Roz is talking dirty to me."

"On a serious note, we're putting the finishing touches on the business. This brownstone has been the headquarters for Operation: Touchstone, and it's a well-oiled machine," Thad declared proudly. "Our own fearless Huey P. Newton, Brother Rush, coined the proper name for our operation at the last investors' meeting. Since we're in the final inning, I'd like Rush to explain the tag again. Brother Rush?"

"Solid." Rush cleared his throat. "A touchstone is a hard, black stone used to test the integrity of gold and silver, and it symbolizes our venture in a way. Each of us is a resilient touchstone, verifying his own character in the face of rhetoric from all those claiming to know better—people with silver tongues and golden ideas of what each of us is destined to be in *their* eyes."

"Right on. Folks like Rush's ex, Trina, Chelsea, my father, Dean Hausbruck, and other non-believers are in for a rude awakening when the new revolution comes," Thad shouted, as cheers erupted from around the table.

"Can I ask our resident Eldridge Cleaver something?" Saadiq inquired. "Why hasn't our Minister of Information informed us in detail about this Hausbruck dude?"

"I've told you the story, right?"

"You called him closed-minded, but never mentioned anything specific," Saadiq replied. "And if anyone should know about this turkey, it is me, Brooklyn's own H. Rapp Brown, so I can speak on it."

"That highly educated man needs a crash course in Salad Bowl Theory 101 to knock him into the new millennium. If nothing else, Hausbruck's laissez-faire attitude burns me. At Columbia, he was a brick wall refusing to let me into places where he felt that I had no right to be."

"Don't let stuff you can't change get to you." Rush advised. "When Hausbruck left old Germany and came to modern America, the man retained *and* adopted the most heinous of international vices, but you can't change everybody's mind."

"True. Anyway, I'm sure our own gun-toting Bobby Seale will vibe with this story," Thad said, looking directly at Virgil. "The last time I was in Hausbruck's office, we were battling back and forth about some issue. All of a sudden, I couldn't take his flippant attitude anymore, and I got juiced with the idea of payback. I jumped up and vowed I'd leave a mark so raw and real and undeniable, that the nearly blind scrooge would be forced to take notice of me and 'those people in my group,' as Hausbruck commonly referred to the Black Business Students' Council."

"See, man, that's exactly why I can't stand those devil crack—"

"Virgil," Rush broke in, "don't even say that word. Please ease up on that poison, doctor. We don't need that kind of energy in our space."

"Now you understand that we're in the process of orchestrating a major play. The game plan is to break our molds and show 'em all. We refuse to settle for just being a nutty professor, a flaky musician, a straight-laced suit, or a thuggish musclehead," Thad barked like a rebel warrior. "Our mantra: *Doubters, beware!*"

His army cheered, "Right on!"

The next day arrived, without a call from Thad.

"Hi," Chelsea spoke softly into the receiver, anxiously curling the phone cord around her finger. "I'm glad that you agreed to see me."

"I'm not speaking with any press people right now, because I know all they want is to make a buck off my heartache," a solemn voice replied through the phone, then paused. In the visitor's room at the Bronx Women's Correctional Facility, a pained face stared back at Chelsea through a pane of bulletproof glass. "But when you said you were a dazzling sister of Delta Alpha Zeta, I had to meet you. I don't have a real, or rather, biological sister."

"I was willing to tell the wardens anything to get you to accept a visit from a stranger, Carolina. Or should I call you Mrs. Smithey?"

"The formalities. Oh yeah, you'll make an excellent journalist all right."

"Uh, thanks…I think. Besides that, I need someone I can talk to…someone who understands the heart's troubles."

"Gee, who needs the therapy session more, me or you?"

"How are you holding up?" Chelsea asked and got no response. "To be honest, the station just cut back my hours. Some of the staff complained that I was 'exhibiting behavior unproductive to the work environment,' which irritates me, because I was really getting into—"

"Because you were really getting into the media madness? You hate to miss a day of work, because then you'll be left behind in the rumor mill of dogshit that used to be someone else's life smeared all over newsprint and the goddamn TV?"

"No," Chelsea insisted. "Ups and downs with my boyfriend are dragging me through hell. Truth is, I was becoming despondent, lapsing into daydream-like spells, my migraines becoming relentless. I'm on the brink of exploding."

"Poor girl, life must just be bloody irksome for you right now, huh? Ya know, between manicure appointments and sorority brunches and all?"

Chelsea paused, watching Carolina mock her with a sickening sympathy full of fake puppy dog eyes and an obnoxious infantile tone. "Carolina, I didn't come here to talk about me. I'm here for you. My best friend Kayla is also a journalist. She went in my place with Adolfo Alvarez to visit the cri—your home."

"The crime scene? Is that what you were going to say? I recall seeing someone who looks like you that day. So that was your best friend traipsing around my house? I could've killed that girl, sniffing around, getting off on my husband and me in our most miserable moment. Why are you so interested in me anyway?"

Carolina's gaze turned to sharp, brown blades, and Chelsea squirmed in her chair, the splits in the old vinyl catching her pleated skirt. The inmate's evil expression made Chelsea thankful they spoke via telephone, separated by unbreakable glass.

"What you're going through is dreadful. After your, uh, unfortunate tragedy, I was researching your story for Channel Two." Chelsea looked down at her hands. "Carolina, we have very similar backgrounds. I feel like I know you."

"Now I'm a damn research topic?" Carolina sneered, then laughed. "Look at you, sweetie. I bet you even smell like you don't belong in this place. I assumed every last snooty little D.A.Z. would turn up her nose at a woman in my situation."

"Normally, I would, but I took the pledge: A dazzling D.A.Z., devoted to the sisters of Delta Alpha Zeta until the day I D.I.E." Chelsea hoped Carolina would laugh at that, but she didn't. "Honestly, my heart goes out to you. I feel sorry for you."

"I won't cash your pity check. Save it." Carolina shook her head brazenly, her side-swept bangs falling into her eyes. "Don't feel sorry for me, kid. Learn from me." She pointed through the glass, her tone adding an Eleventh Commandment.

Chelsea nodded timidly, noticing the diamond ring on Carolina's finger. "The wardens let you keep that?"

Carolina slowly raised her left hand, admiring her ring. "They don't know I have it. I keep it in my pocket and slide it on when I need comfort. Nobody will ever take this from me. It's a part of me," she purred. "Columbia, right?"

Chelsea nodded.

"Vanderbilt."

"I know. From research." Chelsea stood, her thighs peeling away from the gripping vinyl of the seat under her. She peered over the partition at the guard by the door. In the next carrel, a man raged about "the kids" to a teary-eyed woman on Carolina's side of the glass. Chelsea hunkered back down and looked at Carolina intently. "Why'd you do it?" she whispered. "I want to know you and understand." Chelsea watched a solitary drop of sorrow roll down Carolina's magnificent cheekbone and into her trembling lip. "Carolina? I'm trying to understand," Chelsea begged quietly.

"Do those media people have you wired? If they do, I swear—"

"No. Please, I want to know and help you if I can, Carolina."

"Because I loved him! It's downright criminal, hell, sacrilegious how much I loved that man. He filled all my holes, and I couldn't let half of myself walk out on the rest of me—physically tearing me in two? Can you even fathom what I'm talking about?"

Suddenly, the man next to Chelsea turned his volume up. "Mary, I love you, damn it!" His enraged tone, the powerful words, the real emotion shook the cinderblock room. The man roared, mixing nasty words with loving ones, and a thunderous smack shook the Plexiglas shield between the free and the fallen. Chelsea watched more sorrow soak Carolina's face.

"Think you have what I had? Better be goddamn sure before you do anything crazy to hold on to him," Carolina screamed into the mouthpiece, jumping from her chair. "This fades, sweetheart!" She waved her hand around her face to signify beauty. "This doesn't!" She punched the left side of her chest to indicate the heart.

Chelsea dropped the receiver, rubbing her earlobe.

"Hey! Hey, calm down! Let it go, big man!" The security guard bounded over and grabbed the unruly man next to Chelsea, who was now kicking and screaming profanities, pulling him away from the phone. "All right! Everybody out! Play time's over!"

Raising her hands to her mouth, Chelsea watched Carolina fight the guard who appeared on the inmates' side of the glass, the noise on Chelsea's side providing the soundtrack for the silent, nightmarish action on the other.

As the guards carted off their respective hell-raisers, Chelsea mouthed to Carolina, "I understand."

3

SIMPLE SAYINGS AND SECRET-SPILLING

"Virgil has been avoiding the brownstone and not returning my phone calls this week," Thad yelled over the jazz music playing on Chelsea's stereo on Saturday night. He sat stiffly on the edge of the living room sofa. "I had to track him down at his construction work site on Lexington Avenue and convince him to do this double date tonight."

"Typical," Chelsea said to herself in her bedroom. "Runs all over town to track down his friends but goes days without giving me so much as a phone call."

"I pray Virgil and Rozalyn have something, *anything*, in common with you," Thad hollered from the other room. "Chelsea, baby, what are you doing in there? They should be here any minute!"

"Stop rushing perfection. Come in here and zip me up," Chelsea called back.

Thad put down his glass of red wine and stomped to Chelsea's bedroom. "Let's leave before Kayla gets home. I don't feel like dealing with that nosy witch tonight." Suddenly, Thad's shoes welded to the floor as he stood stone-like next to the bed, watching Chelsea's back at the vanity. The room—and dirty feelings about what he sensed had happened there on the night of his graduation—made him pause.

"Well, don't just stand there." Chelsea turned to him. "You have the tickets?"

"Yes," he replied robotically.

"Oh, no, Thaddeus, why didn't you wear your nice blazer? That old leather jacket is so…what's the matter with you?"

Thad's eyes traveled around the wilderness of Chelsea's bedroom, along the endless shades of red fabric and layers of lace. His eyes fell on the red silk scarf that Chelsea used to blindfold him during their wicked lovemaking session days before. He flapped the lapels of his jacket to circulate more air and keep the walls from clamping in on him. To Thad, her room held secrets. "What did you say?"

"What happened to the Italian blazer I bought for you?"

"Chelsea, we're going to see *Bring in 'da Noise, Bring in 'da Funk*. Maybe you should get a little more *funky*."

"I'll stick to *classy*, thank you. Now could you zip me up, honey?"

Thad approached Chelsea, hesitating to touch her. He eased his hand onto Chelsea's skin, and the contact sent a shudder through her that he felt in his fingertips. Slowly, he inched the zipper of her black slip dress up toward the two tiny freckles in the middle of her back as he watched her in the mirror. She closed her eyes, shivering as if touched for the first time, while guilt oozed through Thad.

"I set up this date to patch things up with you after the shaky week we had, Chelsea. Let's try and have a good time tonight, okay?"

"That'll take two of us, no?" Chelsea said as the doorbell chimed. "And it'll take a hell of a lot more than this," she added after Thad left to answer the door.

The cab ride to the Ambassador Theatre was quiet. Sitting up front, Virgil rapped with the cabdriver who, coincidentally, was from his old neighborhood, New Orleans' Seventeenth Ward. But silence remained the fourth passenger in the back seat for a long while.

"So, did y'all hear about that crazy lady from the Bronx—Shippy, or whatever her name is?" Rozalyn eventually asked.

"Smithey. It's Carolina Smithey," Chelsea impatiently corrected her. "We're doing an investigation into her story at Channel Two."

"Well, excuse me," Rozalyn huffed.

Thad groaned. "I can't believe you two are talking about this. Does anybody talk about anything else anymore?"

"Blame it on the media. They're always trashin' people," Rozalyn snapped. "Folks only talk about what's shoved in their faces daily."

"Yes. Chelsea, we'll blame it on you," Thad half-joked. "What exactly do you enjoy about the unmerciful news business anyway?"

"It's like practicing medicine and curing the sick. News is something everybody needs, and there's an endless supply of wrongs that need to be righted...or, at the very least, exposed."

"Well, didn't she, like, kill her husband or something?" Rozalyn returned to the topic. "I heard they were loaded, rich, and that lady just went ballistic when she found out her husband was sleepin' around with a chick from the projects."

"That's not entirely true. See, it's random know-nothings in the public who trash people with rumors! My station's been following the story for a week now. Everybody's trying to paint Carolina as this crazed killer, but it was a self-defense situation. To this day, she claims she loved her husband deeply."

Chelsea's tone dismissed Rozalyn, and she shifted toward Thad, tightly crisscrossing her fingers with his.

In turn, Rozalyn fluffed her auburn hair weave with both hands and much annoyance. She pulled down the hem of her short skirt and turned to face the window, deliberately bumping her meaty hip against Chelsea's little one.

When the couples arrived at the Ambassador, Chelsea insisted on paying the cab fare and made sure that she and Thad walked ahead of their companions all the way to the front row of the theater's balcony.

"Hey, isn't that Karma DePass and Roland Reynolds?" Rozalyn

whispered as they took their seats among the mostly dapper audience. "Over there. Look, Virgil!" She pointed energetically at the famous singing couple in the front row of the orchestra section.

Chelsea rolled her eyes and sighed. "Rozalyn, it's not unusual to see celebrities at such events, okay? It's not about being fabu—it's about the event. Even entertainers want to be entertained."

Thad pinched Chelsea, and Rozalyn pinched Virgil harder, each indicating to their significant other that tensions were rising.

When the house lights finally dimmed, Thad couldn't enjoy the tap dancers' footwork. The tapping, the singing, and the bucket drumming somehow got lost as he sat trapped between Virgil and Chelsea. Virgil's big arm hogged the armrest, and Thad frequently caught Chelsea staring at him. He looked at her. She looked away. She grabbed his hand, pulling it into her lap.

"Relax, I'm not gonna run off or float away, baby," Thad whispered, leaning over to kiss her ear while Chelsea giggled.

Thad looked down at the oneness of their clasped hands in Chelsea's lap, staring at the spot on her hand reserved for a certain sacred ring, wondering whether he had the courage to put it there. With the world around them enchanted by the performance on stage, Thad wanted to ask Chelsea about their passionate night following his graduation and, especially, what he thought he had seen on the floor near her vanity the day after. He wondered, but dared not ask, was that torn condom evidence of a sexual plot?

He looked at her. She looked away.

Questions lingered, but Thad simply played the goo-goo-eye game with Chelsea until the standing ovation. The stage curtain closed, as did Thad's willingness to swallow the possible answers to his questions.

Virgil, Rozalyn, Thad, and Chelsea hiked up the aisle toward the exit. Chelsea suddenly stopped, and Thad, still linked to her at the wrist, was yanked backward. The flow of traffic bottle-necked, bumping into them.

"Chelsea, what—" Thad's words were choked back by Chelsea's tongue rushing into his mouth in a rough kiss full of tender fear. Without a word, she led him through the doors of the Ambassador.

"That show was so damn cool," Rozalyn oozed as the four of them stood outside of the theater. "Oh my God, I've wanted to see it ever since Cheryl and the girls from the salon told me about—"

"Yes, magnificent," Chelsea remarked with authority, clipping Rozalyn's statement like a cheap coupon. "Savion Glover is bring-ing tap back en vogue, because it was a dying art in black circles. And Wolfe's direction is superb, as usual."

"The boys had hip-hop beats and kung-fu flicks at Caesar's place tonight," Virgil whispered close to Thad. "You're gonna pay for this."

"What are everybody's taste buds in the mood for?" Thad asked quickly, detecting Virgil's restlessness with the constant tit for tat between the ladies.

"Wanna go to Justin's?" Rozalyn suggested. "The crowd was talking about it."

"Yeah, who knows, perhaps Sean Puff-Daddy-P-Diddy Combs himself will be there tonight." Chelsea imitated a desperate fan, then swiftly dropped her voice to make the group's decision. "No, I'm in the mood for Chinese. There's a great place called Dragon Plate on Forty-fifth and Seventh."

No one responded, so Chelsea pulled Thad's jacket and began heading toward Seventh Avenue. Rozalyn rolled her eyes and grabbed Virgil to follow them.

A light sprinkle had turned the streets a shiny black. Nightlife was in full swing in Manhattan, the playground for love, adventure, and social pleasures of all design. Thad let Chelsea lead the way through the crowd of trendy young people and moneyed older folks playing under the lights of Broadway theaters and pricey restaurants. It was Chelsea's territory, so she designed the adventure while Thad wished he could blink his eyes and be in Brooklyn where he could be in control.

"This is your kind of place, Chelsea," Thad noted as they were seated at the Dragon Plate, a tiny room dressed in Asian grandeur mixed with gaudy American excess. "Everything in the room is trimmed in gold, and nothing on the menu is under twenty bucks."

After the waiter took their orders, Thad noticed Chelsea chatting with Virgil.

"So, to keep me off the streets, my Grandma Belle taught me to play the flute," Virgil said. "She had no idea how much more trouble she made for me."

"What do you mean? I think it's sweet." Chelsea smiled.

"So did all the neighborhood dudes. All of a sudden, I wasn't the one beatin' up scrubs. They were kickin' my ass for playin' a stick with holes in it, like a ghetto leprechaun. They were callin' me freakin' Flute-of-the-Loom."

Chelsea giggled heartily, as the waiter returned and served their meals.

Thad sat staring at the gold-trimmed plate in front of him for several minutes. "Once again, Chelsea, I have no idea what you've ordered for me."

"Oh, just eat it, Thaddeus. And have some of this," Chelsea shot back dismissively, sliding her glass of red rum in his direction. "I'm sorry, Virgil. You were saying?"

"I stayed with my brother, Melvin, until I was about nineteen.

I got a gig as a bouncer at this calypso joint called Funky Bayou, but the old dudes hated that all their old ladies wanted to take me to bed." Virgil flexed his arm muscle and winked at Chelsea. "So, I moved to D.C. to start over. I was selling gym memberships during the day and bouncing at night. But ever since I served my stint in the big house for aggravated assault charges four years ago, I've had a hard time gettin' anything other than construction work."

"You went to prison?" Chelsea gasped, Carolina Smithey suddenly on her mind.

"I was on lockdown in the big house on some trumped-up shit. I used to rumble in nightclubs back in New O. with chumps who misinterpreted my physical demeanor and rapport with the ladies, dig? I nearly broke a dude's neck, because his fox wanted to leave the bar with me," Virgil boasted. "That punk couldn't accept his loss graciously. It turns out he was an off-duty pig with a complex about his small nightstick, know what I'm sayin'? A freakin' white cop with a fine black fox! You believe that?"

Playing with the lumpy liquid dish on his plate, Thad whispered to Rozalyn, "Behold my stuck-up sorority girlfriend sharing a moment with my ex-con blood brother over dim sum. The odd couple, yakking it up like old neighbors."

"Talk about a Kodak moment," Rozalyn mumbled to Thad, sucking her teeth. "I want to slap Virgil whenever he tells those stupid stories."

"I'm just glad he's making her laugh, Roz." Thad took a slurpy bite of his dinner, longing for a footlong with extra ketchup from the rusty cart on 113th Street. "Besides, Virgil left that life behind when he moved to New York."

"He *claims* he did anyway," Rozalyn whispered, rolling her eyes.

After dinner, Virgil and Rozalyn went on their way, and Thad endured another tense taxicab trip back to the Upper West Side. A tipsy Chelsea wobbled with the motion of the vehicle, mumbling incoherently about the merits of reading to kids while they are still in the mother's womb. In his own world, ignoring her, Thad watched as the picture of the city through the window changed constantly, cafés becoming clothing shops becoming coffee houses. Reflection made him prime for a revealing conversation; the lingering questions needed answers.

Sitting on Chelsea's sofa with the living-room lights off, Thad told her, "That extra glass of red rum has made you delirious, but I wanted to come up and thank you for being so gracious tonight."

"Mmm-hmm," Chelsea hummed, laying her head on his lap.

"What do you think of Virgil? He's a pretty cool cat, right?" Thad played with ringlets of her hair. "Rush and I met him when we were sophomores at Howard. He was a hard-ass bouncer and wouldn't let us underage students into a club. Anyway, we chatted. Rush dug Virgil's musical interests and asked him to join his band."

"Yes, the thug past aside, he's really nice, great sense of humor. That Rozalyn, though, I'm not so sure about. She seems a little jealous."

Thad ignored Chelsea's usual assessment of other women. "Do you like Virgil enough to understand why I'm going into business with him?"

"Well…" Chelsea suddenly lifted up onto her elbows and hit Thad in the chest. "Hey, what's with all the damn secrecy, anyway? All you say is 'this business.' What business? You still haven't told me exactly what the hell you're getting into. Thaddeus, do you realize how that makes me feel?"

"Chelsea, if you want to share in my life after tonight, you best get hip to the neo-soul movement. I'm telling you what I'm doing. I'm trying to ease into it."

"Ease into what, Thaddeus? What is all this jive, seventies flower-power crap? Your father will never agree to some childish gig with your friends. Get real!"

"What the hell are you talking about, bringing up my father all of a sudden?"

"He and I care for you," Chelsea slurred slightly, almost falling off the sofa. "We don't want you making some senseless mistake. Thaddeus, don't stop being a real man now for some foolish boys' game."

With a pang, Thad's blood scalded the underside of his skin. He rose and stomped to the door. "Find me when you're ready to be a real woman that supports her man!"

"Thaddeus, wait!" Chelsea screamed, running after him in the dark and meeting a slamming door head on.

"Is that damn thing ready yet?" Chelsea snapped, applying another coat of polish to her thumbnail.

"A little longer, dear." Kayla went from the bathroom to the kitchen, reemerged with a carton of strawberry sorbet, and joined Chelsea on the sofa.

"It's been two damn weeks! No visit. No phone call. Not even a measly email. How dare that son-of-a-bitch ignore me?" Chelsea scowled. "Now he's screwing up my concentration at work *and* the perfect opportunity his father handed to him!"

"Girlfriend, why do you deal with it? For the umpteenth time, either use your kitty to train that puppy or cut him off like split ends."

"That's what I'm doing, honey." Chelsea blew at her fingernails. "If Thaddeus had a shred of gumption, he'd see that he's so much better than those ruffians."

"Speaking of ruffians, Saadiq is quite yummy." Kayla playfully licked the head of her spoon. "The guy who came to the door the night of Thad's graduation party, right? A dreadlocked dessert."

"Don't even go there, Kay. He is vile." Chelsea stood and placed her hand against a slinky red sundress that hung on the coat rack, making sure the nail-polish color matched.

Kayla rolled her eyes. Her sass bubbled. "Saddiq is vile, but Thad is a grand prize? Gimme a break, sweetie."

"Don't you dare compare the two. Look, Kayla, clearly you've been on edge lately, as have I, but don't speak on my man unless you get it right. Got it, sweetie?"

Kayla slammed her sorbet carton on the end table. "Okay, so what's the next move in your grand scheme, gingersnap?"

"Kay, you know I hate it when you call me that."

"Well, excuse me if I'm still spooked by that god-awful crime scene I saw a few weeks ago, and, on top of that, I have to put up with your Thaddeus shenanigans."

Chelsea sighed and sat next to her. "I'm sorry, Kay. I know you're still freaked out."

Kayla shook her head. "Oh my God, Chelsea. I can't even begin to describe what it felt like being in Carolina Smithey's bedroom. It hid all kinds of dirty secrets."

"Dirty secrets?" Chelsea lightly laughed off the statement. "Don't even dwell on it. Just get it out of your mind." Chelsea patted Kayla's knee. "Right now, I'm going over to Thaddeus's wretched place." She moved to the coat rack, slipped into her red dress and strappy, high-heeled sandals. "He hasn't told his father about his crazy plans. Hell, he hasn't even told me what the hell he's up to."

"He can't *confide* in you. That's what he said, remember?"

"Whatever. Thaddeus wants to pull a stunt and surprise everybody with his special little project." Chelsea fluffed her hair, as she headed down the hallway toward the bathroom. "I'm going to find out what he's up to and I'm gonna blow the lid wide open."

"This scheming, backhanded route is not really your style, Chelsea Elizabeth Fuller." Kayla paused and sighed. "On second thought, it is *so* you."

"The scorecard favors Thaddeus right now, so I need some major points, if only to repair my trust in him." In the bathroom, Chelsea spritzed herself with perfume. She looked at the device on the counter. "I can't wait for this thing. Keep an eye on it, Kay, and I'll call you for the results. Thanks, sweetie." Chelsea raced from the bathroom, grabbed her handbag, and planted a kiss on Kayla's cheek.

"Work him, girl! Wrap him around that pinky, and get the platinum around the finger next to it," Kayla rooted, rolling her eyes at Chelsea's back. "And say hi to Saadiq for me!"

On the subway to Brooklyn, Chelsea longed for the comfort of a Town Car. She would have even settled for the privacy of a taxi's backseat. A man smelling like a pack of cigarettes got on at Fourteenth Street and sat next to her. Holding her breath, Chelsea focused her attention on the children's hospital ad on the wall of the subway car. The baby in the picture smiled at Chelsea, and she smiled back. Chelsea couldn't take her eyes away from the curly-haired brown sugar on the poster, spellbound by a connection she knew would last only as long as the train ride.

When Chelsea arrived at Thad's apartment, a short woman in Afro puffs, a tank top, vintage jeans, and brogans, answered the door. Chelsea looked at her like suspicious women do. She peered inside and saw a familiar girl in a melon-toned kufi lounging on the couch.

"What's up?" the first woman greeted her. "Can I help you?"

"I'm looking for Thaddeus," Chelsea replied coldly.

"Coming in this time, precious?" the pretty, head-wrapped woman on the couch asked.

"The guys stepped out for a minute. They should be back soon. I'm Nenna, Saadiq's girlfriend," the first woman said, pulling the door wider.

"I'm Chelsea."

"Remember me? I'm Arianna." The other woman stood from the couch and turned down the reggae music to a whisper on the stereo. "I think we got off to a rocky start the night of the party."

"Yeah, I'm sorry." Chelsea switched tones, seeing potential allies in the room. "I was a little upset that evening. I had a lot on my mind."

"I live upstairs. I'm good friends with the guys." Arianna offered the visitor a seat. "I've heard a lot about you, Chelsea. You're studying to be a reporter?"

"I prefer broadcast journalist." Chelsea caught herself and put a cap on her attitude. "What do you two do?"

Arianna returned Chelsea's half-smile. "I'm a writer. I freelance for New York's urban magazines, and, right now, I'm also working on a collection of essays on issues relevant to black women."

"I perform with a group called Daughters of Destiny. We combine dramatics and singing," Nenna said, struggling to infuse positivity into her tone. She lit a bidi, watching Chelsea unenthusiastically bat her eyelashes and play with her earring. "So, it's great what the guys are doing, huh?"

Chelsea perked up. "Uh, of course! Tell me what you think about it, Nina."

Slowly and deliberately, Nenna blew a cloud of smoke in Chelsea's direction, and Chelsea hacked on the fumes like an old man.

"Um, Nenna, why don't you help me get drinks for us." Arianna jumped up from the couch, pulling Nenna into the kitchen.

"Girl, I'm not digging that Amazon's funky attitude," Nenna whispered loudly next to the refrigerator. "I want to smack that fake expression off her face."

"I feel you. You almost spit fire in there," Arianna said, cracking ice cubes. "Chelsea's a bit preoccupied, like she's up to something. Be careful what you say. Thad said he hasn't revealed everything about the business to her yet."

"Nina? *Nina!* Is that bitch on crack? I can see why Saadiq loathes her," Nenna seethed, grabbing the glasses. "That priss sickens me, sitting there with her skinny legs crossed like a two-bit supermodel. She'd better put that Ivy League education to use and exercise some respect, before I take her back to grade school."

"Yellow light, Nenna. Slow it down, girl." Arianna led her back to the living room.

"Here you go, *Shelby*." Nenna pushed a glass of ginger ale into Chelsea's hand.

Feeling droplets sprinkle from the glass onto her leg, Chelsea looked down at her lap quizzically. "Uh…thank you, sweetie. And it's *Chelsea*."

"Oh, did I make a little booboo on your dress? Forgive me," Nenna begged sarcastically.

"It's okay. Listen, um, I'll freshen up in the washroom and be right back." Chelsea stood from the sunken cushion of the tattered armchair and walked to the back of the apartment. She heard Arianna and Nenna laughing at her while she eased down the hallway with disclosure still on her mind.

Across from the bathroom, Chelsea spotted opportunity in an empty bedroom. She crept through the half-open door. Her eyes quickly scanned the room, darting from the bed to the bookcase to the concert poster on the wall, until she saw a stack of papers on a corner table. She scooted over to the table, pulled the chain of a tiki-shaped lamp, and rifled nervously through the official-looking documents, scouring for a clue.

"Oh my God!" Chelsea gasped. Under countless sheets of Freeman-Webber letterhead, she found restaurateurs' contracts and a liquor license autographed with the signatures of Rushon McKinney, Saadiq Abdul, Virgil Davies, and Thaddeus Carmichael, Jr. Chelsea's eyes fixed on the last signature, and she was filled with shocked anger.

Suddenly, the apartment's front door squeaked and a gang of male voices drowned out the sound of Chelsea's racing heart. She jerked to look over her shoulder, quickly rearranging the papers as she'd found them. Chelsea scuttled to the door of the bedroom, trying to pray her way out of the compromising position. Unable to see anyone from where she was hiding, she darted across to the bathroom with her breath stuck in her throat.

Once inside, Chelsea tried to compose her frazzled nerves. The sting of betrayal ate her skin as she stared at her warped reflection in the mirror. Suddenly, Carolina Smithey's image was in the mirror, forty and fuming. Chelsea shook her head violently and looked again to find Carolina gone. She pulled a bottle of pills from her purse and popped a couple of the relaxants into her mouth, fighting the urge to barge into the living room and rip Thad's flesh with her freshly painted nails. After a deep-breathing exercise and a lipstick reapplication, she emerged from the bathroom.

"Chelsea?" Thad replied, surprised to see the lover he'd been eluding.

"The ladies were keeping me company until you returned." The slender girl sashayed over to her man, working the sundress that accentuated her bust and buttocks. She grabbed Thad's arm. "Can we talk outside?" Chelsea led Thad out of the room as he handed a bag of take-out from Mekka Café to Saadiq.

Outside, Chelsea brushed a spot clean for herself on the stoop and sat next to Thad. She looked at him intently. Her voice lost the sweet quality that she'd exaggerated in front of his friends, turning sad and desperate. "What's going on, Thaddeus? You make intense love to me, then we argue. We go to a show to make up, we argue again, and then you avoid me, hanging with your ever-groovy friends, conspiring to take over the world. It's been *two* weeks. Tell me *something*."

He looked off into the distance. "I'm at my most comfortable here. It reminds me of my days at Howard where, for the first time, I felt the way the majority must feel every day. There's a certain empowerment in that environment. I split from your scene because those people in there are my link to the world I know."

"What about me? I'm a part of your world now, but you shut me out. For the life of me, I can't see why you're fighting fate. You were always so ambitious. I saw so much ahead for you and me. The path we were on—it shattered all the myths. What's happening to our future? What has our relationship become if we can't talk?" Chelsea put her hand in his. "Thaddeus, I love you. Do you still love me?"

A hope-crushing pause followed.

"Sure, there are things I love about you, but you can't change a person. I was being changed against my will." Thad released a frustrated sigh. "Whereas here, I'm surrounded by the people who don't judge me on my credentials or my lineage or any crap like that. Chelsea, you've got issues you need to deal with."

Chelsea looked away and bit her lip to keep from screaming. "Look, I've been reading Dr. Melanie Berkowitz's *Loving Endlessly*.

It's a modern relationship-building guide. She says all we have to do to make it work is—"

"Enough with the damn books, baby." Thad squeezed Chelsea's hand. "None of those self-righteous, so-called experts know a damn thing about what's happening here. They're talking to the WASP crowd. Chelsea, tell me how *you* feel for once, without holding the hand of some Ph.D. through his bestseller."

Chelsea gazed out into the street. Some of the people passing looked like people she knew, but many didn't because of the way they spoke or carried themselves, or the way they dressed or wore their hair. Somehow, a vast universe separated Chelsea from the barefoot kids playing stickball in the street; the tattooed teen blaring rap music from a boombox perched on his shoulder; the young women with over-styled ponytails and big earrings, licking on lollipops and walking with an extra switch of the hips.

"I know what you're thinking, Chelsea. But looking out there, I see life at its most vivid, energetic, and real. Somehow, I want to make you see what I see—that these people, and my friends inside, different as they are from you, are perfect creations of their Maker."

"But I want better for you than what they can offer, Thaddeus. I want better for us, something stable. Am I wrong for wanting my man to be successful?" Chelsea wept, resting on Thad's shoulder.

"Baby, confidence breeds success, and I'm confident that what I'm doing here makes me happy. I hate to break it to you, but success isn't born out of fairy tales about smart black people, meeting in the hallowed halls of academia, marrying into air-tight careers, and creating eugenically perfect children, all while reading *The Conservative's Guide to Buppie Living*." Thad shifted to look into her soul's windows. "I'm sorry, we're not the Huxtables. Hollywood dreamed up that fantasy in a box. Now, I've confided in you. I truly know what I want. Do you? The ball's in your court, but it's a sin not to go after that thing you want most." Thad kissed Chelsea's forehead and left her on the stoop.

Overcome, Chelsea raced into the brownstone but was halted in the hallway by the power of an imaginary, two-ton stop sign. From the vestibule, she heard Thad's friends laughing, living, sharing. The gates into their world of afro-consciousness, jam sessions, and political poetry were closed to Chelsea because her identity, sense of rhythm, and belief in "the cause" were questioned by each soul in that apartment. Chelsea turned and walked out to find the world she knew.

Heading to the subway in tears, she pulled a cell phone from her tiny purse and called Kayla. "What's the verdict?" Chelsea asked as soon as Kayla answered.

"Congratulations, girlfriend," Kayla replied. "It turned blue. You're having a Thaddeus Junior, *Junior*."

"I'll see you in a few," Chelsea said, choking and folding the phone. She balled her fists to contain her excitement, but she wore a country-fresh grin on her face for the entire train ride home.

Storming into her apartment, Chelsea ran past Kayla on the sofa. She checked the home pregnancy test in the bathroom. "You read this thing right?"

"Yes! Now tell me what happened on your information-gathering mission."

Chelsea released an ear-shattering scream and raced into the living room. She flopped next to Kayla, flailing like a giddy schoolgirl. With greedy eyes, Chelsea grinned, rubbing her flat stomach.

"Calm down, gingersnap," Kayla soothed. "What the hell happened?"

"Oh, Thaddeus wasn't home when I got to the brownstone. So, Saadiq's girlfriend and the girl who lives upstairs, Arianna, are commandeering his living room—"

"Is she cute?"

"Who?"

"Saadiq's girlfriend."

"She's decent. I mean, she's no calendar beauty, but put it this way, she looks like the kind of girl you'd think he would date."

"Oh shoot! One of *those* types?"

"Yes, honey. The very thing I knew Thaddeus would be exposed to living in that place, carousing with artsy, urban chicks into chunky silver rings and hip-hop. Ugh! Anyway, I thought I'd squeeze some dirt out of these chicks. Wrong! These atrocious bitches are diluting my program. Kayla, I wish you were there. We would've served them so much D.A.Z. diva shade, they would've choked on it, honey!" Chelsea spoke so fast she became breathless.

"Slow down, ginger."

"I digress. Anyway, these Angela Davis wannabes were giving up nothing, so I had to think fast. I figured if these chicks had already heard things about me from Thaddeus and Saadiq, I wasn't going to get far with them. Screw them. I decided to use my journalist's skills and get the goods my-damn-self. So, I creep to the bedroom and find all these papers on the game they're running. Kay, I gagged."

"Is it juicy?"

"On levels," Chelsea muttered, grabbing a pad and pen from the stationery kit in the coffee-table drawer. "I'm pissed! I think they're trying to start some sort of corny restaurant."

"That's not so bad. It's legal, depending on the menu. What are you doing?"

"Are you kidding? Can you imagine what kind of greasy-spoon

dive they would start up? I just don't see it working. Kay, he never even had the guts to tell me about this. That hurts like hell. Thaddeus will only be going down with those goons over my dead body." Chelsea scribbled furiously, penning a letter.

Dear Mr. Carmichael,

I have reason to believe your son is involved in questionable activities. You disapprove of his living arrangements with his friends in Brooklyn, and I'm in perfect agreement with you. I thought it fair to warn you of his attempt to undermine your authority by entering into a dubious business venture with his friends.

You're aware that I'm as concerned about his future as you are. I'd certainly hate to see him throw away his invaluable education by passing up the secure and gracious opportunity you provided with your solid family business for what I believe to be a ridiculous, capricious stab at a fly-by-night diner of some sort.

Mr. Carmichael, I implore you to help me dissuade Thaddeus Junior in this undertaking and convince him to reconsider these plans he's keeping from those who really care for him, before he falls deeper into what appears to be a big mistake.

Sincerely,

Chelsea

PS. I hope it was right for me to break this news to you. I could not stand for this deception to continue. Please, let me know how else I can help.

"I have one word for you: 'email.'" Kayla shook her head.

"The situation appears more serious this way." Chelsea sealed the letter in an envelope and put a stamp on it.

"Chelsea…um, I think it's cute how we became friends when we were young, because everyone told us we look alike, but now I'm seeing something in you I don't think I like, qualities and actions even I wouldn't resort to. At first, I blamed it on the pharmacy in your purse, but now I just—"

"Kay, you should've seen him," Chelsea raved, in a desperate-sounding whisper, her gaze pointed at a distant nothing. "The way he looked at me, the conviction in his eyes touched the softest part of me…but his passion wasn't for me." Her glassy eyes dropped to her navel. "But guess what? That's all about to change. Now Thaddeus Carmichael will have to direct some of that excitement toward this new life growing inside of me."

"Chelsea, I'm not sure I can join in this celebration. I was looking for the blouse you borrowed from me, and I found a ripped, used condom in your top drawer. I let you and Thad have the apartment to yourselves a couple of weeks ago so you could make up from the fight you had. But…is that condom what I think it is?"

"Kayla, Thaddeus drew the battle lines. Now, it's war." Chelsea stood, walked to her bedroom like a zombie, fell against her pillow, and sobbed uncontrollably until she sank into a heavy sleep.

4

SUPPER CLUBS AND SUCKER PUNCHES

"Birdie's visit is this weekend," Thad reminded his mother over the phone.

"That's all she talks about lately—" Mrs. Carmichael was interrupted by Thaddeus Senior yelling in the background. "Dad wants to know if you've been reviewing the company logs and registries he sent you. You know he's still upset about your living situation, Junior."

"Tell him I've looked over the damn books," Thad squawked, staring at the stack of material on Perennial Private Car and Limousine Service in the corner where it had been since he had received it. "How much longer must I speak to him *through* you?"

Close to the receiver, Mrs. Carmichael whispered, "He threatened not to allow Cynthia to visit you, but I convinced him that wouldn't help matters. Hold on."

An angry voice bellowed, "Junior, how's that apartment of yours?"

"Things are fine, Dad. I'm pleased that you can address me directly."

"Don't patronize me, son. Listen, I'll call you in a few more days to set up a meeting with a market researcher, so be prepared," Thaddeus Senior said without feeling. "Hold on for your sister."

Thad made silly faces at the people gathered in his living room stuffing invitations into envelopes. "Wow, that deep, father-son conversation lasted a record-breaking *two seconds*," he told them.

"Hey, Junior, I can't wait to see you. I've written two more originals, and I've been rehearsing when Dad's at work," Cynthia squealed in a whisper.

"You'll stay upstairs with Arianna. She and Nenna will prepare you for the big night. Are you up to it?"

"Better believe it," Cynthia replied. "Thank you, Junior. You don't know…no, you *do* know how much this means to me."

"I'll see you when you get here, Birdie." Thad smiled.

He put down the receiver and resumed helping Rush, Saadiq, Nenna, Virgil, and Rozalyn prepare notices with the date, time, and location of the launch of their arts and nightlife revolution. Benny and Kahlil had already rounded up a unit of soldiers to distribute countless flyers on the avenues of Manhattan and Brooklyn. José and Caesar had leaked the plan of attack via an email campaign. Arianna had used her media contacts to disseminate news of the pending invasion.

"Judgment Day is on its way. Armageddon is inevitable," Rush said, tossing another stack of notices Thad's way. "Tell Daddy to get hip to Soul. It's about to slap him in the face."

The weekend arrived, along with the mail. Heading to her fifth-floor apartment from the mailroom, Chelsea flipped through an assortment of junk mail and postal goodies. Suddenly entranced by a greeting-card-sized envelope from Thad, she dropped her bills, magazines, and coupon circulars on her coffee table. Meanwhile, an intruder entered the apartment and crept up behind her soundlessly. As she reached for a letter opener, Chelsea felt a jabbing thrust penetrate the center of her back.

Releasing a piercing scream, Chelsea jerked, swinging her arms wildly.

"Damn, girl." Kayla, in a pink sweatsuit, laughed hysterically, dropping her gym bag. "Be glad it was me. You left the door wide open. This is New York, honey. You can't do that."

"You scared the hell out of me," Chelsea snapped, her eyes inflamed.

"Saturday is cardio-funk class with the girls. Shola was pissed that you missed. She wanted to show you these hideous earrings Walé gave her. Don't tell her I said that, though." Kayla plopped onto the sofa and picked up the new issue of *Essence* magazine from the coffee table. "Where'd you go this morning?"

"Oh…I took that black Byron Lars trench back to Bloomie's."

"You said you loved it! You got a great deal on it off-season."

Chelsea's eyes remained on the envelope in her hand. "Right, um…"

Kayla put down the magazine and looked over at the coat rack where the black trench coat hung draped by a red silk scarf. "Girl, you didn't take Byron Lars back to Bloomingdale's, did you?"

"Huh?" Chelsea glanced at the coat rack.

"Next time, if you're going to lie, hide the evidence. Spill it, ginger!"

Chelsea stared at Thad's envelope, scratching her head and tapping her foot.

"Why on earth did Virgil Davies call here this morning and ask for you? What's going on in your world that I don't know about?"

Chelsea's mind snapped back to reality. "Oh, Virgil's call was innocent. After our double date at the theater a few weeks ago, we've kept in touch."

"Why?" Kayla's question made it seem inconceivable.

"Never mind that. I'll tell you where I went this morning, but you have to swear you won't tell a soul. Swear?"

Kayla's eyes narrowed. She slowly crossed her arms. "Tell me."

"I've been visiting Carolina Smithey in prison."

"What? You've gone to the Bronx to see that woman?" Kayla leapt from the couch and rushed over to Chelsea. "You went to see her, and she spoke to you? Everyone says she won't speak to the press."

"I didn't approach her as a journalist looking for a scoop." Chelsea backed away. "I wanted to get to know her. I identify with her in a lot of ways, as a person."

"She's a murderer! I went to her home and saw the bloody aftermath of what she did!" Kayla backed Chelsea all the way around the sofa. "How in the hell do you *identify* with her? Because she has money?"

Chelsea fell onto the sofa. "Well, no, not only that. Kay, when I saw this woman, the glass wall between us in the prison's visitor's room turned into a mirror. I saw my aged reflection staring back at me."

"I can't believe you. Chelsea, don't start this crap about seeing yourself in other people. That drives me crazy! That's how we so-called lookalike best friends ended up here together, remember?"

"I'm not kidding. When our eyes connected, woman to woman, we were ensnared in this wicked parallelism. I think Carolina felt it, too. I became more intrigued, because it was like getting a good look at myself in about twenty years, minus the tacky orange jumpsuit, of course."

"Chelsea, stop it."

"Get this. Carolina is a member of Delta Alpha Zeta. She's an only child, a Capricorn, and her husband was the only man she'd ever been with intimately."

"So?" Kayla sat next to Chelsea. "She killed the man. Now you feel this spiritual bond because she's in our sorority? Chelsea, I'm sure this breaks some sort of code or law or something. If anyone from the station finds out, you better believe they'll fire your ass."

Chelsea met Kayla's eyes. "That's exactly why they won't find out, right, Kayla?" She looked back down. "See, that's Carolina's beef with the media. They just want to get their claws into her, get some goddamn juicy exclusive and exploit her like the next tabloid headline of the week."

"Chelsea, I still have nightmares about the blood on the mirror and the white penthouse burned half-black," Kayla whispered. "Now you go and befriend some criminal who also tried to kill her murdered husband's mistress?"

"She didn't do that!" Chelsea sprang from the sofa and went to the window. She peeled back the sheer drapery and gazed out. The shooting pains in the lobes of her brain intensified as the sun went into her eyes. "Somebody tried to frame her."

"Yeah, right. Who?"

"She wouldn't tell me."

"Chelsea, the woman—"

"The woman was *raped*!" Chelsea screamed at the window. The sinful word sounded as if it had passed through a megaphone in a naked tunnel decades long, echoing in the space between them before fading out. Chelsea turned to Kayla. "Feel bad enough now? Or maybe if I told you that her daughter died of sickle cell anemia at the age of twelve?"

Kayla was quiet.

"After her daughter's death, Carolina folded into herself and wouldn't let her husband touch her for nearly three years." Chelsea spoke through tears. "She told him she was tired of being left all alone in that fancy penthouse, but he was too busy with business to care. Turns out he was also busy digging in the slums for the sex she wouldn't give him, and Carolina found out about it a few months ago. She told her husband she was willing to forgive him for the affair in time, but he couldn't wait and forced himself on her."

"I'm sorry." Kayla sank back into the sofa, shaking her head in utter confusion. "How can a husband rape his own wife?"

"It's possible. Michael told Carolina she could no longer control the right he had to her body as her husband. He told her that she couldn't have it both ways. She couldn't tell him not to get sex somewhere else and then tell him he had to 'turn himself off' when he climbed into their bed. But she just wasn't ready to welcome love back in her life, especially forced love."

"I feel like such a jerk." Kayla softly pounded her palm against her own forehead. "I'm so sorry, Chelsea."

"Keep it between us, and don't worry about it." Chelsea sighed, slowly opening the mysterious envelope and pulling out the card inside. "Oh my God!"

"What's that?"

"Read it," Chelsea snapped, throwing the card at Kayla.

Kayla threw Chelsea a pissy look as the card bounced off her chest. "Wow, this is cute." Kayla admired the card's front decorated with a design of an African mask on a wooden table before a microphone stand. On the table, a bowl containing a half-eaten mango sat next to a wine goblet. The letters *NRK* were carved on the table's surface. Opening the card, Kayla read aloud:

You are cordially invited to the Grand Opening of
Nubian Rhythm Kitchen
A New Perspective on the Cosmopolitan Supper Club
Dine on the universal flavors of
African, Caribbean, Spanish, Creole,
and American Soul Cuisine.

Unleash your inner cultural enthusiast every evening
with instrumental roots music, performance poetry, soul concerts,
orchestrated oratory, and acoustic a cappella.
Experience the scintillating vibes of
Subconscious Soul
and the showcasing of raw, radiant talent.
Saturday, July 4 at 8 p.m.
1220 Seventh Avenue in Brooklyn's Park Slope
Nubian Rhythm Kitchen: A Nubian Eden with an Urban Edge

"Chelsea, I'm the last person to throw kudos at Thad's feet, believe me, but, honey, this is amazing. If the actual supper club is as classy and professionally done as this invitation, then—"

"I know, damn it!" Chelsea screamed, gripping tufts of her hair in her hands. "The thing looks freaking fantastic. That's the problem. His new-age, black-hippie shit is so top-of-the-line glorious, he'll impress everyone and convince them he knows what the hell he's doing. And I'm supposed to do back flips? Ugh, I can see it now—some aboriginal hole-in-the-wall, where tragically hip folks gather to vibe to groovy compositions, and eat gumbo with forks shaped like afro picks. I just don't get it." Chelsea was frantic, pacing and yelling incoherently.

With thinning patience, Kayla chirped, "Um, gingersnap, the wild outbursts? You need to hold it down and get a hold on yourself. We do have neighbors."

"Could you stop with the *gingersnap* shit?"

"Excuse me?"

"Look, I'm sorry, Kay." Chelsea went over to the window and peered out onto the city again.

Kayla stood behind her. "I've seen the ballistic bitch come out of you before, but this is definitely a new level of fanatical. I mean, this psychodrama and the little girl's victim act is pathetic. We're not going to have another Earl episode, are we?"

"That was a long time ago, sophomore year of undergrad. This is different."

"You lost it with that one, ginger. Chelsea, you chased that boy, but you weren't giving Earl anything in the sack to stay for. You know how men think, or now you should after what Carolina Smithey told you. Earl didn't deserve you, but you still pined for that sucker until King Thaddeus came along. Now look at you."

Chelsea faced Kayla with blood-red eyes. "In the beginning, it was me pushing Thaddeus along. I fed his damn ego and laid out all our future plans, when he couldn't even face his father. Now he wants to pursue something that spits in the face of everything I worked for. I'm supposed to shut up and back him up? Hell no!"

"You got what you wanted. You're pregnant. Now, he gets what he wants. That's how life works, honey. You can't get something for nothing."

"Kay, he wants what he wants *without me*."

"Girl, you are well aware that I'm a fourteen-carat dog trainer, but a diamond leash can't fit every man's neck. Thad's a stubborn ox with his head stuck in a creativity cloud. You know this. So his capers should no longer put your panties in a tizzy. Now, you can either have your platinum diva card revoked and give Thad his props, or shorten that skirt and go fight for your man. Just quit trying to win an Oscar with this dramatic performance."

"That's your pep talk?" Chelsea wiped her eyes.

"I respect your problem, but I don't have the answer. Nikki broke up with Tyler like last week, because he was paying her no attention. Follow her example and eliminate the stress, girl. It turns out Tyler has become fascinated with a culture other than his own, and, according to Nikki, Thad's crew influenced him.

Look, I have to get ready for my date with Kendall," Kayla said, heading to the bathroom. "I hope you heed my second set of advice. Just eliminate the stress."

Chelsea's brain pains multiplied. The phone rang, and she let it ring, digging through her purse for her precious pills.

"Chelsea, I received your letter," a commanding voice called over the speaker of the answering machine.

Chelsea jumped at the phone, yanking it up. "Mr. Carmichael?"

"Chelsea, I got your letter. I had a sinking suspicion Junior was up to something when he moved in with those guys in Brooklyn."

"I've tried to talk to him."

"I know you have. Listen, I'm catching a morning flight to New York tomorrow. We'll straighten this out." He paused. "Damn, I could just kill that boy!"

"Me, too. I'll do anything to save Thaddeus from making a grave error where his future is concerned. I know you've tried hard to make sure he's responsible enough to help your family business grow."

"Well, I try my damnedest." Thaddeus Senior sighed with anguish. "I realize you've been a stable support for him, Chelsea. Junior's always had this godforsaken rebel quality, which he got from his mother. He's always got something to prove!"

"Have you heard anything else from him lately?" Chelsea asked, looking at the card in her hands and hoping her letter had reached Virginia before one of the impressive supper club invitations did.

"No! And now he's got my teenage daughter out there, filling her head with all kinds of fluff. I don't want her being exposed to all of this bullsh—" Thaddeus Senior managed to stop himself. "Look, I'll see you tomorrow, okay?"

"Okay, I'll be waiting, Mr. Carmichael." Chelsea popped her

pills and settled herself deeper into the sofa, rejoining the second chapter of *Eating for Two: A New Mother's Guide to Positive Prenatal Practices*.

The next day, Brooklyn's streets still sizzled with its authentic sights and sounds. Chelsea and Thaddeus Senior burned under the Sunday sun, encountering barking dogs, bare feet, bass-bumping stereos, and barbarous laughter, as they walked uncomfortably along the block from the train station to Thad's more subdued street. They climbed the dingy stairs to the entrance of the brownstone. Chelsea pointed to the door where loud, jazzy music was coming from and allowed Thaddeus Senior to proceed in front of her. Thaddeus Senior pounded on the door with brute force, but to no avail.

"Is it always like this?"

Chelsea nodded resolutely to fuel the old man's assumptions. Thaddeus Senior turned the knob, and they entered Subconscious Soul's rehearsal session. The air throbbed with competing tribal drumbeats, unctuous blares from a sax, a fluttering flute and mellow musings in a velvety baritone voice. The flow faded, and the band members stopped mid-number, staring at the uptight visitors in their loose landscape—Thaddeus Senior in a linen suit and straw fedora, Chelsea in a spruce white outfit and big sunglasses.

"Mr. Carmichael," Rush said, as women poked their heads in from the kitchen to see why the drumming and poetry reciting had stopped.

"Rushon, where is my son?"

"He's upstairs at Arianna's."

As the visitors turned to leave, Chelsea removed her glasses, rolling her eyes at Saadiq with enough venom to kill the soul of every soul brother in Brooklyn. All the young men exchanged glances.

"Damn, you cats feel that negative energy? That man sucked all the good vibes out of the room." Virgil shook his head in disbelief.

"It was the kiss of the spider-woman with him," Saadiq replied.

"The uprising starts early. Thad better take this opportunity to stand up to his old man, because it's too late to punk out now. Resume play!" Rush called. "Keep it focused, Benny. I want to hear you French-kissing that flute this time, Virgil!"

In the brownstone's upstairs apartment, Arianna yanked her headwrap from her head and threw it at the monitor as her braids spilled from the unraveling cocoon. She jumped up from in front of her computer. "Who the heck is ringing my doorbell so incessantly? You killed my thought!" She opened the door. "Chelsea?"

Thad turned from his stack of business papers on the dining room table.

"Arianna, this is Mr. Carmichael. Mr. Carmichael, this is Arianna." Chelsea introduced them as though they were dinner party guests.

"How's this one?" Cynthia asked, strolling out from the bedroom, holding a black gown to her chest. She halted at the sight of her huffing father. "Daddy?"

"Let's leave them alone to talk," Arianna suggested nervously, holding Cynthia by the shoulders and leading her back into the bedroom.

Thad rose from the chair as the two men, alike only in name, locked eyes. An even match for once, Thaddeus Senior consumed the room with his stature, while Thad counterattacked with confidence.

"I guess she's shown you the invitation, Dad," Thad spoke

coolly, glaring at Chelsea. "You couldn't have received the one I sent home to Virginia already."

"Damn an invitation! I received a frantic letter from this poor girl, begging me to get out here immediately because you're involved in all kinds of craziness. Junior, I want to know what the hell is going on here, and I want to know *now*!"

"Letter?"

"Are you opening some foolish diner or something?"

"What letter, Chelsea?" Thad hissed at Chelsea, who cowered behind Thaddeus Senior like a tattling sibling. "What? Are you two in cahoots with each other?"

"Junior! You need to be more concerned about me right now!" Thaddeus Senior shouted, inching closer to his son. "The goddamn point is you've been lying to everyone! How long did you think you'd keep this from me? What the hell were you thinking?!"

"Dad, first of all, it's not a diner. It's a supper club. Let me explain."

"I don't give a flip if it's a supper club or a diner's club or a damn dinner theater! Junior, you've been hiding this whole underground operation. Did you honestly believe—"

"Shut up and listen for once, damn it!" Thad pointed a finger square in his father's face. His voice trembled as his words hit Thaddeus Senior like a Mack truck. "Yes, it was wrong to keep my plans from you, but that's all ex post facto! This was something you never could've stopped. And you sure as hell can't stop it now. You can't live my life. I won't let you!"

"We've been through this! You got your way when it was time to go to college. I backed off and let you go to Howard, for godsake."

"'Let me,' hell! I *chose* that! I was being brainwashed into becoming a stiff-shirt, bourgeois Republican. I needed a sanctuary and a dose of hard-boiled reality!"

"Junior, I've had enough of this guilt trip!"

"I colored outside of the lines, and you'll never let me forget I turned Daddy's well-defined maps into a comic book. Well, I'm bringing something of my own to the table, rather than settling for what's handed to me. But if that MBA I just got pleases you, then so be it. The two of you can go sit on it!"

"Damn you, Junior! You ingrate!" Thaddeus Senior exploded. He was in his son's face. "What about Perennial? You had me busting my ass to help you expand the damn company for your sake!"

"Oh, no you don't. That family business expansion was *your* plan! For so long, you couldn't separate Thaddeus Carmichael, Sr., from Thaddeus Carmichael, Jr.! According to my tally sheet, it's my turn to control my life again!"

Like a bullet, Cynthia shot out of the bedroom and jumped between the two most important men in her life, fearing the big man would strike the spunky one. She gave Chelsea a foul look. "Why are you just standing there doing nothing to stop this?" Cynthia struggled to push her towering father backward and onto the couch. "Would you two stop? I can't take it anymore!"

"Sorry, baby girl. Your brother is stabbing your father in the heart."

"Daddy, don't say that." Cynthia snatched an invitation from the table and stuffed it into her father's hand. "Look at it. Junior did this all on his own. The card is for *his* business. You want him to be just like you, Daddy, but he's not. Be proud of him. He's doing a good thing," She got up, grabbed Thad's hand and led him over to his father. "Daddy, meet your successfully independent son," she said, forcing their hands together, introducing them for the second time in their lives. "After what happened to Brandon, don't let our memory of his tragedy be in vain," Cynthia whispered with her dewy eyes closed.

In a vise grip with his son, Thaddeus Senior stood slowly. He couldn't bear to look Thad in the eye.

"From one Columbia man to another, one businessman to another, one Thaddeus C. Carmichael to another, I just want your respect. That's all. Will you be on hand for the opening of my business, like I was there for yours?" Thad's sincerity rang a crystal clarity into the room; the resounding hush begged an answer from the big man.

Chelsea waited with bated breath.

"Junior, your mother and I will fly up on Saturday to see this empire you've built, albeit out of spite. But, if it crumbles, if you fall, I won't be there to pick up the pieces." Thaddeus Senior faced his son with a mixture of anger and defeat in his eyes. "A Columbia man, a true businessman, a strong-willed Carmichael would do that for himself." He released his son's hand, kissed his daughter's cheek, and left the room, taking his doubt with him.

Thad wrapped his arms around Cynthia, squeezed hard and sighed long. "It wasn't a pledge of full support, but I didn't expect that. Thank you, Birdie," Thad kissed her. "This is for you and Brandon and me, all of us."

"Thaddeus, I have something to say," Chelsea shyly interrupted.

"So much for confidence in a traitor! I don't want to hear a goddamn thing you have to say, you conniving bitch!" Thad grabbed his papers from the table and slammed the door on his way out of the apartment.

Chelsea dropped into an armchair. "Can you believe the vicious thing he just said to me?"

"You don't even realize what just happened, do you?" Cynthia asked as she sat across from Chelsea. "I mean, didn't you feel the mountain of emotions being stirred up between those two?"

"Who's Brandon?" Chelsea whispered, leaning into Cynthia.

"Help me make sense of this situation. Why do I feel so outside of everything?"

"Oh my God. Thad never told you?"

"Here we go again." Chelsea lowered her head. "No."

"Daddy's been grooming us into a dynasty. Brandon, the oldest, would have been the politician. Thad was the business tycoon, and Daddy still thinks I want to go to medical school. But he doesn't know when to stop, you know, like where his life ends and ours begin. Anyway, Brandon would rather have been the most valuable player than the senate majority leader." Cynthia picked up the supper club invitation from the table and studied it. "It exploded when it was time for Brandon to go to college. Grambling State wanted Brandon for their football team, but Daddy refused, because his contact at Columbia could get Brandon in good with their political science department."

Her eyes full of questions, Chelsea stared at the teen girl.

Cynthia sniffled. "It was a sunny Sunday like today. Daddy and Brandon had been fighting all morning, because Brandon never put the Columbia application in the mail. Brandon couldn't take the weight of Daddy's iron hand anymore. So he overdosed on steroids and committed suicide. He was so pumped with bad blood he ran headfirst in a Heisman stance, with his favorite football tucked under his arm…right smack into an oncoming truck on a Virginia freeway."

Cynthia paused to dry her eyes. "Brandon wanted to go out with glory, in his own way. That's why the Nubian Rhythm Kitchen is necessary. Thad says if he must go, he wants to do it *his* way." Cynthia placed the invitation in Chelsea's French-manicured fingers and left the room, leaving Chelsea alone with her tears.

Independence Day. Underneath a blue-black sky speckled with stars, the air was still. The smell of exotic dishes fanned out from the supper club's kitchen and caressed that air, stealing it from the strength of after shave and fragrant body oil. Jittery nerves hid under cotton shirts and fine dress pants. Hands danced in pockets, wiping sweat from palms and reaching for keys or coins to jangle.

"I never really celebrated the Fourth of July until today," Saadiq thought aloud, looking up into the dark sky.

"There was nothing to celebrate before," Virgil replied. "Just a bunch of firecrackers and bogus parades that don't mean a damn thing to people like us."

"Today, our Revolution begins. The neo-soul nation celebrates our independence," Rush explained.

"We did it." Thad grabbed each of his blood brothers for a hug.

The past week had been hectic, preparing for battle: finalizing last-minute details, signing up performing acts, assembling a staff, purchasing supplies, and approving menus. That night, the first cannon was fired, and the doors of Nubian Rhythm Kitchen opened for business. Saadiq's aunts managed the kitchen crew. Kahlil's and Benny's friends served as the waiters, and Virgil convinced Rozalyn to moonlight as the hostess.

Meanwhile, in crisp new threads, pacing in slick shoes on the grit of their newly colonized sidewalk in the trendy section of Brooklyn, Thad, Saadiq, Virgil, and Rush stood guard outside of NRK. They greeted refugees seeking asylum from the interment camps of "the other side."

Thad straightened up when he saw his parents amongst an approaching crowd. "Good evening. Welcome to Nubian Rhythm Kitchen. Enjoy a unique dining and entertainment experience," he spoke with the smoothest diction, ushering his folks to the door.

"Hi, honey." Mrs. Carmichael smiled, tossing her shawl over her bare shoulders.

"Junior." Thaddeus Senior grabbed the lapels of his suit and popped his blazer tight, nodding a salute.

"Go ahead. Get inside and see what I've been hiding from you."

"Okay, okay." Mrs. Carmichael patted Thad's chest and grabbed her husband's hand, pulling him inside. Crossing the threshold, they were neither in Norfolk nor New York anymore, but in Nubia, a land handsomely furnished in an endless blend of fine woods.

Resting on a gleaming hardwood floor that stretched to all corners of the room, an arrangement of mahogany tables set with bamboo chairs faced an unassuming lacquered stage. A lone microphone stood center stage, and a faint red spotlight warmed the area artists would soon grace.

A cherrywood bar lined with antique cast iron stools sat on an elevated deck in the back of the club. The back wall of the bar was a watery landscape, an illuminated wall-sized glass tank, housing a bevy of tropical fish. Intricate carvings of African-inspired motifs adorned wood panels lining the rustic mud brick walls. Reproductions of the carvings were engraved on the pine doors of the men's and ladies' rooms, where a Masai warrior statue guarded one side of the entranceway. A Sphinx of Gizeh protected the other.

Ethnic art was featured in a mini-gallery to the right of the club's entrance. A teak rack and a small glass showcase displayed handmade crafts for sale by local artists. Buttery leather cushions rested on the chairs and kente print placemats lay on the tables. Vine plants crept up walls, hugged the lip of the stage, and wrapped around table legs. Palms sprouted from Egyptian urns in every corner. Overhead, Art Deco lamps powdered spots of the room in soft light. Completing the ambiance, faint, infectious drumming crept from speakers on the stage and sweet incense burned in pewter dishes on the bar.

Thaddeus Senior reemerged from the club's entrance. He marched outside and faced Thad with an expression of reserved pride. "How did you do it, son?"

"Those guys who were 'doing nothing' had time on their hands and figured they'd help me. Virgil controls the bar. Saadiq books acts for the stage. Rush manages the gallery." Thad pointed to his troops who were conversing with their own families. "It also took a lot of dreaming, praying, secrecy, and, since I oversee the books, a Columbia education."

A gleam filled Thaddeus Senior's eyes. "I can respect that, Junior."

Mrs. Carmichael appeared outside just in time to hear those words she and Thad had longed to hear. She touched Thad's face with the gentlest kiss. "Honey, I don't recall a funeral, but I feel like I'm already in heaven."

"Me, too." Thad grabbed his mother close to him while his father folded large arms around both of them. For Thad, the moment could've lasted forever as he thought of Reggie's desires for his own son. Thad cursed himself for forgetting to invite the old security guard at the Exchange Building to join in the celebration. "Go on inside. I have a table near the stage waiting for you."

"What the hell?" Saadiq whispered as a well-dressed huddle of three couples approached the club. "Check this out, Thad."

"She can't be serious," Thad grunted, staring at the group led by his woman.

Chelsea's hair was pulled back in a tight shiny bun. Her make-up was flawless, creating a glamour doll come to life. Her tawny, spaghetti-strapped dress was a second skin blending so perfectly with the first, Thad could tell she was wearing no underwear.

"Who the hell is this?" Thad referred to the white man escorting Chelsea. As they got closer, he realized the man was Tyler. A changed man, the new Tyler sported a deep tan, buzzed haircut, and goatee.

Chelsea purposefully ignored Thad, introducing her entourage to his colleagues. "Hi, guys. These are my friends from Columbia. Kayla Harmon, a fellow journalism student, and Shola Oyamolé is studying nursing. These are their escorts Kendall Washington and Walé Akinsola. They're med students. And you all know Tyler McDermott." Chelsea finally looked in Thad's direction. "Tyler's going into the textiles industry."

Rush, Virgil, and Saadiq greeted the women and shook hands with their dates. An overanxious Tyler gave them a grip handshake like the soul-brothers use, but he said nothing to Thad, who glared at Tyler with visceral anger.

"Congratulations, Thaddeus. Thanks for having us," Chelsea whispered extremely close to his face, as she walked into the club on Tyler's arm.

"I knew that was coming," Saadiq grumbled. "She's officially crossed over."

"Thad, your boy played you like a punk. *And in your own house?* Want me to take care of milk boy for you?" Virgil pounded his fist into his palm, laughing hysterically.

Thad shooed Virgil away. Rush shook his head and walked into the supper club with Virgil.

"Wipe that crooked smile off your face, Saadiq."

"I'm not taking pleasure in your pain." Saadiq rested his arm on Thad's shoulder. "But let's face it, we all had a feeling Chelsea preferred vanilla shakes. Don't sweat it. You needed to cut her loose a long time ago."

"I know," Thad mumbled. "I can't take her hot-and-cold games anymore."

Saadiq led Thad inside. "Trust me, don't lose your cool on this exceptional night. I've been thinking about your plight all week, especially after Chelsea summoned Daddy to New York to give you a spanking. Come with me. I want to introduce you to someone." Saadiq took Thad backstage where the evening's performers warmed up.

"What are you up to? I just want to be left alone right now."

"Thad, this is Asha Dare," Saadiq said.

A leggy woman in a body-length, batik-print sarong that tied at the nape of her neck and revealed her defined back and arms, rifled through a duffel bag. She turned around in a graceful spin.

"Asha, this is Thad Carmichael."

"Hi, Thad." The willowy girl with doe eyes and silky eyelashes offered him her hand. "It's nice to finally meet you."

"Hi, Asha. It's a pleasure meeting you," Thad replied, noting how her shortly cropped, natural hair gave her cheekbones to the world. Her mocha skin had an endless sheen, and she smelled like fresh cocoa butter and apples.

"She's the genuine article, baby," Saadiq whispered in Thad's ear and slipped away.

"So, Saadiq's been ragging on me already?"

"More like *bragging* on you. He mentioned something about intelligence and a big heart. Does that sound about right?"

"He's been *lying* about me?" Thad said, making Asha giggle.

"Thanks, I need to laugh. I'm so nervous."

"What are you doing this evening?"

"I'm a dancer."

"'*Dancer*.' I love the way you say the word, with that air of artistic credibility. Calm your delicate nerves. You're home. Relax and your talent will flourish."

"It's the New York crowd. I'm a transplant from Atlanta, about a month now. I met Saadiq and Nenna at BAM, and Nenna invited me to join Daughters of Destiny. So, I choreographed routines inspired by the pieces the Daughters are performing tonight. I feel like the standards are so much higher here." Asha sat in a folding chair, nervously playing with the wooden bracelets on her arm.

"No, that's *your* audience out there, Asha. Don't focus on regional affiliation, just the universality of art, okay? It's all love here. I'll be rooting for you." Thad winked at her as he headed back to the club's main room.

Asha smiled. "Thanks."

Thad passed Cynthia and Arianna on their way backstage. "Good luck, Birdie," he whispered.

Thad joined his partners in the club, and they circulated through the sea of supporters in host mode, introducing themselves, asking if meals were satisfactory, and thanking people for their patronage. Suddenly, the drumbeats in the club gave way to a jazzy avant-garde suite. Thad smiled, looking over the clientele as they swayed to the milky sounds soaking the room. He was pleased that the event had materialized just as he had pictured it. A veritable grab bag of New York's nightlife crowd was in attendance—high-society types, neighborhood folks, hip-hop enthusiasts, artists, college students, culture buffs, entertainment industry insiders, and a few buppies thrown in for good measure. The atmosphere was electric and beautiful.

"Excuse me, Thaddeus?"

Thad strolled toward the booth from where the voice had drifted, and he came face to face with Chelsea and Tyler. He glared at them as an angry volcano within him began to bubble.

"My goodness, Thaddeus! Can we get some decent help around here?" a tipsy Chelsea snapped. "I needed another red rum and a Beaujolais ages ago!"

"This isn't the damn Primrose Café, Chelsea! Wait for your server to put up with your crap." Thad walked off, hearing the insidious laughter of Kayla, Kendall, Shola and Walé erupt from their booth.

Witnessing the scene, Rush approached Thad. "I see Chelsea and her cronies are overdoing the splendid time routine, yapping about meaningless drivel and faking arrogant chuckles."

"I ought to kick those peckerwood and Pollyanna asses out of here." The expanding veins in his neck made Thad's collar tighter than a headlock.

"Now you sound like Virgil. Let it go. Remember where you are. Just keep the parents and the phony cronies separated, and try to enjoy yourself a little, too. Deal?"

"You're right, Rush. I won't play her game. Not tonight. No, sir. I'm in Heaven." Thad heard footsteps running up behind him and felt a tug on his coat. He turned around. "What the hell do you want, Judas?"

"Yo, Thad. Let me explain, man." Tyler's face was red, his eyes big.

"Cut the *urban* act, Ty! You've already got the black Barbie doll to play with. What else do you want?"

"Thad, don't be like that, man." Tyler reached for his shoulder. Thad pulled back. "Damn. How could you, man? All the time I was sharing a black perspective with you, I never thought you'd up and adopt my freakin' lifestyle, and my leftovers at that! What would your Christian Right parents say if they saw you right now?"

"Chelsea begged me to come as her date." Tyler perspired, pleading his case. "She said you insisted I be her escort tonight, because you'd be busy working. I thought you were cool with it until I saw your heated reaction when we first arrived and then just a minute ago."

"Even if I never trusted you, at least I used to respect you, Tyler."

"Thad, man, you've got to believe me. The longer I sat there with those fools, I realized what was going down. I had no idea she was playing me to play *you*!" Tyler struggled to spit out his sentences. His tanned face was apologetic as his arms worked in stilted gestures. "It's not even like that with Chelsea and me. I had to break out from there. It was getting weird. Chelsea's been downing gallons of red rum, and she keeps watching your every move, saying crazy stuff to Kayla about how tonight's *the* night."

Thad put his hands in his pockets and shook his head. He sighed. "I believe you. At this point, I'll believe anyone before I defend Chelsea."

"I guess you two are on the skids. Thad, I think she's up to no good."

"Ty, I'm sorry. The girl makes me paranoid, and now you see why. Come here, fool." Thad grabbed Tyler close to him and rubbed his shaved head. "What is this? Why are you going *homeboy* on me?" He laughed, heading toward the stage.

"I respect the culture." Tyler used Rush's favorite words, relieved to see Thad smiling again.

"Where the hell is Nikki?"

"I had to let that go, man. Nikki couldn't hang." Tyler shrugged. "I'm opening my eyes to a lot of things, man. She wasn't ready."

"Sounds familiar," Thad mumbled, walking Tyler to his parents' table. "Is the smoked salmon to your liking?"

Mrs. Carmichael nodded, while Thaddeus Senior gave the meal a thumbs-up.

"You remember Tyler."

"Hi, Tyler," Mrs. Carmichael said, offering him a seat.

"Junior, where on earth is Cynthia?" Thaddeus Senior inquired roughly, wiping his mouth.

"I'll go get her right now." Suddenly, Thad appeared on stage, smiling and summoning his partners to join him. "Welcome to Nubian Rhythm Kitchen. My partners and I invite you to kick back, relax, and marinate in the artistry on this stage tonight. I'd like to christen the supper club's grand opening with a very special first act. Ladies and gentlemen, fly away with the enchanting Ms. Birdie!"

The audience applauded as a woman sauntered on stage and held them in a teasing moment. Her red gown and ruby-studded headwrap glowing, she raised an arm with the slowness of molasses. Then Benny's sax pushed its sexy, sweaty burn into the club. With the mood right, Ms. Birdie captivated the crowd with two jazzy numbers, serving kitten purrs, snazzy scat, and candy-sweet cadenza like a classic diva. In one fell swoop, the songbird's closing dedication, "Daddy's Daughter," lifted the emotion in her throat on angels' wings and earned Ms. Birdie her name.

"I've come to the end of my vocal journey," Ms. Birdie announced, fanning herself. "I'd like to thank my brother Thad for helping this young bird to spread her wings. I flew to Mt. Happiness and back, and he provided the sky. I'd also like to thank my parents for their love and Brandon for his inspiration. Good night." Ms. Birdie left the stage in a whirl, a bit older than her seventeen years.

Mrs. Carmichael was misty-eyed and Thaddeus Senior searched for words as Thad rejoined their table.

"Junior, who was that and where's her St. Katherine's of Hope school uniform?" Thaddeus Senior finally asked, putting an arm around his trembling wife. "Barbara, you okay?"

"Relish this moment. You just saw Birdie's dream realized. She was incredibly nervous about your reaction, Dad. Please don't take this away from her."

"That's why she was tweeting around the house last week." Mrs. Carmichael rubbed her husband's fingers, their golden circles of commitment reconnecting on the table. "She's a woman now, Cole. With her songs, Birdie was trying to say a lot of things she hasn't been able to express, to you in particular. I hope you listened."

The spotlight dawned again, bathing the stage in a golden glow. Rush, Saadiq, Virgil, Benny, and Kahlil surfaced in the light in dashikis and white linen. They introduced themselves as the featured act, Subconscious Soul. Their family, friends, and local fans went wild, showering them with a genuine love.

Deepening the love vibe, Rush performed a libation "in honor of lost loves and high hopes" before donning his poet's cap. "And now, righteous brothas and sistas, cool cats and foxes, Subconscious Soul will bring the house down with rhythmic, ancestral grooves. Saadiq's and Kahlil's meaty drumming will pump the heartbeat. Big Virgil's playful flute will tickle your ears. Little Benny's liquid-like sax will rub the whole thing down, as I, prophet of Gil Scott-Heron, stir you with potent vocal stylistics," Rush declared, as the younger women in the club swooned. "I shall recite 'n' ignite, preach 'n' teach, as I describe the vibe, and rhyme on-time, taking the soul on a hip trip, with powerful poetry, lucid lyrics, and veracious verses."

The crowd's applause was deafening.

"Subconscious Soul is composed of disciples of the neo-soul movement, spearheading another renaissance of black expression. The only membership requirements are openness, creativity, and common values in the struggle for consciousness. Join us," Rush invited. "My first piece is called 'Seeing Is Believing.' See if you believe what I spit."

The instruments' sounds tiptoed in, ready for the words.

Rush cleared his throat. "Seeing is believing. See, cloudy vision can screw you like a power drill if you let it. Believe it, you can get drunk off anything, party people—hegemony, haberdashery, hot toddies, hot 'n' horny horseplay. The big H-bomb is ticking while you drown in your own Heaven or your own Hell. For yours truly, my penchant is for a cool dip in euphoric hash hedonism…in hemp for days, esoteric bliss in the form of jazz at midnight and existentialist chit-chat under blue lights. But don't be fooled by the features or blinded by the bomb-diggitiness. There's a brain in this pretty head. And I, for one, know that even the prettiest party people can be pushed to the edge…to the utter boundary of irrationality…to the critical point where atrocity and Christmas parties are one and the same…where black-berry wine and a kick in the ribs are a sensible combination… consequence is a foreign word…and two scoops of vengeance sprinkled with violence is a justifiable dessert. We all ain't truly happy at this party, people. So, keep your eyes open. Believe."

In a bold, nasty performance, the band displayed its artistic guts to the audience—words, spoken and sung, over drumbeats subconsciously bursting skin, sax squeals subliminally ripping flesh and flute notes psychically peeling back the raw excess to expose every listener's soul to the burning acid of emotion.

By the time Subconscious Soul closed its set, Thad had ascended to another place, riding on a comfort cloud. He remained on that higher plateau until his eyes fell on Chelsea across the room. Then he gave up the driver's seat as she took the reins, forcing her sexiness, and the things she could do with it, into his mind.

"Damn, the last time I saw eyes like that was graduation night, when she lured me back to her apartment and screwed my brains out," Thad whispered to Tyler. "She knows exactly what she's doing. See, this is where I'm supposed to get itchy in the privates, explode, rip her clothes off and give her an angry bounce right there on the table. That's what she wants."

"That's how she kept eyeing you earlier, man. That's it!" Tyler insisted through stiff lips. "Man, if looks could kill…"

Thad watched Chelsea whisper to Kayla. While everyone else in the club had just been ripped open and had their souls bared by Subconscious Soul, the expression that Thad considered Chelsea's mask of insensitivity to black rage had remained intact. Her gaze stayed affixed on him—fire in her eyes, sex on her lips and booze in her posture.

Suddenly, Thad awoke to Saadiq at the mike, explaining how he had helped to groom the next act. "My brothers and sisters, please welcome a troupe of wise women on the move, Daughters of Destiny!"

The lights came up on Nenna, draped in African garb, Jackie, in a power suit, and Felicia, in a sporty windbreaker, assuming poses relevant to their attire.

Nenna stepped into the spotlight, reciting a poem about rising from the salts of the Motherland. Asha leapt out from the darkness, swirling and stretching in spider-like movements—a panther in a black catsuit, the slick fabric hugging every inch of her frame, accentuating each line and curve. Thad watched Asha's eyes, her lips, her hips. He stole a look at Chelsea, who was looking at him look at Asha.

Onstage, Felicia stepped forward, rapping fiercely about female membership in the hip-hop generation. Asha shifted to a funky mood, replete with jerky thrusts and sultry pumps. Mesmerized by Asha's taut, gleaming muscles, Thad felt himself stiffen below the belt. With each extra-low dip or exaggerated back bend of the limber dancer, more hot thunderbolts of agitated blood hardened the awareness in her admirer's briefs.

Jackie then took to the front and methodically read a business report, "Top Story—Women in the Workplace: The Trials and Tribulations." Asha became a cyborg with sharp robotic movements, abrupt gestures making her breasts and tight buns bounce. By then, Thad was in an awe-stricken trance. His appreciation bordered on gawking. He shifted tensely in his seat to hide his arousal, realizing ashamedly that he was sitting with his parents.

Reluctantly relieved to watch Asha end her performance, her skin aglow with a well-earned, womanly sweat, Thad applauded, thinking piss-rotten thoughts to bring his privates back to normal in that public situation. He glanced over and saw Chelsea stumble to the ladies' room just as his parents stood from their table.

"Junior, honey, your father wants to leave."

"So soon, Mom?" Thad whined. "Birdie's still backstage."

"We'll wait for her at the hotel. I don't want to get back to Manhattan too late. I have some business calls to make to the West Coast. I'll send the driver back for her," Thaddeus Senior said, pushing in his chair. "It's a shame we didn't get to see Chelsea tonight."

"Yes, something came up." Thad laughed nervously, throwing eyes at Tyler.

"Thad, the place is gorgeous. We're so proud of you." Mrs. Carmichael gave him a kiss. "And Birdie, her voice has grown tremendously. She was fantastic!"

While Saadiq introduced the evening's final act, Thad hustled his parents to the front door, keeping an eye out for Chelsea. Once Mr. and Mrs. Carmichael were gone, Thad wiped his brow. He spotted Asha at the bar. "You were outstanding."

"Thank you. You didn't see my legs shaking, did you?"

"Believe me, you were incredible. Name your drink. Something exotic?" Thad asked, walking behind the bar.

"Just water, thanks." Asha leaned over the bar, trying not to smile too much.

Thad slid Asha a glass of ice water and positioned himself to study her. "Where did you learn to move like that?" He leaned in a little closer.

Asha looked away with schoolgirl coyness and froze with her eyes still averted. "Um, Thad, do you know this girl staring at us?"

"Yes, I know her." Thad sighed and came out from behind the bar.

Chelsea supported herself against a stool and peered at them. She slowly inched toward them, teetering and tottering with a drink in her hand. She was obviously coming apart at the seams. Wisps of her hair fell out of their place in her bun, a strap of her sexy skin-dress hung off-shoulder, and lipstick stained her pearly white teeth.

"I need to talk to you," Chelsea snapped.

"Go talk to your country-club clique," Thad replied through clenched teeth. "I'm speaking with a real *lady* right now."

"You. Who the hell are *you*?" Chelsea tripped as she spun around, looking Asha up and down with venomous eyes.

Asha waited a second or two, weighing her options. Then she stood and scooted past Chelsea with her head hung low. Looking apologetically at Thad, she whispered, "I better take off. Saadiq has my number. Maybe we can talk some other time." Asha trotted off hurriedly, leaving cocoa butter and apples on Thad's mind.

"Who is that bitch?" Chelsea slammed her drink against the bar, shattering the dainty glass, as Saadiq appeared, grabbed Thad by the arm, and led him away. "Thaddeus!" Chelsea shrieked, red rum coating her forearm and dripping from her trembling fingers.

Stuffing two more tens in his back pocket instead of in the cash register, the bartender, Melvin, looked at Chelsea from behind the counter as if she were crazy.

Meanwhile, Saadiq pulled Thad into a huddle with Rush and Virgil. "Asha's the sun dipped in black, right? She's groovier than a jazz record. Don't deny it. Her down-home aura is a refreshing antidote to Chelsea's uptown attitude."

"All right, Asha's cool. And Chelsea's turning into less of a prize every day, but only I can give the woman her official walking papers, Saadiq. So don't celebrate like you just won a bet with yourself." As the four men walked to the stage, Thad explained the Chelsea-Tyler situation. "I have a conscience, so before I get involved in anything new, I've got to tell Chelsea things are over."

"Are you for real? You're letting Chelsea go?" Virgil asked. "I like her, man. She's got a lot of fire."

"That's what I'm afraid of." Thad sighed, as they climbed onto the stage.

Rush took the mike. "Looking over this supper club, I can't help but marvel. For, in this pocket of Brooklyn, New York, a collection of minds and souls gathered to bask in the non-toxic rays of culture and community and cuisine. In one breath, folks beckoned here were listening and learning and eating and laughing and conversing and connecting. It's truly beautiful. We'd like to thank our patrons, friends, and families for celebrating a successful opening of Nubian Rhythm Kitchen with us. Thanks to our wonderful performers and staff, and everyone is invited back to dine and vibe at NRK. This place is for you, my people. Thank you."

As a throng of people left their tables and migrated around the stage for hugs and handshakes, Chelsea trudged onto the stage, pushing past Saadiq and Rush. She cleared her throat at the mike. "Um, excuse me, everyone. Excuse me. Tonight, we're celebrating more than one special occasion," she slurred, as Thad tried to silence her with one hand and escort her away with the other. "I'm Chelsea Fuller, Thaddeus's fiancée, and I'm pregnant with our first baby! We did it, honey!" Chelsea yelled, toppling onto

Thad in a sloppy embrace. She wet his cheek with saliva-drenched kisses, while the microphone crashed to the stage floor and awakened the room with an ear-piercing feedback squeal.

The group of bystanders cheered for what seemed to be charming news. Thad looked at his friends as shock tried to fight its way past the paralyzed layers of the rest of him. Suddenly the universe spun unforgivably. Thad was yanked out of his mind and body and, from outside himself, watched the swirling chaos— his friends' drop-jawed expressions, Chelsea's alcoholic breath on his face, the crowd's clueless cheers, the stinging words that seem to echo endlessly. Thad determined that madness was destined to be his best friend. Formal introductions had just been made.

5

SIN AND EVEN MORE SIN

Brooklyn awoke to the sounds of clapping thunder the next day. The sky had opened its bellows, belching a wrathful boom, and the world's roof, ashy and angry, spat wet needles against every New York borough. Inside, barely guarded from the rain's spikes by the brownstone's walls, Thad wondered whether the news from the night before had brought it on, had caused the heavens to cry a descending wall of thorny tears onto the earth, had aggravated the impulse for the sad, sad Sunday.

"Man, I knew it. I knew it. I knew it. I knew it."

Thad rested his face in his hands. "Shut up with the *I told you so's*, Saadiq—"

"Where's Virgil? He said he was coming by this morning," Saadiq interrupted Thad's frustrated patter. "The rain probably scared him off."

Rush closed his tiny box of performance-enhancing grass and placed it back on the windowsill. "So, what are you going to do, Thad? This is major. One minute you say you're ending the relationship, and the next, Chelsea's your pregnant fiancée?"

"That fiancée business is crap!" Thad shot up from the couch and paced around the room, catching incense ashes and pizza crumbs on his bare feet. "I'm glad my parents weren't there for that twisted exhibition. Or Asha, for that matter."

"Which head are you thinking with, Thad?" Rush declared.

"The one popping seeds in one woman and pulling up to the bumper of another? Or the one trying to run our supper club and please your parents?"

"Yeah, and who's to say she's telling the truth?" Saadiq ranted. "I mean, weren't you taking precautionary measures?"

"The kid's mine. I'm the only one she's been sleeping with." Thad walked slowly to the window. "I was expecting this any day now."

"Funny, when she announced it last night, you looked like you'd been struck by lightning."

"Rush, Chelsea planned the whole thing! She set me up the night of my graduation party. She got me back to her place and seduced me!"

"Seduced you?" Rush threw his hands up. "Why would your own woman, who's giving you skins anyway, have to *seduce* you?"

"The blindfold. The condom. I knew she was up to something!" Thad turned to yell at the window. "She's been off the pill due to side effects from her migraine medication. Since the rubber's mandatory, I get pleasure from having Chelsea put it on."

"You don't just pull out?" Saadiq was horrified.

"No, all right? We both felt that condoms were safer."

"A man can't feel a damn thing with those raincoats on! I mean—"

"Shut up, Saadiq," Rush interjected, eyebrow arched. "Wait a minute, Thad. Go back to the blindfold part."

"Chelsea's into rough sex. That night, we got hot and heavy. She whips out a blindfold, ties me up, and turns out the lights. I heard her rip open the rubber with her teeth. Later, I thought I felt her take the thing off, but we were so into it, and she was working like she wanted to break me in half. Damn her!" Thad smacked the glass. "You know how it is when women intoxicate men with their authority. You can't think straight. I couldn't stop! We argued the next morning and when I stormed out...I thought I saw a cut-up condom next to her vanity. I just didn't want to believe it."

"Blindfolded and blindsided," Rush sighed.

"You literally got screwed by this girl. She made sure this would happen, one way or another. The psycho tried to play Tyler against you last night, now this?"

"Saadiq, you should watch out too," Rush warned, lacing up his shoes. "Kayla was checking you out last night. She's got an evil love jones to whip on you."

"No way. I won't let a bourgeois girl sex me up so she can steal my jimmy hat while we're doing it, and then tell me she's having my love child as some sick way of keeping our ankles chained together."

Thad spun around. "Shut the hell up, Saadiq!"

Rush hopped to his feet. "Thad, I'm going with Saadiq on this one. Between love and madness lies obsession. Chelsea is mad about you and obsessed with you. Even if you don't buy the science fiction of it, deal with the reality before you get blindsided with another suckerpunch. She was determined to have you, and now she does."

Thad sighed, his friends' words rubbing coconut-sized grains of salt into his wounds. "I'm going to have a serious talk with Chelsea right now."

"Do that. We'll be at the club setting up for open mike tonight. We'll be expecting you, Thad. And Virgil, if we can find him." Rush grabbed his keys and walked out of the apartment.

"When you see Chelsea, be sweeter than syrup, dig? Baby-talk her, mentally wine and dine her. Hell, suck her toes if you have to. Just convince her not to have this kid. You're not ready, and especially not with that nutcase." Saadiq scribbled on a chewing gum wrapper, handed it to Thad and walked out with an order:

"When you finish wiping Chelsea's nose, make use of that."

Alone, Thad felt smothered by the enormous silence. The sky cracked a whip of lightning, and more rainy daggers beat the side of the brownstone.

Crack! Again, moist nails thumped against the outside walls, and a mind-busting slideshow was on fast-flash in Thad's head: *Chelsea with a huge belly; Chelsea on a gurney, screaming with her legs spread wide open; a baldheaded baby girl with a golden spoon in her mouth; his own ankle chained to Chelsea's; himself on the ledge of a tall building with the crowd below yelling, "Jump!"…*

Falling against the couch, Thad jolted back into reality. "There's no way in hell Chelsea Fuller's giving up a baby my seed created," he whispered into the air, as his vision focused on the wooden mask on the opposite wall. Its sharp features staring back at him, the mask tilted precariously, silently daring Thad to drop his mask first. Instead, Thad looked at the crumpled wrapper in his hand. From within its folds, Asha's phone number blazed in red ink.

As Thad approached Chelsea's apartment building, he saw Virgil dashing across the street and into a cab. Or, rather, from where Thad stood underneath a big umbrella, under falling sheets of water, the man's jacket and body size closely resembled that of his friend. *But why would Virgil be in this area?* he thought.

Breezing through the building's lobby, Thad barely waved at the rotund doorman who hardly nodded back from under his cap. Thad didn't connect with the Norwegian counterpart of Reggie the security guard—no small talk about the weather, no chats about politics, no laughs about life. Whenever Thad visited Chelsea's apartment, a weak wave was all he gave the doorman, and a flimsy nod was all he got in return. Somehow, it was enough for both of them.

In the small, mirrored elevator, Thad only had five floors to assemble the necessary guise and coat of armor to deflect the on-slaught of his lover turned enemy. He watched the lighted numbers change. Two. Three. By the fourth floor, he was ready. On the fifth floor, he marched down the hall, shield and mission in tow.

In a pretty peach tank and shorts, Kayla opened the door and quickly slammed it shut in Thad's face. "Chelsea, come get this person away from our doorstep!"

Chelsea, slightly crusty in mid-hangover and a red robe, opened the door, grabbed Thad's hand, and kissed him. "Good morning, honey."

"Kayla, I'm in no mood for your crap today," Thad muttered as Chelsea led him past the sofa to the back of the apartment.

"Kiss my ass," Kayla spat, flipping channels to the Style Network.

Chelsea closed her bedroom door and sat next to Thad on her bed, playing with his ear between her fingers until he jerked away.

"What the hell were you thinking bringing Tyler to the club last night?"

"He's applying to be an honorary blood *brother*. I figured I'd initiate him, give him a little taste of jungle fever to get him in good with your associates."

"Don't screw with me, Chelsea!"

"Thaddeus, I'm joking. Look, I did it to make you jealous, okay? I wanted your attention…because I love you. You know, forevermore, like we promised?"

"All you did was make me look like a fool the entire night, first with Tyler, then with the girl at the bar, and then your crazy announcement on stage! Fiancée, my foot! Luckily, my parents weren't there to hear that shit."

"Stop it, Thaddeus."

"What's with all these damn pills?" Thad asked, pointing to the pastel tablets sprinkled across Chelsea's bed. "And what's in this stupid journal you're always scribbling in?" He snatched up her sacred diary.

"Stop interrogating me! And give me that back," Chelsea screamed, retrieving her private printed thoughts from him.

"Was Virgil just up here?"

Thunder crackled outside, and a breeze pushed through the open window and up against the ghostly dancing curtains.

"No, uh, why? What would Virgil be doing up here?"

"We use protection when we're together. Who else have you been laying up with? Tell me!" Thad knew the answer, seeing her physical evidence against him laid out on the night table—the home pregnancy test; the ripped, aging condom; the red, silk blindfold.

"When we made love on your graduation night, the condom broke!" Chelsea threw herself on him, sobbing. "You know I haven't been with anyone else!"

"Yes, you have," he said in a whisper, his eyes on the red scarf. "A blind me."

Meanwhile, Kayla crept to Chelsea's bedroom door. Overhearing Chelsea's pleas and promises of fidelity, Kayla, too, wanted to know why Virgil had been in the apartment when she woke up.

"So what do you want to do about the pregnancy, Chelsea?" Thad struggled to stand and free himself from her grip, falling against a stack of Chelsea's books on the desk. Her recipes on how to love, live, think, eat, and breathe crashed to the floor, along with a picture frame.

"What kind of question is that? I just called my parents. They're upset about the timing, but they're expecting us to get married, which we were going to do anyway. That's the kind of family I come from. Thaddeus, I'm keeping this baby."

Outside, a whip cracked, and more water poured from the sky.

While the ghost at the window danced wildly, bits of glass crunched under Thad's shoes so he couldn't move. The rain outside washed impurities out from beneath the city's concrete shell, suddenly exposing truth clearer than glass. Thad looked down at the broken picture frame that had fallen to the floor. It held a photograph taken at the height of their romance, a flashback to earlier strawberry-and-cream days—Chelsea's hair a little longer, Thad's eyes a little wider. Though jagged cracks cut across their two-dimensional smiles, a guise broken made Thad feel lighter.

On that rainy Sunday, Thad's eyes were as wide open as they could get, and Chelsea's hair was a mess.

"Once upon a time, your love was strong enough to blind me. Like you did that night. But now I see you, Chelsea. I see you." He smiled. "My mind's been fighting what my heart already knew. Now, reality's rocking me with a brain-quake the size of your lies, baby. It's heavy, but, hey, now I know what I've got to do. So, it's great. I'm officially a father, and I'm proud of that, despite the circumstances under which this child was conceived. I want you to have the baby, Chelsea, and I'll tell my parents the news—myself!"

"Oh, honey, you'll see; the three of us will be so happy together."

"Oh no." Thad ducked out of the way of Chelsea's embrace. "There's no 'three of us.' Our child will have two loving parents; we just won't be together."

"Thaddeus!" Chelsea was stung. "Your little cat-and-mouse game is really ticking me off. This news was supposed to pull us closer together!" Again, Chelsea attempted to get her hands on Thad's body, but his denial pinched her nerves and crossed signals in her mind.

"Face it, Chelsea. We're through, finished! Forget forevermore! It's over between us, except for my child you're carrying. Damn it, I'm sick of playing emotional hardball with you. You downed my friends and my aspirations. You betrayed a trust, and you get off on playing jealousy games. I can't be in that kind of sick relationship!"

"Get real. You don't respect *my* friends or my 'highbrow' goals. You've deceived me since we met, and you get off on playing hard to get—always wanting me to chase you!" She brought her voice down. "I'm willing to forgive you, so you should do the same. Thaddeus, let's put all this behind us and focus on rebuilding."

Outside, the storm raged on. Inside, in her eyes, Thad saw the Chelsea Fuller with whom he'd fallen in love—the innocent girl who believed in fantasies, waited until twenty-two, and trusted him enough to let him take her precious pearl. Daddy had told Chelsea to wait for a good one, a strong, ambitious one. Thad was all of that to her and vice versa. But, suddenly, truth rubbed alcohol on the open wounds of newly unmasked hearts, because neither knew whose façade had tricked whom. Thad shook away the candy-coated nostalgia, warding off his inner romantic fool who just wanted to wrap his arms around Chelsea and kiss her eyelids.

"I'm sorry. I'm no saint, but, Chelsea, you've been even less of an angel. It could never last. I'm wood, and you're fire. And I'm tired of getting burned."

Kayla took her ear and herself away from Chelsea's closed bedroom door.

Astonished, Chelsea dropped to the floor. "You sinner," she whispered, gazing at the bruised memory in the picture frame at her feet.

"What?"

"I said you're a sinner," Chelsea spoke in the softest voice. She looked up at him, her eyes wetter than the rain. "Remember your big philosophical speech? You said it was a sin not to go after that which you want most, and that means in *all* ways. Right? I tried. You didn't. So, you're the goddamn sinner, Thaddeus Carmichael, Jr."

"Chelsea, baby, I tried, but…" Thad's mind was a yo-yo. His integrity was attacked, and the verbal judgment hurt more than a physical flogging. "Look, I'm not sure what you're accusing me of, but you've done some really twisted things. Something's different about you, and I can't be around you right now. Maybe one day down the road I'll resolve this so-called 'sin' within myself, but, as of today, I guess what I want most is something else. Not you."

Thad reached for the doorknob, his soul doubting his words, as Chelsea grabbed Dr. Rubenstein's *You're a Winner, Now Prove It!* and hurled the book at Thad's back. The sting in his spine spun him around. Surprise etched on his face, Thad looked into Chelsea's rabid eyes.

Suddenly, Chelsea sprung up from the floor and leapt onto Thad like an attack dog, beating and slapping and clawing him, screaming bloody solecisms. "You sinner! You can't deny me, Thaddeus!"

Thad wrestled with Chelsea, squirming until he finally wrenched her off of him and onto the bed, round tablets of relief flying in all directions. With her face in his, Chelsea leaned into Thad, biting into the flesh of his lip. Grimacing, Thad yanked away, leaving strains of blood in her mouth and strands of his shirt under her fingernails. He slammed the bedroom door in a frenzied flight toward the living room and ran smack into Kayla.

"She's crazy! The girl is out of control," Thad wheezed, rubbing his throbbing lip. "She attacked me! She's lost her mind!"

"Get the hell out of here, now!" Kayla plowed into Thad's chest, barreling him down the hallway.

"She's crazy."

"Get out, you sorry son-of-a-bitch!"

As the sky deepened to gunmetal gray, streetlamps flickered on like birthday candles in celebration of the rain's end. Still tense, Thad walked down Seventh Avenue, tucking in a new shirt that had replaced his devoured one. Over the horizon, he saw Nubian Rhythm Kitchen. The golden neon sign rested on a hut-like awning, and a marquee announced "Spoken Word Open Mike Night."

Suddenly, his shoes could fly again. Thad's pace quickened to a sprint, his boots licking the wet sidewalk in time with his heartbeat. He skillfully dodged random puddles oozing from the cracked sores of the pavement like pus filled with more of Chelsea's accusations and assaults. Reaching NRK's entrance out of breath, Thad admired his personal Jerusalem from the outside until the aroma of Jamaican sausage lured him inside.

Stacking glasses and coasters at the bar, Melvin insisted, "Virgil, when are you gonna slip me some of the bread you cats are makin' with this place? Let me get some of that stash."

"Stash? Fool, we opened the place *yesterday*," Virgil snapped, fiddling with the cash register. "We're not even turning a real profit yet. Besides, it's not just my money, so I'm not giving you a damn thing."

Melvin threw a stack of napkins at the back of Virgil's head. "You've got brass balls now that you're hangin' with these pretty college cats?" Melvin snatched Virgil around, pushing his five-foot-seven frame against Virgil's six-foot-two mass until the register slammed shut. "You betta watch the tone you take with me, sucker!"

"Chill out, Mel," Virgil whispered through frozen lips, his breaths turning to quick heaves. "Look, the guys are right over there. Don't make a scene."

Melvin looked across the room, where Thad stood talking to Kahlil and Saadiq as they dragged big couches from backstage and arranged them around a microphone and stool in the center of the club. Melvin slowly took the heat off Virgil, backing away and wiping the spit from his lips with his sleeve. "You may be three times bigger than me, but I'm still your big bro, Virgil, and I'll kick your ass if you keep poppin' off at the mouth."

Virgil stared into his brother's beady eyes. "You're already living with me and Roz. I got you this bartending gig. What else do you want from me, Mel?"

"First off, don't forget who was feedin' your ass back home, before you went big-time bourgeois, playin' that sissy music with the Boys' Choir of Harlem over there. Yeah, I'm livin' off of you and your bitch now, but I'll be gettin' out of y'all's place in a minute. As a matter of fact, my boys Cedric and Jojo mentioned comin' up north to start somethin' over in Jersey."

"Something like what?"

"Never mind that! All that matters is I'm strapped for cash, baby bro." Melvin's eyes got tighter as he extended a hand low under the counter and waited with a frown on his face.

Breathing deeply, Virgil waited in a useless standoff for Melvin to drop his hand. The hand stayed. Virgil turned around and punched the register. The drawer shot out. Virgil snatched up two hundreds from the tray, slammed it shut, and slapped the crisp bills into Melvin's palm.

"That's right, baby bro. You call those cats your blood brothers, but we're *real* brothers, *real* blood. We're family, and blood's got to look out for blood." Melvin snickered as Virgil stomped away.

Saadiq adjusted the mike stand in the center of the club. "Talk to me, Thad."

"I called my parents and told them everything."

"What? Why the hell did you do that?"

"Because I want Chelsea to have the baby, and don't give me any lip about it, Saadiq! I got enough of it from them. They think I should marry her."

"I didn't say a word," Saadiq sang. "But I bet Big Pappy Carmichael lost it."

"My father's convinced I'm officially a crazy, rebellious child. Like I planned this," Thad replied, helping Kahlil set a bamboo bench before the mike.

"Are you going to marry her?" Kahlil asked, roping off the presentation area.

"I can't do that and be happy. I'll be in my child's life, not Chelsea's. It's over."

With a satisfied smile, Saadiq went to the bar to burn incense as the leaders of the dinner crowd dwindled into the supper club. Ignoring the customers as they walked into the entrance, Virgil stood at the front door with his hands in his pockets, cussing like a sailor under his breath.

"Hey, Virgil, what's up?" Thad asked, easing next to him.

"Nothing!" Virgil's eyes didn't leave the front door.

"*O*-kay." Thad paused. "Oh! This morning, we were looking for you—"

"Why are you guys always trying to trail me? I'm not obligated to check in with anybody. I'm not the one you need to keep tabs on anyway. Your man Rush is in the alley, and guess what he's doing. That's right. Puffing on hay. Why don't you go chase him for a little while, huh?"

Virgil's defensiveness prompted Thad to back off and approach Saadiq in the club instead. "What's wrong with Virgil?"

"Don't know. Why?"

"Never mind. Where's Rush?"

"He's out back with Benny partaking in a little ganja action."

"He knows I don't like that, especially not here."

"Cut him a little slack. He told us not to tell you anyway." Saadiq pulled Thad aside. "Look, forget Rush. Did you make use of what I gave you this morning?"

"Why are you treating me like I'm in need of some kind of fix?" Thad gazed pensively at the entrance of the club. "The answer is yes. She's supposed to meet me here tonight. I hope she shows. On second thought, I don't." Thad pulled away from Saadiq. "I don't know why the heck I called that girl."

"Sure you do." Saadiq patted Thad's back. "When I met Asha, I knew she was perfect for you, man—sexy, good energy, talented, from worthy roots, right?"

"Most definitely, Asha's good people. But I feel like I'm skipping the mourning period. I just ended a serious relationship. Saadiq, there's a lot of emotionally charged stuff left between Chelsea and me."

"Explain that to that pretty little face over there." Saadiq pointed to the front door where Asha stood.

Thad barely moved. His feet took slow, uncertain steps, telling him to stop and think twice; but his leg muscles told his feet to pick up the pace, to walk him over and escort Asha away from the swelling crowd to a table in the corner.

After they ordered drinks, Thad cleared his throat and waited to see who should start. He sighed. "Asha, about last night…"

"You don't owe me any explanations, Thad."

"Yes, I do. Chelsea and I just ended a long relationship, and I just discovered that she's having my child. She feels she has a right to my time and attention, whereas I'm trying to move on from the idea of us as a couple."

"Well, are you going to support the baby?"

"Of course, by all means. Just clearing up any confusion."

"Oh, thank you." Asha smiled at the waitress who set a jumbo daiquiri in front of her. "I'm actually fresh out of a relationship myself. He was a real easygoing man from Nigeria. We danced together in Atlanta, and he taught me everything I know." Asha crossed her chocolate legs and looked down at her leather sandals. "Turns out, he was giving private lessons to a number of other girls in his class."

"Sorry to hear that. None of my relationships have ended due to the wandering eye. I guess that's something to be proud of." Thad slid his mug of lager back and forth across the wood grain of the table. "Anyway, we're both at similar junctions, right? Live and learn." He lifted his glass. "To new beginnings?"

Asha raised her daiquiri with both hands and clanked Thad's mug. "Definitely. To new beginnings."

Thad sipped his drink, staring at Asha's silver jewelry glinting in the mood lighting of the club. He bit his sore lip, trying to fight the feeling below his belt. "Tonight is open mike for poets. You do the spoken word thing?"

"Oh, no, no, no. I'm strictly dance. I express myself best through my body." Asha raised her arms in a swan-like motion, while Thad's eyes agreed with her. "I don't do words. That's Nenna's thing. She's doing a couple of pieces tonight."

"Rush is reading, too. The man's a lyrical genius, a real poetic soldier. It's such a cool talent to flow like that. His next project is an urban poet's society of spoken word artists called Vocal Cords that'll teach kids the value of poetry. Kahlil will be drumming between sets and accompanying the poets' performances."

"That should be a nice touch, the drumming and the words dancing together. We held readings like that at Spelman. The brothers from Morehouse College would come over, and we'd gather in the student union and just vibe. It was deep, seeing those men open up like that and share. The flavor was so *real*, you know?"

"I love your connection to the basics. I mean, conversations were never like this with Chelsea. Asha, you don't understand. Debating the nutritional value in soul food versus the Primrose Café menu, or the spring selection at Barney's versus Saks, or vacationing in the Hamptons versus Colorado Springs, gets old." Thad paused. "Asha, listen to me, ranting about the ex already. I'm sorry. So, you attended Spelman? What's it like going to school with all those other women?"

"Of course, there were instances of major drama, but I found a place for myself and met some cool sisters. Morehouse is right next door, so we weren't sheltered, but it was a big change from living under my parents' roof and going to a performing arts high school. I learned a lot. I just graduated, early actually."

"Early?" His voice changed. "How ol—um, what did you study?"

"Philosophy. Took summer classes to finish in three years. All I want to do is dance. Came to New York to see how the big kids do it before I conquer a dance academy in Paris that I dream about attending. My dad didn't want me to leave. He's scared for his little girl. You know, bright lights, big city? I'm getting all of my adventure-seeking out of my system while I'm still young. I'll be twenty next Saturday."

Twenty. He swallowed the number. "Oh…cool. Well, I went to Howard undergrad. I studied business, and just got my MBA from Columbia."

"I know. Saadiq told me. Columbia, that's impressive."

"Thanks. I'll be twenty-six next month. Fortunately, I've already created my dream business, so I'm feeling pretty good about this accomplishment."

"This place is totally righteous, Thad. Gosh, sometimes I wish the whole world was just like this place. You know what I mean? Like, I wish people didn't have to travel to discover—what do you call it, African Heaven?"

"A Nubian Eden with an Urban Edge." Thad smiled.

"Ah, yes, a Nubian Eden. I dig that! But I wish we just lived in this, like, in a Nubian Rhythm *World*, you know?"

"Exactly! Me, too! I can't believe you're reading my mind like that. On second thought, I hope you're not reading my mind; otherwise, you'd leave this table quicker than you sat down." Thad laughed with Asha while his eyes traveled up and down her legs. Then a chill suddenly breezed along the nape of his neck. Thad lost his smile as he looked toward a table a few feet away where Chelsea and Kayla waved mockingly at him. "Would you excuse me for a moment, Asha?" Thad charged over to Chelsea's table. "What the hell are you doing here?"

"Is that the little skank from last night?" Kayla asked.

"Chelsea, why are you here? Didn't you beat me up enough already?"

"It's a public place." Chelsea's stare was hard and glazed. She sipped her red rum leisurely, leaving red lipstick traces on the rim of the glass. "Just couldn't wait, could you, Thaddeus? Dropped a real woman, carrying your unborn child, no less, and ran straight into the arms of an *actual* child. Just look at that young, tender thing."

"What's her curfew, or is it already past her bedtime?" Kayla snickered.

"Tell me, Thaddeus. Does that mystical creature have special powers? No, let me guess. Does she have a ring or a bone piercing her nose? It's always one of the two. And can't you lose your license for serving alcohol to minors? But I guess she moves pretty fast for her age. What is it they say, Kay? *Earthy* girls are *easy*?"

"Shut the hell up! This is childish. You two are the real immature ones. Why the hell are you dressed like hookers?" Thad surveyed their short, low-cut outfits, attire thoroughly out of place among the largely collegiate crowd that had gathered among local poets and rappers at the supper club that evening. "I don't want this kind of lasciviousness here! Have some respect, at least for yourselves."

"*Lasciviousness*? Oh, now you want to be *my* daddy. Oooh, scold me," Chelsea cooed. Her eyes were like deep freezers, and her batting eyelashes fanned an icy air that cooled the entire club.

"Cut the filthy little vamp routine and get the hell out of here now!"

"I want to be bad, Daddy. We came here to get a little action just like you."

"Go to hell, Chelsea!"

Chelsea grabbed the tail of Thad's shirt before he could get away, pulling him back toward her. She uncrossed her legs in slow motion, spreading her caramel thighs. While Chelsea firmly clutched Thad's tightening buttocks in her right hand, a long, red fingernail on her left lifted her short skirt, just high enough to reveal that she wore nothing underneath. Chelsea's feminine power pulsated while she made small circles at her waist. Thad felt the freezer burn. He couldn't take his eyes away from Chelsea's crotch as the excruciating moment turned lethal. She dug her nails deeper into his tense cheeks until he flinched from the pain.

Meanwhile, Asha turned in her chair to look for her date. From the corner of her eye, Asha watched Chelsea lick her lips at Thad with a lingering tongue roll.

Then Thad heard Saadiq on the house microphone, calling for

poets to sign his clipboard. Thad snapped out of his lusty daze. He looked at Chelsea's heavily made-up face. "Damn, how can I still get worked up by the same woman who tried to rip my eyeballs out earlier today?" Thad's question was a heavy breath. "You're pulling out all the stops tonight, aren't you?"

"Just forget you ever saw that tonight, because there's no way to relieve yourself now." Chelsea closed her legs, depriving Thad's undeserving eyes of a glorious view. She mouthed silently, "Sinner."

"I wish to God I never said what I said to you. It was a simple saying. Now you're gonna haunt me with my own words? You're deranged." Thad yanked away from his tormentor. He took his seat across from Asha, shaking the image of Chelsea's pretty privates from his mind. "I'm sorry I kept you waiting, Asha," Thad apologized, rubbing the awakening excitement in his slacks under the table.

Suddenly, confusion wrinkled Thad's forehead, as soft toes under the table reached from Asha's direction, crept up the hem of his pants and gently caressed his calf muscle. Asha leaned back in her chair with a new ease that had hid under a mask of shyness minutes before. She removed the straw from her goblet and placed it in her mouth. Slowly, she pulled the straw through her glistening lips and licked its tip. Warm toes, phallic gestures, come-hither eyes that told him to go thither—these mixed-messages made Thad's condition worse.

"I want to show you something," Asha purred, fanning herself lazily so her bangles rattled an ethereal mating call. She looked over her shoulder and waited until Chelsea and Kayla glanced in her direction. Then, grabbing Thad's hand, Asha led him like a mindless animal right past their table—close enough to cut her competitor with switch-knife eyes and a quick whiff of cocoa butter and apples.

"Oh no, she didn't," Chelsea and Kayla chimed together in pure disbelief.

In the dimly lit, unfamiliar supper club, Asha invented the expedition as it unfolded. She searched for a secluded place. Heading for the only bright lights in sight, Asha dragged Thad through the double doors of the kitchen and past Saadiq's aunts frying meat pies and catfish fritters on the grill. An unlit storeroom in the kitchen's far reaches presented itself as the perfect destination. Still clasping hands, Asha lured Thad through the deep black rectangle on the stark white wall and drew the curtains over the entrance closed.

As a dash of blue moonlight through a high window barely shared its shine, Thad looked into what he could see of Asha's eyes. "You wanted to show me something?"

"Thad, you're an intelligent man." Asha took his shoulders and rested him against a stainless steel counter. "I'm sure you've figured out what it is by now."

"Well, I have an idea, but, I mean, I just met you."

"That's okay, sweetheart." Asha stepped closer to him, pressing her cheek to his and rubbing her pelvis on his hardness in a thick, deliberate grind. She whispered, "I feel like I've known you all my life. We think a lot alike. I feel a real connection, don't you?"

"Yes. Sure," he whispered back, feeling her breath on his ear, its warmth melting the wax, his brain, and everything else inside of it. He laughed nervously. "Look, uh, I'm totally lost. I don't know what to make of this night or this entire day. Asha, you're a very attractive girl, but don't you think it's too soon for this? I think maybe we should wait or—"

"*Shhh.*" Asha placed her finger over his lips. She stepped back into the blue box of light that the high window dropped to the floor. "It's never too early between two souls like ours. Two minds, two bodies, dancing to the melody of heartbeats. Like the drums and the poetry."

Thad gripped the counter and shook his head like the son of a preacher man on the ledge of devilish peer pressure.

"You mean to tell me you don't want to see this, Thad?" Asha slithered out of her jungle-print skirt and removed her black halter. The light re-dressed her body in nothing but a metallic purple glow. Each perfect breast beckoned him, and her quiescent, feathery cove begged to be invaded.

"I don't have any protection," Thad whispered.

"Don't worry, baby. I know what to do."

Thad waited, full of steam, full of a familiar hunger, starving for a spot to pile drive his storage of anger for Chelsea. He squeezed his throbbing arousal. About to explode with agitation, he grabbed Asha, groping her, kissing her, licking her. She squirmed out of his hungry grip and shoved him away. She kept him at arm's length.

"Naughty boy," Asha scolded, pushing him back against the counter. "I don't work that way."

"Oh my God. I'm sorry." Thad chuckled, bashfully, crossing his arms, turning his body to hide his stiff shame. "This didn't feel right, Asha, but, it's just that you offered, and what you're offering looks scrumptious as hell." He laughed again, scratching his head and backing away. "I guess I should've checked myself. Every woman isn't into aggressive sex."

"Sex? Is that Chelsea's thing, rough sex? I'm not into *sex* at all, Thad," Asha replied, drawing him back toward her by the collar. "I'm into *love-making*. There's a big difference." She kissed his forehead. "Now, let's try this again."

Asha slowly stripped Thad of his clothing, his desire building with each layer removed. She laid him flat on the counter, and the cold steel sent a shockwave through his naked body. She dotted him with tender kisses from head to other head to toe, while he savored the sensation of her soft lips against his skin. She climbed onto the counter and crawled over him. She traced a wet trail around his neck and chest with her tongue. The electricity in her mouth sent a current to his hands, which impulsively hugged her waist. He gripped the small of her back, as she mounted him and allowed him to gently glide inside.

Their lips locked. Their bodies rocked in symbiotic undulations.

The sizzling grill, kitchen crew's voices, and clanking dishes barely masked her wailing or his moaning, making the sensuous act all the more exciting—the turn-on heightened, knowing that, at any moment, they could be caught, pleasuring each other's bodies.

Thad shifted on top of Asha and kissed her heaving bosom. He caressed her hips as he played in her naval with his tongue, before easing lower, pushing the muscle in his mouth past tangled vines until it reached sweet wetness and stayed awhile.

Thad rose again, plunging his vessel into her sea, and, as Asha swallowed him in her waves, a solitary drop of passion trailed back up her system, spilling as a single tear from her eye. At the same time, Thad closed his eyes to fight back what came naturally—the urge to dig her out with force. Instead, he worked her terrain with keen concentration, thrusting rhythmically, in sync with the tribal drumming that drifted in from the club.

Good for the body. Swaying. Swimming. Swishing.

Bad for the mind. Drifting. Drowning. Draining.

At the almighty point of human connection, an invisible foot, heavy with hidden motives, pressed the gas pedal of eroticism's dingy side, until Asha and Thad smacked into one another's un-spoken places. Outside of the storeroom's high window a cannon of thunder exploded. Streaks of lightning crackled. The sky started its war of monstrous rain again. Simultaneously, inside the secluded room, lust's momentum sent pots and pans from the shelf below crashing to the floor. The tumultuous clangor sounded just as Asha's and Thad's mounting urges climaxed like the surge of gigantic geysers. Thad signaled Asha. She quickly released him from her grip, digging her nails into his thighs, as he sprayed shame onto her abdomen in an orgasmic frenzy.

Feeling like a filthy, empty basement, Asha cradled Thad as he fell on top of her.

In the meantime, Chelsea had fought her way past the horde of college men that had swarmed around her table in the club to flirt with her and Kayla. She had found her way to the back of the kitchen. She had watched.

Chelsea stood paralyzed by disbelief, staring at Asha and Thad locked in a shadowy maze of sweaty arms and legs. Chelsea shook herself out of the shock. She snatched the curtain closed and staggered back into the club. Suddenly, disgust pinched her innards, burning the back of her throat. She dashed to the ladies' room, fumbled into the last stall, hoisted up the toilet seat and dropped to her knees. One convulsion, then two, a heave and a half, and the water in the bowl splattered with the salmon tint of vomit, as Chelsea revisited her lunch—and images of Thad's emotionless skin-play with Asha—in violent gags.

Kayla, meanwhile, had wandered over to the poets lounge and eased her way to the end of a bamboo bench. "Hi."

"Hi." Saadiq looked up from the clipboard in his lap. "Kayla, right?"

"Yep." Kayla looked at the stage, then down at her hands.

"Are you interested in sharing a piece tonight, or…"

"No. I'm no Maya Angelou." Kayla chuckled, her eyes straying. "Besides, I'm more into music than poetry, which I guess is the same thing, except that what's recited becomes resonated and complemented by the rhythm of instruments." She finally glanced up at Saadiq. "Why are you looking at me like that?"

"Uh, no reason." Saadiq returned his bottom lip to its upright position.

"Surprised that I can actually hold a conversation?" Kayla smiled.

"Sorry. Was I that obvious?" Saadiq covered his face, groaning apologies. "I didn't mean to be rude. All I know about you is what Thad tells me and, I guess, what I see in your friend Chelsea."

"Well, I'm *not* Chelsea." Kayla scooted closer to him. "Besides, that's not a fair way to judge someone. What if I said all I knew about you was what Chelsea tells me and what I see in Thad, and then held that against *you*?"

"*Touché*, mademoiselle."

"Oh. *Tu parle français?*"

"Just a little. I mean, I'm no regular on the French Riviera." Saadiq ran his fingers through his dreadlocks. "So, you dig music?"

A chocoholic wickedly tempted by fields of milky brown kingdom come, Kayla watched Saadiq's locks snake through his fingers and fall back against his broad shoulders—his supernatural cool, a walk on the wild side of her usual candy cravings. "Heavily. I'm a music video junkie." She tugged at her gold drop earring. "Actually, after news media, I think music is the world's greatest communicator."

"Right on, sister. Now that I know we're eating from the same sum-and-substance, I'd love to share one of my many cultural theories with you."

"Please." Kayla casually draped an arm over the part of the bench behind his back.

"Okay." Saadiq's face brightened as he shifted toward Kayla to explain his mind's work. "I've conceptualized theories that I want Arianna to help me compile in a written volume once she publishes her own book. The most prominent is my belief that black music will eventually bring unity to humanity. Hear me out. See, it's evident in the universal appeal of black music—hip-hop, rhythm and blues, jazz, reggae, gospel, rock, funk, soul—as the musical choice of our generation."

"Wow, you know, I read a recent article about this phenomenon."

"Yes. Cultural studies circles are buzzing with this. Anyway, I'm predicting that the new millennium will witness the flourishing of a new society at the hands of the Neo-Soul and Hip-Hop Nations, due, in part, to a unification under the shared values of Generation X—the most multiculturally open-minded in our nation's history. These values are influenced, in part, by music, and the music that happens to be created by black people speaks to the generation of this 'new world order.' You dig it?"

Kayla pretended to absorb Saadiq's theorems, watching with intense intrigue the prophet's lips under his nappy goatee as he spoke. She was lost in the sway of Saadiq's locks, each seeming to contain fibers of rich intellect, cultural prowess and historical pride, sealed into the kinky rope sprouting from his fertile crown. Up at the mike reciting theorems of her own, Nenna watched Kayla poke her perky chest out and cross her long, bare leg toward Saadiq, tossing it seductively to the funky rhythm of Kahlil's drumbeats.

Just as Saadiq noticed Kayla's bullet bra peeking from under her super-tight top, Chelsea appeared, grabbed Kayla and dragged her out of the club.

6

SCANDAL AND EVEN MORE SCANDAL

Blood was everywhere.

Kayla covered her mouth as she walked down the never-ending, white hallway. She tried to steady her trembling legs, reaching for the walls. They were scalding hot to the touch. Kayla yanked her hands away, leaving smears of lipstick that blended into the crimson crusts streaking the walls, forming a gruesome, psychedelic pattern.

"You're not allowed in here," the reprimand came in Alberto Alvarez's wrathfully stern whisper. "But it's too late now."

"I'm sorry," Kayla said through her cotton-clogged throat.

Hundred-dollar bills rained down from the roof, payment for playing the game. She walked faster along the narrowing walls, ducking as screaming newspaper and magazine headlines written in vital fluid zoomed past her. It was like something she'd seen but never wanted to see again.

Vwoosh! A giant television with her face on it whizzed past, nearly severing her head. Crash! It smashed against the wall. A sea of blood flowed from the screen.

"I'm sorry," Kayla screamed, as two uniformed cops ran toward her with behemoth cameras on their shoulders aimed at her skull. They ran through Kayla knocking the breath out of her and, then, disappeared.

"Murder. Media. Mayhem. Money. Here's your chance to do this," Alvarez's voice echoed with hellish retribution. "Scandalous tragedy, up-to-the-minute eyewitness news—hot, fresh, and ready-to-eat!"

Suddenly, a man draped in white appeared at the summit of the hallway, surrounded by a blinding glow. A breeze blew the butterfly wings sprouting from his back and the river of wooly locks framing his bronzed face.

"Come," he summoned, holding out his hand to her. "Come unto me, and you shall have everlasting peace, sister—an infinite supply of music, guiltless jobs and no competition among friends."

Kayla was dizzy. She wanted to reach him, but he seemed so far away. She heard clomping footsteps behind her and turned to find the camera-toting cops had returned, charging toward her. She screamed. The illuminated spirit man called for her. She ran. She ran toward the light like a lost lamb to its savior. He was far. She saw his hand. The Cyclopes on either side grabbed greedily at her, their slobbering snouts splattering blood on her back. She ran. Faster. Faster. She reached for the waiting hand...

Kayla jerked up from her pillow, gasping for air. She wiped her wet forehead, looking anxiously around her bedroom. It was still and quiet, except for her rapid breathing. Reaching for her heart, Kayla felt the quick, nervous rhythm in her chest jar her entire body. She fell back against the pillow, wheezing out the imaginary fright from her stomach in deep sighs.

"Shola, I had another one," Kayla whispered into the Channel Two studio lounge phone. "These horrible images are harassing my mind. I don't need this crap on a Monday morning."

"Another nightmare? Kay, what you saw that day at the crime scene in the Bronx can be pretty traumatizing. Maybe you need to take some time off?"

"No. I may be losing my mind, but I don't want these hardcore journalists here to think I'm cracking under the pressure. That just doesn't fly here. This business is not for the emotionally weak, or the morally strong for that matter. These people here are like wolves perched for the next bloody scoop."

"Agonizing over this media guilt thing again? 'News is objective,' or, at least, that's what you told me once," Shola replied. "It's not about frivolous emotions or moral blasé blah. Media people just tell us what's going on in the world, right? You don't create all the madness that goes on, so you're not necessarily responsible for what it means to people. That's how I see it anyway."

"I know, but there is a certain way things are covered in the media that only contributes to the madness, to the point where the public feels justified in despising the message as well as the so-called 'innocent' messenger—that would be me."

"Well, honey, if you're having any second thoughts about your career choice, then we could always use some help over here in the maternity ward. The hospital is always hiring and the other nursing interns and I would love a day off."

"No, I don't think I'll leave the business. I'll just try and change it."

"Good luck, superwoman."

"Anyway, girl, I think Saadiq was in this last dream…I mean, nightmare." Kayla's voice went soft and gossipy, as she sat down in one of the big blue chairs at the large oval table. "He was dressed as—well, he looked like—never mind."

"Oh, Jesus."

"Well, yeah—" Kayla recalled the image of the divine man draped in white in her dream.

"What?"

"Forget it."

"Kayla, tripping on crushes is *so* ninth grade."

"Whatever, Shola," Kayla replied, sketching on a *Channel Two*

Eyewitness News notepad. "Saadiq intrigues me. He's a bit militant, but he's mature about it. He's different from the bogus buppie boys I've dated like Kendall. Anyway, I actually spoke to Saadiq last night."

"You're kidding. *In your dream*?!" Shola inquired with exaggerated interest.

"You are so dead next time I see you."

"More drama at the club? Did Chelsea show her tail to the world again?"

"Literally, honey. She flashed Thad and showed him that she'd left her panties at home. It was classic Chelsea Fuller." Kayla stopped giggling. "All jokes aside, it's happening again, Shola. Chelsea is tormenting her conscience over a man, lashing out when her emotional investment isn't getting the returns she feels it rightfully deserves."

"You told me. Back in California, in high school, right?"

"When I started dating guys and spending my time with them, all of a sudden Chelsea went into this fit of jealousy—threatening these guys. And remember that worthless Gamma Phi Gamma stud, Earl, she dated freshman year at Columbia?"

"Vividly. Now she's a walking medicine cabinet."

"Tragic. But that's my girl, and I have to be there for Chelsea, because she was there for me, when both sets of my grandparents passed away within two years of each other. I seriously feel like she's suffocating me, but, at the same time, I'm scared for her."

"What's Thad running from? Why is he hurting her like this?"

"I don't know. Last night, Chelsea said while she was puking, 'a voice spoke the *Eleventh* Commandment,' directing her to 'collect' on the love she's invested in a 'sinner'—whatever that means. Chelsea has her Queen of Sheba thing going on, and Thad is somewhere else."

"Chelsea wants cocktail parties and caviar paste."

"Precisely, and Thad wants block parties and bean pies."

"They're polar opposites, which I guess you know a little about, Ms. Dream Lover." Shola laughed. "Let's get you a pillow with Saadiq's name on it."

"Not cute, Shola. Anyway, I prayed Chelsea wouldn't break down and start chasing Thad like a lovesick fool, but now she's got this catty, possessive thing happening, and her mania follows me like secondhand smoke."

"Stunningly deep. Kay, I've got to hustle. Dr. Bridges is calling, so I've got to go running. *Mmm.* Tasty!"

"*Ooh*, I'm going to tell Walé. Let's get you a bedpan with Dr. Bridges's name."

"Bye, girl."

It was deathly quiet until a force spoke. "Kayla, you were late this morning."

His voice punched the air out of her aching body. Kayla jumped up from her chair and turned around, crumpling the paper with little hearts drawn on it in her hand. Alvarez stood at the door of the lounge with his arms folded, filling the entrance with his height. His tanned jaw came to a point at his chin, and devil's horns sprung from his plastic, wavy, black hair. Then, Kayla blinked hard, her vision cleared, and Alvarez appeared normal—still tan, still plastic.

"The Smithey murder story is burning like a wild flame. The woman from the Soundview Projects may step forward and start speaking. There's word of an exclusive to *News Now TV*." His exuberance faded. "Chelsea called, said she's not feeling well and can't come in today. I'm sorry, Kayla. I know you hate when this happens, but I need you to do double duty with Internet research and tape editing."

Kayla released an irritated sigh and stomped her foot. "Damn."

"What's the matter with you? I'm the one locked in this cage, and you're the one looking like a rag doll, albeit in a fierce outfit. Is that Fescuzza?"

"Yes," Chelsea replied, as the scenario's freakiness set in. She was sitting in a cheap, green chair in a green room guarded by a piggish, gun-toting, badge-wearing ringleader of a peculiar circus—where weeping men, kids and mothers talked to glass portraits of their loved ones. Yet, Chelsea was drawn to the place. She sat across from Carolina, admiring the jailbird diva's perfectly coifed hair and light makeup through the glass divider. "You look fantastic, as usual."

"Sweetie, I don't care where I am. I will *never* let myself go to Shitsville," Carolina asserted, fluffing her bangs. She paused, tilting her head. "Chelsea, I was worried you wouldn't show up today, especially after our last phone conversation."

"I called to check on you, because you were so upset the last time we were face to face. I wasn't sure if it was something I had said or done."

"No, it wasn't you. I was releasing my bottled hostility. The jail shrink came knocking on my cage door to *e-val-uate* me. Me! The 'Wine-Tasting at Wave Hill' organizer, Links chapter president, the socialite of Riverdale who hosted dinner parties so the wealthy neighborhood whores could gossip in my living room—I still wasn't a good enough wife. I don't even know who I am anymore," Carolina whispered. She adjusted the phone to her other ear. "I miss Michael. All I do is cry. I'm so lonely."

"Me, too. My life becomes more like yours every day."

"How dare you?! You have *no* clue what I endure in here, debutante!"

"Carolina, I'm sorry," Chelsea apologized, shaking her head. "That came out wrong. Please, forgive me. The guards said I could only stay if we both keep our cool this time."

"Well, call me the coolest Ice Queen, honey, but don't pretend to know what you don't. My arraignment is tomorrow, and my lawyer says the attorney for Michael's family plans to throw not only the book, but the whole library, at me." Carolina was about to cry, but the Ice Queen tooketh over, and she flipped her head high. "They're freezing all of our assets and joint accounts until after the trial. I have no family, so I can't bail myself out of this hideous place, and I—I—"

"Carolina, you say the word. I'll talk to my parents and have the check in your hands in a matter of seconds."

"Please!" Carolina rolled her eyes, raising her left hand to study the ice on her finger. "I don't need your handout, dear heart."

Chelsea looked down at her own left hand. A tiny friendship ring on her pinky twinkled to the left of a naked finger. "Last night, I was treated to a free peepshow." Chelsea looked up and into Carolina's dead stare. "I saw the final moments of an encounter between my soon-to-be fiancé and another woman."

Behind the glass—silence.

"Carolina, I told Thaddeus I'm pregnant with his first child, which, in my eyes, is a promise, a bond. Then, I walk in on him screwing this young, country girl he doesn't even know!" Chelsea dropped her voice. "I saw him—*touch* her, and, as God is above me…"

"You poor thing." Carolina raised her hand to the glass, and Chelsea placed her hand on the divider to connect with Carolina's warmth. "I plan to plead 'not guilty.' Chelsea, my defense won't be insanity. It's going to be pure, unadulterated passion—the good kind that makes people defend their hearts. I'm going to stand before that damn judge and say that to his face."

"Carolina, how do you know that will work? This world doesn't take romantic passion seriously. I mean, I do, but that's only because I have rage swarming in my head, and I know it's because I'm right in my heart. What I feel is right. Like you, I'm willing to go all the way for love."

"Like me, you better be sure he's worth it, honey. Michael was *everything* to me—especially after we lost Miranda."

"If you could go back, would you do it again?"

"Absolutely."

The certainty in Carolina Smithey's hardy voice was sharper than cactus needles, and its honesty prickled the landscape of Chelsea's skin until the pathos made her itch.

"I found out he was seeing—*that woman*—and I confronted him. Sure, there were signs, but you overlook those when he's a good man otherwise, and especially when every jealous neighbor is watching, waiting for the fall of your storybook marriage. So, you put on your game face, and you make it work. Well, the mask made my face hurt, and I could no longer stand the infidelity, or, even more, the crush of my ego. My heart hurt, my pride hurt more. My image of how things were supposed to be was smashed to bits of ridiculous hope. Yes, I ignored his needs, but I still didn't expect him to get his satisfaction elsewhere."

"So you stood your ground?"

"Ultimatums don't work, Chelsea. After he strayed, all I had for Michael was conditional forgiveness, but he wanted more. Now, I realize it was just me that he wanted—without the put-ons or the perfect-wife rep. But I had pushed him to the point of having to steal it—steal *me*—from me. My fears and his force just made me snap that day. He was stealing love I should've just given to him freely. Chelsea, I—"

Behind the glass—more silence.

"Like I said, if you have with this man even half of what I had with my Michael, then you should learn from me, dear—don't let some undeserving, lowlife tramp steal away your soul mate with the stuff between her legs!" Carolina cautioned. "But, at the same time, don't make the same mistake I did. Don't rush to judgment, because the pinnacle of prerogative can lead to a sojourn of hell. Yes, I went all the way, and did something I never thought myself capable of. Now, I'm paying for it with my life. Honey, I know you're intrigued by my story, but, Chelsea, mine is a real life soap opera—no commercial breaks, and killed-off characters don't come back next season."

"I can't help my feelings." Tears escorted Chelsea's whimpers. "This man is tearing me apart. I refused to go to work this morning. After puking twice, I wrote page after page of rage in my journal." She fingered her blurry eyes. "I can't shake the image of their moistened bodies twisted together like a wet, human pretzel!"

"Chelsea, I still haven't told how I did it or how much it hurts like an endless hell. You're young. What seems so right, right now, has to be left to chance sometimes. You can't force it. At times, fate is a better judge of life than you are." Carolina's eyes looked through the glass and through Chelsea. "If we have the understanding that I think we do, then I think I'm ready to tell you what this life can really do to even the most dazzling of us, Chelsea."

Behind the glass—extended silence.

"Chelsea, I want you to tell my story," Carolina whispered at last.

"Come again?" Chelsea wiped her dripping nose.

"I see that you're hurting, and hurt is my middle name. Chelsea, I feel ready to open up my bruised heart and maimed soul. I want to tell you every last grotesque detail and free myself of this scorching heartache I've been suppressing in these suffocating walls."

"Carolina, I thought you didn't want to disgrace what you've been through by giving it away to strangers."

"Listen to me, Chelsea. I don't want you to take my pain and carelessly fling out as a shitty sensationalized diversion for people to read over their morning decaf coffee or to watch over their cheap TV dinners. In case I never get out of here or Michael's family puts me in my grave early, I want you to tell the world the truth. I want you to capture it in a meaningful memoir for me, and I want you to bring this same understanding and passion you're showing me now to my story. Maybe we can help other women survive this misery, maybe I can warn them about the booby traps and pitfalls that await them, if they choose to travel the road of real, utterly stupid-blind love."

Carolina's genuine expression took her out of the orange jail-suit, so she wore only her sincerity and sorrow. Chelsea looked at Carolina's bitter, beautiful face until the glass and the guard and the green walls disappeared. Reality was only comprised of the desire to be understood, both of their tears and the pain in Chelsea's swollen womb.

"I understand."

The session with Carolina and the two-hour shopping spree on Madison Avenue had drained Chelsea, but neither the advice nor the spending helped to ease her grief. She dragged big shopping bags through her apartment door, wobbled to her bedroom, and fell onto her mattress like dead weight. From her bed, she stared at the full-length mirror on the wall, mentally cursing Thad and Asha.

"Carolina wants me to tell the world who she is, but who the hell am I?" Chelsea thought aloud, watching her reflection pose the question, too. An hour into mulling over Carolina's proposal and cheating in her staring match with the mirror, Chelsea finally went over to it and slipped out of her little chartreuse dress. Examining herself from the front, Chelsea played with her hair, poked her lips out, smiled and experimented with a variety of facial expressions.

"Okay, cute hair, pretty face," Chelsea told herself.

Moving on, she studied her breasts. "Medium-sized, but perky and just enough for cleavage," she said, pushing them together with her hands to form a sufficient twin set. "Flat stomach, and I love my belly button." Her voice trailed. "Even though my tummy will soon be the size of a beach ball."

She examined her hips and thighs. "*Health For Now, Forever* is working." Stepping on her tiptoes for the high-heel effect, Chelsea spun around and stared at what she could see of her rear end— a bad viewing angle and minimal rump made analysis difficult. Besides, she had always told Kayla: "I wish my tushy looked like those girls' butts in the music videos, you know, perfectly round and lifted."

Chelsea threw her hands up, yelling at the woman in the mirror. "I gave myself a full self-examination like Dr. Rubenstein's book says, and I can't find anything wrong with me!"

Perfection's frustration was fatiguing, until Chelsea stepped down from the tips of her toes, stopped holding in her stomach, and quit sucking in her cheeks. Taking in reality's slow vaccination, she crossed her right arm to cover her breasts and placed her left hand under her navel. She contorted her body to hide from the woman named Truth in the mirror who stared at her exposed flesh, judging her nakedness.

Chelsea gasped. She quickly approached her nightstand, flipped to the next chapter behind the bookmark in *You're a Winner* and read the title, "The Inner You."

She slipped into her silk nightgown and paced the room, pondering ways to examine the inner Chelsea. She impulsively dashed over to her bed and pulled out a pine chest from under it. She fumbled the lock hurriedly as if the answers Truth sought were inside. Opening the chest, she was hit with the gravity of its memories.

Makeshift awards, honoring J.P. Anderson Academy's spelling bee winner for two years in a row, were on top. Chelsea chuckled at the infantile writing on the certificates, admiring the modesty of honors seemingly more deserved than her agony. Sifting through the pile of stuff, she found purple pompoms and a cheerleader picture from days filled with self-esteem lessons she had promised herself she would never forget—*promises, promises*.

Chelsea pulled a silky sash from under a tarnished tiara and gently draped it around her neck. The first black *Miss J.P. Anderson Prep* in the school's history had been catapulted into a beauty-pageant career that thrilled her mother more than herself. The old crown's crusting jewels and sash's peeling letters were painful symbols of how she felt at that very moment.

Digging deeper, Chelsea found her Columbia dorm council badge under her dean's list letter and Women in Journalism Award for Community Service. Setting those aside, she slowly unrolled a year-old *Columbia Daily Spectator* announcing the Homecoming Queen nominees and featuring her picture. Never certain whether popularity or politics was to blame for a loss she had never fully accepted, she sighed. "Damn, Gretchen!"

Hunting through a happier heyday drained her; so, she decided not to rummage through the other chest—the one dedicated solely to Thad, containing all of his pictures, little notes, cards, gifts and his underwear from their first time.

Chelsea prepared to put away her memories for another time when she came across an old photograph of her parents. In the yellowing snapshot, Terrence and Paula Fuller sat on the hood of an ugly car on the side of a California highway, looking young and carefree, happy and unaffected. It was the photograph Chelsea pulled out occasionally when love and longing were on her mind.

The photograph was almost a mirror image of the photo of Thad and Chelsea in the broken picture frame. She was her mother, and Chelsea's chiseled, wide-eyed father was the spitting image of Thad. Déjà vu on semi-glossy paper, Terrence and Paula were Thad and Chelsea; except, Thad's elegant business suit and Chelsea's anchorwoman smile were stand-ins for Terrence's afro and Paula's tacky, yellow bellbottoms.

Nostalgia boxed with Chelsea's feelings, her eyes filling with tears she could not fight off. The photograph was her entire world, for she was in the photo in more ways than one. It was a recorded moment in time containing her whole family—taken after Terrence learned Paula was pregnant with Chelsea, four months *after* their fairy-tale wedding.

"That's how it's *supposed* to be," Chelsea screamed, her anger echoing throughout the quiet apartment—*promises, promises*.

Chelsea shoved her inner self back into the makeshift, peeling, yellowing heap of history in the chest and slammed it shut. As her aching outer self limped to the kitchen, she wore depression over her nightgown like a mink in the dead of a summer solstice and carried her diary and parents' photo like security blankets. Bringing a bottle of brandy and a goblet into the living room, Chelsea downed about four migraine pills and two of the big blue tablets the girl at The Health Stop called "guaranteed pick-you-ups."

She set the photo down on the table and tried to compose an entry in her diary but couldn't concentrate enough to do it. The photo kept haunting her. She set the photo of Terrence and Paula on the floor to get it out of her eyesight and closed her diary. She grabbed the TV clicker, flipped on the *Oprah* show and tried to glean something from the guests discussing the topic, "Putting Yourself First." Despite the compelling expert advice, Chelsea could only think of Thad first. Plus, the brandy was feeling and tasting too good to her.

Eventually, Chelsea sipped herself into a drunken sleep.

Kayla stood over Chelsea two-and-a-half hours later, shaking her. "Girl, wake up! What have you been doing in here all day?!"

"What?"

"People in the newsroom were asking about you today."

"Oh," Chelsea whispered, rubbing her eyes. "Hey, Kay."

"Are you okay?"

"Well, physically I feel like crap, but, emotionally, I just feel like shit, that's all. Kay, can you believe what Thaddeus did last night?"

"Gingersnap, while I'd really love to figure out what new foolishness Thad is kicking up now, I've got a date," Kayla apologized, petting Chelsea's head.

"Kay, don't. Please sit and talk to me."

"I'm in no mood for a pity party, Chelsea." Kayla sighed, rolling her eyes. "You want to talk? Allow me to start. Why are you playing hooky to mope around here, doodling in your diary all day?"

"Kay!" Chelsea sat up, clumsily collecting her robe over her shoulders. "That's not fair. I'm depressed."

"We're supposed to be helping each other through this summer internship, but your depression's got them heaping more responsibilities on me. I'm still part of the superwoman's club, while you've got Oprah's Book Club and a half-empty bottle of brandy keeping you company." Kayla picked up Chelsea's prized photograph from the floor. "Why is this here?"

"I was just looking at it," Chelsea muttered.

"This reminiscing is not good for moving on. Why do you do this to yourself?" Kayla scolded softly.

"Kay, I'm trying to piece my world back together and—"

"No." Kayla stopped her flow. "Enough with the excuses, Chelsea. Your obssession with the past makes you unwilling to change, and your desperation to be perfect makes it worse. For godsake, what's going through your mind?"

Chelsea looked down at her parents' picture in Kayla's fingers. "When I was a girl, I desperately wanted a sister, but my mother couldn't have any more children."

"I know. You told me."

"To appease me, my mother told me that I had a sister out in the world who I didn't know yet. She said every person has some-one else somewhere in the world who looks like him or her." Chelsea's red eyes met Kayla's. "She said some people are born twins, but others don't realize it until they pass their 'other selves' walking down the street. When I met you the first day of first grade, it all made sense. You were like my twin sister. And when I met Thaddeus, well…wait here." Chelsea stumbled to her bed-room and returned with a frame. "Look at those pictures."

"Oh my God. Chelsea, the resemblance." Kayla swallowed hard, placing the two pictures side by side. "It's downright scary, but you realize that your mom's twin theory is just an innocent myth, right?"

Chelsea giggled through the pain. "Sure, but it gave me hope to hold on to."

"They're…like…two halves," Kayla said, though the pictures didn't match exactly—the one of Thaddeus and Chelsea was broken, cracks running through the glass and splintering across their smiles. "I remember you mentioning it before, but I never really made the connection, but now I really see it. Chelsea, this is totally bizarre. A Daddy's girl like you madly in love with a man who—"

"Don't say 'madly'!" Chelsea snapped.

"Sorry," Kayla recanted.

The tears came back to Chelsea. "Daddy protected me from everything when I was a girl, including those nasty little boys who only wanted to get in my panties."

"Thad is Daddy in a newer, sleeker package," Kayla concluded in an airy whisper with a hint of epiphany. "He's safety for you."

"Kay, when I met Thaddeus at that campus social, I knew he was the one. I opened up to him and allowed him to be the first I knew of romantic love."

"Chelsea, I give you props for holding on to that virginity thing. Lord knows I couldn't do it, and yes, you had a good upbringing, but you've developed a demented outlook. You can't stick people in little slots and duplicate what once was. Life doesn't work that way. Get used to it—lovey-dovey romance isn't hereditary."

"I don't care. Even if that knucklehead Thaddeus can't find it in his heart to forgive me, our baby will. Our love will be strengthened by someone we can't even see yet. But this baby will exist only because I trusted Thaddeus with my heart and body. My only true happiness will be to have what my parents have."

"Girl, I wish I could save you from this self-destruction. Why do you hold on so tight to fantasies? Come back to reality before it's too late, Chelsea. This picture is nothing but a memory."

"I'm so confused."

"Because you're a traditional girl in love with a man on a save-the-world trip. Damn, why do I suddenly feel hypocrisy tapping

me on the shoulder?" Kayla bit her lip and shook her head.
"Look, I'm probably more confused than you are right now. I
was at the bookstore today reading up on the black arts movement when I suddenly realized that I've disliked Thad for ages,
but I hardly know the man. Yet, I give him the shadiest of treat-
ment. I'm not being fair to him and neither are you. Think about
how much you're asking him to give up. The man respects our
culture and dedicates his time to its uplift. I think that's a good
thing," Kayla said, rubbing Chelsea's back. "Now, I've got to get
ready to go."

"Thanks, girl." Chelsea kissed Kayla's cheek, trying to smile.
"You see, that wasn't so bad. You can make Kendall wait while
you cheer up your best friend. Hold on, I thought you two were
taking an 'I-need-space' break."

"Oh, yeah…uh, right." Kayla quickly stood and walked to the
hallway. "I'm hooking up with a cutie I met at the bookstore today,"
she lied. "See ya."

In his comfy nest of an office, Thad sat in his leather chair
behind a big mahogany desk next to a straw cabinet housing an
old-school record player and a collection of vinyl albums. He
drew inspiration from his wall collage of picket signs, protest
message buttons, and old black-and-white pictures of platform-
heeled sisters and soul brothers in zoot suits, beads, and tie-dyed
dashikis.

Thad had spent hours upstairs in the supper club's office that
Monday evening, counting the contents of the moneybags in the
safe, agonizing over his idea, and practicing his pitch several times.
He had listened to the rhthym-and-blues and classic soul station

for motivation, even singing along when he could. Finally, he turned down the stereo, took a deep breath, and dialed his parents' Virginia home.

"Carmichael residence."

"Hi, Mom."

"Hello, Junior."

"How's everything on your side?"

"Fine. Perennial has picked new clients with the summer conventions and all. You know how it gets. How are things with you?"

"The supper club is great, but Chelsea's not taking our breakup well. I think it's affecting her mentally."

"I always thought that girl was a little loopy, but I hoped you'd marry the woman who bore your children. For all Chelsea's quirkiness, I'm impressed that she yanked your father to New York because she was worried about you. I admire her willingness to try anything to get you back in our good graces."

"Mom, other motives drove Chelsea to do that. You saw what she was so worried about. The supper club. You saw it, and you said you love NRK."

"Oh, excuse me, 'NRK'? Is that the hip way you refer to it? Well, I do love NRK, Junior." Then her voice changed. "But I think it was the dishonesty that robbed us, including Chelsea, of some of the joy in it. Your father says, with or without you, he plans to push forward with the New York expansion of his business."

"Good for him. I don't want his plans thwarted because of me. How's Birdie?"

"All she can do is rant and rave about performing at your club."

"Great. Hey, have you finished that urban landscape painting?"

"Almost. I still work on it in the basement on weekends."

"Tell Dad to pick up the line, too. I have a proposition."

"Cole, grab the phone. It's Junior."

Thaddeus Senior came on the line. "Hi, Junior. How's business?"

"Things couldn't be better, Dad." Replying with exaggerated enthusiasm helped to quench Thad's feeling that maybe his father had expected to hear a negative update. "Subconscious Soul is arranging meetings with music industry contacts, bringing major publicity to the club."

"Have you boys looked into the fire and theft insurance like I told you?"

"Yes, Saadiq is on top of that," Thad lied, hoping Saadiq had, in fact, responded to his repeated requests to research the insurance policies.

"What's this talk about Cynthia performing up there again?" Thaddeus Senior asked. "I've had my fill of her neverending chatter."

"Cole, don't start." Mrs. Carmichael sighed.

"I thought you enjoyed her performance. Weren't you proud of Birdie?"

"Well, of course, but I assumed it was a one-time thing. I want her to concentrate on finishing St. Katherine's and applying to colleges. Junior, I don't want her distracted with all of this glitzy showbiz jazz."

"No disrespect, Dad, but have you asked Birdie what *she* wants?"

"No disrespect, Junior, but you do whatever *you* want, and that includes keeping your plans secret from your family and impregnating a woman to whom you're not married. You're in no position to question how I raise my daughter."

"One has nothing to do with the other, Cole, and you know that." Mrs. Carmichael stepped in. "Let's not start the blame game."

"Dad, Chelsea's an emotional mess. I want nothing to do with her right now, but that won't prevent me from taking care of my responsibilities as a man." Thad exhaled. "Listen, that's not what

I called to discuss, Dad. Don't spoil this for me. Okay, the reason Birdie is so stirred up is because I've planned a big night for the whole family at the supper club. Nothing official, just something I thought up. Tell Birdie to pick up the line. I want everyone to hear this."

"What are you up to, Junior?" His mom chuckled. "Birdie, Thad's on the phone!"

Cynthia dashed to her bedroom to take the call. "You told them?"

"More mysterious plans?" Thaddeus Senior grunted. "Junior, you realize what happened the last time I received news you'd been keeping from me?"

"Cole, let the boy speak!"

Thad sighed before pressing on. "Next Saturday is unofficially 'Carmichael Family Night' at Nubian Rhythm Kitchen. It's part of my new spread-the-wealth philosophy, to make the woe that went into NRK worth it. So I asked Birdie to prepare two new songs. The V.P. of Mystic Music will be here checking out some of the acts, including Subconscious Soul and Birdie."

"Gosh, you didn't tell me that yet, Thad!" Cynthia shrieked.

"It was just confirmed. In addition to that, NRK will feature the work of an undiscovered artist in our gallery every month, and I want you to be the first, Mom."

"Wow." Mrs. Carmichael was flustered. "Junior, I don't know what to say. I've never publicly displayed most of my work before, but I guess I could finish my current piece and dig out my old college portfolio."

"Mom, your modesty is too sweet. I'd love if you would do that for me," Thad said. "The other night Rush met Carmella Boyd at the supper club. She's on the committees for several SoHo and Harlem galleries, and she selects the traveling exhibits for the Af-Am Museum Consortium. She'll be on hand to meet you."

"Okay," Mrs. Carmichael replied, as if giving in to a reluctant pleasure.

"And finally," Thad cleared his throat, "Arianna is writing a magazine article on nightlife and dining, and she's invited a food critic to rate our establishment and its cuisine for her story." Thad paused. "Dad, I'd like you to honor our kitchen as our special guest chef for the evening, preparing some of your best Creole dishes."

There was a silence that lasted a century.

"If you don't have your old recipe file, I'll purchase a cookbook for your convenience." Thad negotiated, meeting his father eye to eye as a sharp businessman, presenting the stakes. "You'll get marquee billing and a salary if necessary."

No one spoke, but Thad could tell his father held his breath, prepared to shoot down the idea, if only to thwart the possibility of Thad looking like a hero in their power struggle.

"Dad?"

Silence.

"Do it for Brandon, Dad. He fell short of his chance to shine at what he loved because *someone* who was supposed to help him didn't. I'm trying to help the rest of us live out what he couldn't." Thad tried to appeal to his father's sentimental side, in defiance of everything Thaddeus Senior had done to show he didn't have one. "Before you reject it completely, think about what this will mean for all of us."

"Junior, I've come to realize that Brandon was right. I've never blamed him. Believe me, I know where the blame lies." Thaddeus Senior choked on his words. "The thought of what could've been is so damn debilitating." He let loose, bawling helplessly. Manly grunts melted into girly gasps as he pushed tears through barren eyes. "I guess I'm willing to do anything to make sure all my kids can hold their heads high. I want you to have the best, but not at the expense of your lives."

The grief and guilt in Thaddeus Senior's voice set the entire family on a tearful deluge. Thaddeus Senior's sobs were a pain and a joy to hear, and Thad wished that he were in Virginia at that moment to see the big man cry those elusive tears, and then, wrap his arms around his father.

"Cole. It's okay, honey. It's hard to understand, but it is possible to love *too* much, and that's all you did," Mrs. Carmichael said softly. "We can't dwell on what Brandon chose, but I think one night, with all of the family shining, sharing our gifts and doing what we love, is a start in the real healing process."

"I want to prepare a masterpiece meal so bad, son. I thought you'd never ask. I'd be honored, and, let me say this—if there's one thing I've learned from my children, it's that unfulfilled dreams only become unnecessary regrets. I have enough regrets, Junior. I'm ready to dream."

"Thanks, Dad. You don't know how much that means," Thad professed with the only strength his voice could muster, since his staunch opponent had finally laid down arms and offered to break bread. "I'll call you later. 'Bye, everybody."

A knock rattled the door, and Rush slid into the office wearing a grin. "I'm jazzed that I told Saadiq I'd go in his place to meet with the A&R guy at Mystic Music. He referred me to a producer who can hook up Subconscious Soul with studio time to cut a demo. Anyway, he really digs our concept and…what's up, Thad?"

Thad's glassy eyes didn't blink. "A truce is in sight."

"Oh, you told your folks about the family thing you're planning? They dig it?"

Thad nodded. "Everything's falling into place."

"The War of the Worlds between the nouveau riche and neo-soul is seeing the makings of a cease fire. That's proper," Rush commended. "I'm glad your family finally transcended that soul cover-up syndrome to connect with the bare naked beauty of expressing the self."

"Damn, you can put anything in pretty words." Thad laughed. "Honestly, it was a benchmark moment. My dad cried, man."

"See, it's all about communication. Words can erase a thousand miles of distance, if the synergy's right. I know your dad, and to get him to be vulnerable is the culmination of years of Herculean effort on your part, man."

"Now, if I could only get my personal life together."

"Chelsea or Asha?"

"Both. I'm trying to come to terms with Chelsea's wicked fixation on me and separate that from the joy of my unborn child. And Asha's a cool, foxy girl in a real organic sort of way, but what do I make of her willingness to get physical so early in the relationship? Chelsea waited for the sex, and Asha didn't. But Asha understands me, while Chelsea underestimates me."

"Are you sure about that last part? Yes, Chelsea flips out sometimes, but the two of you have this unique thing. I picked up on it. It's like this subterranean connection beyond the physical. Thad, do you know what the hardest thing for a man to make for himself is, besides a three-course meal?"

"What's that?"

"Choices."

"Damn, that's real. Choices and promises."

"The bittersweet dame dilemma. Those sweet chocolates make a man cuckoo for the cocoa stuff. The power of the pussycat can steal the spotlight from the deep connection thing. A woman has the power to make a man change his religion!"

"So, you went from humping honey bees to huffing hemp?"

"Ouch, what a pot shot. No pun intended."

"Seriously, Rush, weed is a gateway drug."

"Thad, don't start coming down on weed. I give the advice around here. I told you I need it for my lyrics. Besides, I think that's the least of my problems—"

"Wait!" Thad exclaimed, punching the buttons on his calculator furiously.

"What is it?"

"I've counted this money three times to verify my calculations, and the treasury is way under the projected profit books. The receipts don't match the safe."

"That doesn't sound good," Rush said, wrinkling his forehead.

"Worse yet, this isn't the first time. Before, I figured it was a paperwork error, because it wasn't off by this much. I have to account for this mess before I can make any deposits. If NRK's losing money, I have to get to the bottom of this PDQ."

"You have a lot of responsibilities on you, so don't stress about it right now. You just had a major family moment. Let's go downstairs and celebrate."

"Rush, I can't just ignore this."

"We'll figure it out. Come on."

Thad locked the safe and the door to the office, checking them twice. Descending the stairs toward the club, he hesitated. "Hey, man, I just got this funky feeling all of a sudden. Either the farina and stew I had for lunch is disagreeing with me, or you-know-who is somewhere around here."

"You're losing it. Puffing on a big fat joint would calm you down, paranoid boy." Rush led Thad through the empty club, past Kahlil's friends clearing tables to create a space for dancing. "Saadiq is hosting a Reggae-House-Hop Shindig tonight." Rush gave a nod to the DJ doing mike check and mixing up dancehall cuts. "It's billed as a party featuring the latest reggae, house, and hip-hop. Half off admission with a canned food donation for the homeless shelter."

"Cool. Where is Saadiq?" Thad went into the kitchen and then over to the gallery. "Where the heck is Saadiq? Is everything ready to go?" Thad asked Rush again.

"He's probably outside collecting the cover charge." Rush replied, spotting the man who he wanted to see. "Hey, Benny, got the smoke?"

Thad walked out the front doors to find a line of students, hip hop clubbers, and trendy regulars waiting outside of the club. "Have you seen Saadiq?" he asked Virgil, who blocked the entrance in a solid, muscle-bound bouncer's stance.

"The last time I saw him, he was sneaking backstage with a chick, but I didn't get a good look at her," Virgil replied with a sleazy wink. "I told him I'd cover the door while he showed the fox around, know what I mean?"

"Well, if you're watching the door, who's watching the bar?"

"Melvin's got it. He knows the routine. Damn, why are you so high-strung?"

"I don't know." The thought of Virgil's brother, Melvin, overseeing money unmonitored made Thad's stomach feel queasier. "I think something I ate is bothering me," he said, peering around anxiously as he walked back into the club.

Suddenly, the DJ on the mike chanted something in a jumbled Jamaican accent, and ear-busting beats blasted from the monster-sized speakers. Simultaneously, a crowd of hyper party people charged through the entrance and gravitated toward the stage as if magnetically attracted to the bass-driven rhythm of the music. Instantly, the place was a scene from a hip music video, with young people chattering in the latest lingo, bodies in natty New

York fashions vibrating to the thumping groove, and the DJ spinning and scratching records for dear life.

Thad excused himself from the rambunctious blowout and retreated to the backstage area. "Saadiq is slipping, passing off all of his work on to other people," he mumbled to himself, finding the backstage area empty.

The feeling that had repelled Thad earlier suddenly intensified in his intestines. He turned to leave, then mysterious bumps in the far corner of the room called him back. The noises invited him to find out who or what was hiding in the darkness. Sickness swelling in him, Thad slowly walked toward the muffled sounds coming from behind the partition of the dressing room.

"*Oooh*, yeah. *Mmmm*. Yes." The female approval was hushed but definite.

The male response was low but strong. "Oh, yeah. I like that."

Thad eased over and peeked through a slit in the dressing room door. A naughty vision assaulted his eyes. His initial thought, that his eyes were deceiving him, was doused by real and raw reality.

Saadiq and Kayla were fully dressed except for the body parts necessary to satisfy animal appetites—he, pulsating against her while his dreads flopped wildly to and fro…she, squirming underneath him, trying to contain her salacious squeals, grabbing his buns tightly to her skin, twisting his locks between her fingers. He and she, attempting to merge their gyrating bodies into one, rocking madly, stealing all the pleasure possible from each other's body in the space and time with which they were forced to work.

What should have been part forbidden romance with no witnesses, and part frisky romp with no consequences was exposed for what it was.

Betrayal, Thad thought as his eyes met Saddiq's.

Thad scurried away with a pang of embarrassment shooting

through him, unsure how to react to the random things occurring so quickly around him. Sweat forming on his brow, he stumbled back into the club. He navigated through the surging sea of young bodies grinding to a rapturous rhythm, guys rolling their things against girls' backsides and girls rubbing their things on guys' legs.

As the dancing crowd's anonymous breasts and butts bounced off him, the evil disquietude of late consumed Thad's thoughts. A slideshow flashed to the beat of the confusion in his mind: *He and Asha interlocked on the sizzling kitchen grill, a pregnant Chelsea on a street corner in nothing but red garters, Saadiq and Kayla screwing in a broom closet, an orgy of chocolate bodies engaged in physically impossible acts, spilling out onto the front sidewalk of Nubian Rhythm Kitchen…*

To steady himself, Thad took a stool at the bar. He ordered a beer, to wash down the vomit bubbling in his throat and to keep an eye on Melvin. In his spinning mind, Thad tried to sort out the dastardly deeds occurring in his place of business.

"Hey, Thad, how are you, man?" Tyler greeted, holding the hand of a pretty, blonde-haired, blue-eyed woman. "You look like you just saw a ghost."

"I'm just stressing," Thad apologized.

"I know. I was a contributing party in your stress for a minute, remember?" Tyler cracked, and they both laughed. "That Chelsea thing was so ridiculous, man. I'm just glad we cleared that up quickly. Hey, I want to introduce you to someone. This is my new lady, Gretchen." Tyler gestured to the woman accompanying him. "Gretchen, this is my buddy, Thad Carmichael."

"Nice to meet you, Gretchen." Thad extended his hand, trying to forget what he'd seen backstage. "Name your drink. It's on me."

"I'll have a martini," Gretchen told Melvin with a smile.

"This is the man I told you about, Gretchen. He owns this cool club."

"It's amazing," Gretchen commended, nodding to the music.

"Thank you. This is what my partners and I wanted." Thad turned to look at the crowd thoroughly enjoying the garden of nubian Eden in the name of the groove, the beat, and the damn-near-holy spirits. "Gretchen, what do you do?"

"Right now, I'm a personnel clerk at a Manhattan credit union, which I detest." She sipped her martini. "My first love is singing."

"Gretchen's on my wavelength." Tyler elbowed Thad, putting his other arm around Gretchen. "She recognizes and respects the beauty of all cultures and artistic expressions, so I really wanted her to meet you."

"Oh, she's a disciple, too, huh?"

"Don't go there," Tyler said, as they all laughed. "Gretchen's into R&B, heavy on the B, and she's looking for a stage to do her thing."

Noticing Thad's skeptical expression, Gretchen pleaded her case, "Thad, I'm legit. Look, I'll audition if I have to, but I would just *love* to get on stage again."

"Thad, do it for a fellow C.U. Lion. You'll never guess who Gretchen's grandfather is." Tyler beamed. "Go on, babe. Tell him."

"My grandfather heads the business school you guys just graduated from—Dr. Hausbruck." Gretchen kissed Tyler, celebrating their point of commonality.

Meanwhile, Thad froze as the name she'd uttered so casually took him back to bitter days. "You're kidding me! Hausbruck is your old man's old man?"

"Yep. I graduated from Columbia three years ago. I only got in because Granddad had 'years of dedicated service to the university.'" Gretchen used a deep, official tone to recall why her family had pressured her to attend her alma mater. "Four years of college was all I could take, though. I was never really into it, so I changed my major from history to music history. I passed the time away getting involved in homecoming activities and things like that. See, I'm an honest, privileged trust-fund kid for a change."

"And you're into R&B?" Thad asked, bells going off in his brain.

"Thad, the girl is good." Tyler rubbed Gretchen's back.

"Ty, you've obviously mastered the art of fishing for a hook-up," Thad joked. "But this is more like a case of you scratch my back, I'll scratch yours."

Tyler looked confused. "Um, okay, what do I have to do for you?"

Thad's smile emerged slowly. "You've already done it."

Gretchen chimed in, "I grew up near Motown. My childhood best friend, Tamika Walker, and I sang, pretending to be all of the famous girl groups. We competed in local talent shows in Detroit, and we won a couple of them. I guess it was the novelty of our act. Ever since then, I've loved singing, but I don't get the chance to do it anymore."

"Well, Gretchen Hausbruck, I'm going to give you that chance. I'd like to invite you to perform next Saturday. I'll get Saadiq to call Tyler with booking procedures for you. We'd love to see what you're made of." Thad raised his mug. "And be sure to invite supporters to your performance, *especially* Dr. H."

"Thank you, Thad." Gretchen clinked glasses in a congratulatory toast. "This means the world to me, and I'll guarantee that Granddad is here Saturday!"

"We're going to jam to this song. Thanks for hooking my girl up, Thad." Tyler escorted Gretchen toward the dance floor, boasting about his "connections."

Glancing at the club's entrance, Thad saw Kayla slither out, shielding her face with her handbag. Her body language screamed guilt. Shaking his head, Thad chugged the last of his beer as someone sat on the barstool next to him. He turned to find Saadiq, smelling of sex. "I guess that explains my nausea."

"Thad, you weren't supposed to see that. Actually, it wasn't even supposed to happen, but it did, you know—the urges?" Saadiq played with a matchbook on the bar, focusing on the embossed NRK on it. Unable to face Thad, he found friends in the fire sticks in his fingers.

"Supposed to be just a kinky quickie, huh?"

"Don't lecture me, Thad."

"I should leave that to Nenna, your woman, right? Real classy, man."

"Look, I know what you're thinking."

"Tell me what I'm thinking, or, rather, what I'm *supposed* to think? Should I feel guilty for spying on your conquest or pissed you conquered anything associated with Chelsea?" Thad brought his voice down. "You were screwing Kayla Harmon! Here! Is Kayla *real* enough for you, *brother*? I guess she's real enough to screw."

"Come on, Thad. Relax, man."

"Look, I don't have any loyalties to Kayla, Saadiq. As a matter of fact, I can't stand the witch, from her tits to her toes. But I recall you saying the same about Chelsea, and they're, like, practically the same damn person!"

Saadiq said nothing for a while. He slumped over, staring at the matchbook, and sighed with childlike regret for the naughty thing he'd done. "Okay," Saadiq finally said, "I'm taking my spanking like a man. What the hell do you want me say, Thad? It was nothing more than what it looked like. She came to me and said she's going through a lot, that Chelsea's driving her crazy, so I figured I'd ease her troubles. There's no explaining. Kayla's cute and horny. She wanted me and let me know it. I wanted a piece of pie, and I got it."

"I'm not playing moral police, okay? It's just that you did everything in your power to drive a bigger wedge between Chelsea and me than the one we'd already created ourselves, and then you go and mix juices with her even eviler twin?" Thad waited for Saadiq to finally ignore the matchbook in his hands and look at him again. "By the way, did you have control of your condom the whole time you were sticking that stuck-up witch?" Thad stood up to leave. "Or did you even use one?"

7

SEPARATION AND STOOL WARS

Thad met Asha at Prospect Park the following day, toting lunch in a picnic basket and wearing his heart on his sleeve. On a large, camel-hair blanket, under a soft spray of sunshine, they shared shrimp kabobs, baby strawberries, and white Zinfandel. Asha's portable stereo and Thad's collection of rare acid jazz and soul classics completed the afternoon's atmosphere. On their private island, surrounded by summer's lazy goings-on, they mellowed out with music and fed each other, trying to make every carefree moment count.

Slowly, Thad leaned over and kissed Asha's shoulder, her neck, her ear. He sat back, drinking her in. The sunlight coated her skin, and since she had spent the morning in dance rehearsal, her svelte muscles were perfectly taut under the straps of her long white dress and silver choker.

"Ever consider the life of a supermodel?"

Asha looked down at the hem of her dress. "No, I can't say that I have."

"You're probably not interested in that sort of thing."

"Well, the aesthetically limited world of fashion isn't ready for too many girls with my look—too black, too strong."

"I see." Thad lowered his voice and stopped staring, sensing that he had hit the nerve that reacts to the politics of female beauty. The rustle of leaves in nearby trees filled the silence between them. Thad tried again. "Well, I'm no expert, but I see a bona fide goddess. Has anyone ever told you that?"

"Thank you, Thad. That's very sweet." Asha looked away to play with a blade of grass. "Come to think of it, Zeké used to say this embarrassing thing to me."

"What?"

"I can't tell you. It's so embarrassing." Asha giggled, fixing her dress strap.

"Tell me." Thad playfully took her strap back down.

"He used to say...oh my God, I can't believe I'm telling you this. Okay, he used to say I was 'a divine ebony statuette, carved by an exacting artist who captured the essence of pure beauty.'"

"Wow." Thad's grin shortened. "Well, he didn't lie."

With a berry on her lips, Asha mumbled, "Yeah, he's sweet."

Thad leaned back onto his elbows and rolled his eyes. Hearing laughter, he looked over his shoulder and saw a set of kids playing tag. "What a life! Children come with a refreshing, built-in innocence that I wish they could share with jaded grown-ups who take the time to see the world through their untouched eyes," he mused aloud, watching a little boy steal a kiss from a little girl. "I need one of those in my life—the kid *and* the kiss." His thoughts went unanswered. "Asha, where do you see yourself in about five or ten years?"

Asha awakened from her daydream. "Huh?"

"I asked you where you see your life going."

"Gosh, I hate that question, because I really don't know, Thad. At nineteen, I feel like I have forever to decide."

"You do think about it, don't you?" Thad looked at her quizzically. "I mean, you must have some idea of where you want to be."

Asha rested on her back and gazed into a sky just as limitless as she believed her time on the very earth beneath her to be. "Zeké used to joke that I had absolutely no sense of true direction in my life. So I told him I'd strap myself to his back and let him lead the way." Asha chuckled, until reflection set in again. "The free spirit in me came to New York on a whim, looking for adventure, I guess. Wait until I tell my dad I met a respectable, upstanding man like you. One with a 'real job,' as he would say."

"Yeah, tell that to *my* father—the aristocrat driven only by Ivy League degrees, executive offices, and passes to join the upper middle class," Thad said, pouring another glass of Zinfandel. "It's okay to have your head in the clouds sometimes, but you shouldn't forget to let your feet touch the ground when it's time to run. You know what I mean?"

"Well, I guess the next phase of my life will probably involve dancing in some way, but right now I'll just see where it takes me."

"Sooner or later, you need to spot a horizon and articulate your path to it."

"I know that, Thad." Asha sat up. "Okay, for instance, I used to think about going to dance in Paris, but Zeké would always tell me how the competition is fierce and I should stay in Atlanta, and…" She slouched back down. "Whatever. I know he was just trying to hold me back. I was hip to his game."

As the afternoon passed and the sun with it, Thad tried to tell Asha about how special the upcoming Saturday would be for his family or how he'd love to see Daughters of Destiny tackle new issues in their stage shows, anything to get her to change the subject. Yet, with each effort to dialogue about other things, Asha's true interest slipped out.

"So Zeké could never understand why my dance style had evolved…" Asha read Thad's contemplative expression. "What's on your mind?"

"I'm adrift in a sea of confusion. It's the supper club business. We had all these good intentions, but, little by little, things are happening lately that have made me wonder what's becoming of that place."

"Things will go wrong while you're adjusting. It's like me coming to New York. I'm new to the city and things have been cool, but I know something's bound to go wrong before it's all over with. Are you sensing evil spirits that won't go away hanging around the club?" Asha giggled, grabbing his hands in hers.

"As funny as it sounds, I *am* feeling something like that. Things are swinging on a gigantic pendulum with a spastic twitch. The minute something good happens, something bad happens just to balance it out. Damn near mechanically, things seem to swing from positive to negative. Back and forth, flip-flop, tick-tock. Something's warning me to put up my emotional and physical security gates. But I keep asking myself: What is this damn clock counting down?"

"That's deep, Thad." Asha squeezed his trembling hand. "But there's no need to go through it alone. Besides, you've got me. I'm not going anywhere."

"Thanks."

Along with the wind and rustling leaves, doubt was in the silence that followed.

"Why is Chelsea determined to make such an absolute fool of herself the way she does?" Asha inquired, playing with Thad's eyebrows. "Is your attention a gift?"

"She told me I remind her of her father. She showed me an old photo of her parents once, and we do look amazingly alike."

"Isn't that a little Freudian-type freaky? She wants to sleep with you and be with you, because you remind of her of her *father*? Ugh!"

"I think she means it on a deeper level, too."

"Oh, like the whole moneyed, Talented Tenth, bourgeois black intelligentsia thing?"

Thad's face contorted as each word, tinged with nasty sarcasm, emptied from Asha's lips. He looked at her and waited. "Chelsea's convinced of something she wants to prove to herself, to me and to the world." He glanced pensively at the children frolicking, wondering about his own unborn wonder. "And, like you said, I know something's bound to go wrong before it's all over with."

Saadiq bombarded Thad the minute he set foot in the supper club that evening. "Thad, I need to talk to you."

Rush looked disturbed as well. "Thad, man, we need to talk."

"Whose tragedy is more tragic?" Thad asked, breaking through their human barricade and heading for the stairs.

"My news requires urgent attention." Rush followed Thad as he ascended toward the office.

Saadiq clamored right behind them. "I'll only be a minute."

"Saadiq, step into the office." Thad turned to put a hand on Rush's shoulder. "I'll be right with you, Rush." Thad closed the door and threw his keys on the desk. "Damn! The answering machine message light is flashing like an emergency siren!"

"I wanted to clear the air about what went down yesterday," Saadiq insisted.

"Takes a while to clear the smell of hot sex from the air. Your heat almost burned the place down. But hey, you don't owe me any explanations about how you conduct your sex life. If you're feeling guilty, that's *your* issue."

"Thad, I want to be sure that this thing won't get amped up into an unnecessary federal case," he said suspiciously. "Besides, you seem awfully concerned with the purity of the club, but, if I recall correctly, it was you who was feeding his primordial passions in *paradise* recently."

"I know what you're getting at, and you can rest easy, lover boy. I won't say anything to Nenna. That's on you. I'm your friend, not your moral parole officer. It's ironic, with as much scrutiny as you dumped on Chelsea, that's one thing she and I always had when we were together—we were faithful in our relationship."

Saadiq swallowed Thad's statement like a punishment pill. "All right, Thad. I deserved that." He looked down at his hands. "Want the real deal, man?"

"I'm over it, Saadiq."

"I never gave Chelsea the benefit of the doubt, because, believe it or not, I wasn't the hippest cat in high school, and girls like her didn't dig dudes like me. You know, the ones into music? It was all about the ballplayers. Basically, I was dissing her to get back at all those chicks who dissed me. Now I realize that wasn't fair. And maybe the thing with Kayla was, like, a sick form of revenge, 'love them and leave them' like the jocks in my school did. I guess I wanted the power to do that myself. Hell, I don't know."

"Let's get off of this subject before it drives us both crazy."

"Agreed. Nenna has a temper, and it would get ugly if she found out."

"God, I feel like my father, playing the righteous ruler around here. Anyway, I've been out of the loop. What's on tonight's itinerary?"

"It's Cool Classics Night. Dirty Dishrags, a local band that plays real down-and-dirty swing music, is opening for the main attraction, Momo's Mo' Down Revue—four older cats who do covers of all the old-school Motown records. They go out into the audience, lay roses on the lovely ladies, and the whole nine yards."

"Good," Thad commended him. "Saadiq, you always manage to become genuine all over again whenever you're talking about music."

"They call me the charmer for a reason."

"I'll get on your case about your other responsibilities later, snake charmer."

"Oh, how'd the date with Asha go?"

"In the ambition department, Chelsea has Asha beat hands down. I hope Asha isn't falling for me too fast as a rebound thing or in her quest to *find herself*."

"Or vice versa. You're in rebound mode, too."

"Right. Well, I still didn't tell her how her all-too-forward behavior on the second night we met bothers me."

"Hmmm, *her* all-too-forward behavior? Let me guess. Did she seduce you, too? First the crafty journalist entraps you, and now the dangerous dancer snares you. Thad, I'm sensing a pattern here."

"Just send Rush in for me, would you?"

As Thad was about to play the million messages bursting to get out of the answering machine, Rush walked into the office with a grave expression and closed the door behind himself. "Which do you want first, the bad news or the worst news?"

"I guess the bad, as if I need any more."

"I found this note taped to the door when I arrived early this morning."

Thad took the red paper from Rush and read the skewed writing:

My Dearest Thaddeus,
I need desperately to speak with you and be with you. I have been in such a quandary since last I saw you. I need you, and I fear what I am

capable of, if I do not win you back. Thaddeus, you know what we shared in the beginning was good, damn good! I have come to see the error of my ways, and I want to explain. You owe me (and our baby) at least that. "Let him without SIN cast the first stone."

Your Lost and Now Found,

Chelsea

After a long pause, Thad looked up at Rush. "I don't know if I should take this seriously, or if it's another one of her theatrical cries for attention."

Rush shrugged. "She came in after I opened the place. I told her you wouldn't be in until this evening, but she insisted on waiting for you. She sat at the bar all morning like a nervous wreck, fidgeting and chewing on her fingernails."

"I don't like this. This note is a cursed clue to a wicked game that I'm supposed to figure out—damned if I do, and damned if I don't. And I have a creepy hunch that all of these messages…" Thad's voice trailed off, and he hit the play button on the answering machine.

Beep. Message One: "Thaddeus? It's Chelsea. Coming to see you this morning. I really need to see you. Don't shut me out. Okay?"

Beep. Message Two: "Thaddeus? Chelsea. You weren't there. I guess it was too early, but I need you. Call when you get my note."

Beep. Message Three: "Thaddeus? Chelsea. I waited for you. I need you. Call me."

Beep. Message Four: "Thaddeus? Chelsea. Where are you? Call me."

Beep. Message Five: "Thaddeus? Chelsea. Call me."

Beep. Message Six: "Thaddeus? Chelsea."

Beep. Click.

"She drives me crazy. Should I be worried?"

"I don't know."

"A part of me wants to run to her, but I have to keep her at bay, teach her a lesson," Thad mumbled, slumping over and resting his head on his arms.

"And, now, it gets worse." Rush took a deep breath. "I witnessed something last night, after everyone left, and it wasn't cool at all."

Thad looked up. "Now what?"

"I saw Melvin take a big cut of the bartender's till without accounting for it."

"You think he stole it?"

"He gave it to Virgil on the sly."

"You think *he* stole it?"

"That's what it looked like to me."

Thad felt his insides twist. The tension in his stomach exploded and spread to the far reaches of his limbs until it consumed him. "On top of everything else going on around here, this is the type of crap I won't tolerate. Why would Virgil destroy something we all worked like slaves to build?"

"Hold on, Thad. Let it sink in first. Have you pinpointed where those discrepancies in the books have been showing up?"

"Now that I think about it, the numbers get screwed up when I'm tallying up the bar's cash register!" Thad jumped up and punched the wall. "I can't believe Virgil would do some shit like this!"

"I hate the idea as much as you do, but maybe there's another explanation for the shortages. We'll confront him in a civilized manner, and see where his head is. Tomorrow, at our place or his place, just not here, okay? I'll see you downstairs."

Rush left the office, and Thad plopped back down onto his chair. He replayed Chelsea's messages—each progressively shorter and more desperate than the one before it. He rubbed his temples. "What the hell is wrong with everyone around here?"

Meanwhile, Chelsea had floundered into the supper club down-stairs, toting a small attaché case. She anxiously galloped over to Rush. "Is Thaddeus here?"

"He's upstairs in the office, but, Chelsea, you should wait until—"

Chelsea was gone. She bounded the stairs in her dainty heels and ran straight into Thad on his way out of the office. She stopped and dropped her shoulders, looking at him for a long time. "Where have you been?"

"I just got your messages, Chelsea, but I won't explain my whereabouts."

"Thaddeus, I don't expect that. I thought something had hap-pened to you."

"Well, you're looking dapper, so what's with all the goddamn red flags?" Hiding his worry for her under anger about the money issue, Thad walked past Chelsea, who looked all the part of the broadcaster in her lime-green power suit.

"Thaddeus, I need to talk to you." Chelsea shuffled behind him, following Thad downstairs to a table near the bar.

Onstage, Saadiq introduced the Dirty Dishrags. The customers in the club hooted and hollered as the quintet burst into a good old swinging number.

"Thaddeus, my supervisors at Channel Two were going to fire me from my internship." Chelsea sighed, sitting across from him. "I begged them to let me stay on."

"I'm sorry to hear that, Chelsea."

"Me, too, but I saw it coming. Thaddeus, you're constantly on my mind, so much so that I can't concentrate on my work—*not* that I'm blaming you. So, please don't say that." She looked away. "It's ironic. I spent so much energy telling you to focus on your future, now I'm jeopardizing my own."

Thad kept his thoughts to himself and let Chelsea spill her guts, hoping to figure out what had gone so wrong. While his heart felt her sincerity, his mind harbored a sneaking suspicion of her emotional instability. He felt that *she* was operating the invisible clock counting down his time to make serious moves. With wariness, he studied her.

"I've been thinking about a lot of other things, Thaddeus. Like how I stupidly got your father involved before you could tell him about your supper club. Yes, I screwed up, but prior to that I asked you if you loved me, and you said there were things about me you still loved, but not all of me. That hurt."

"Chelsea, our relationship wasn't working. Your temper is toxic."

"I can't explain why I tend to expose the worst parts of myself. I can't even fully explain what Caro—" Chelsea stopped before she revealed something she wasn't contractually permitted to share. "Look, I'm just headstrong about stuff like security and the man that I love. Thaddeus, did you forget what we had?"

"I'm no fool, Chelsea. I remember the good times we had in the beginning, too—when you'd come to my campus apartment, and we'd sit on my couch and we'd talk all night. Then, we'd just kiss until the next morning. I liked that." Thad saw Chelsea try to smile through her pain, while he continued through his own. "But you wouldn't even let me touch you. You wouldn't let me go any further until after I met your father and he approved of me. When your mother pointed out our resemblance to one another, you felt safe trusting me." Thad slipped into the sentimental throes of nostalgia, and he wanted to pull back. "I liked that, too."

"Aside from your drive and smile and commitment and strong hands, that's what drew me to you—enough to let you be my first. Then things started to change. When I trusted you, I found things out by accident. I wasn't a part of this grand dream of yours." Chelsea gestured to the customers whooping it up to the Dirty

Dishrags. "You never even told me about the horrific thing that happened to Brandon. Cynthia did. Jesus, I felt more and more like an afterthought."

"You admired my ambition, so my ego wouldn't let me admit that my motivation came from a family tragedy. But when I entrusted you with the dawning of this"—Thad pointed to the African-garbed couple next to them eating curried goat and plantains—"you wanted no part of it. You tried to use my father against me. What am I supposed to make of that?"

"Thaddeus, you said you can't change a person and I agree with that, but I think a person can change himself or herself, if he or she wants to, and I want to. Like I wrote in my note, I've come to see the error of my ways." Chelsea was on the verge of tears. With the most heartrending look in her hazel eyes, she clutched her attaché case, which contained the surprise she'd brought for him. "Thaddeus, please, before you dive into a premature relationship with some young girl you don't even care about or who doesn't care about you, please, think about our child."

"I'm prepared to provide for my baby."

"*Our* baby," Chelsea corrected him, reaching to rub his hands across the table. "Thaddeus, I want to show you something, and—"

"I appreciate your new outlook. It seems genuine, not like an epilogue to one of your self-improvement books, but your humility still needs work. Things with Asha are tentative, but I'm supposed to tell you that. So, frankly, I resent your unbiased advice. Chelsea, my heart belongs to me, and only I can choose whom to share it with. Right now, you're not one of those people."

A poisoned arrow shot through Chelsea's weakened heart, as her property rights to Thad's love were revoked in a heartbeat. The effects of rejection's poison showed on her cracking face.

And there, amidst the rowdy party, were two ships, sailing in opposite directions, but attached by an anchor inside her that would be bigger and more important than both of them in the coming months. The winds blowing her silky cashmere sail and his sturdy canvas sail were cross-currents: betrayal and betrothal, distrust and devotion, misunderstanding and misty memories. Yet, it seemed the tides in the Sea of Love were not strong enough to turn either ship around to rest at a common dock called Forever.

A stoic Thad butchered his burgeoning empathy for the woman who masqueraded as the sweet-faced Chelsea from over a year ago. "I still have questions about the conception of our child, but I won't dwell on that. I'll love my child just the same. But, speaking of Asha, she'll be here any minute. I don't want her to see us together and get any ideas. So, can we close this conversation?"

"Is that it?" Chelsea gasped. "Close the conversation?"

"Oh, one more thing, and I'm serious about this. While you're pregnant, stay off the red rum and stay off my property until my child is born. Now the conversation is closed."

"I'm not one of your goddamn business deals, Thaddeus Carmichael! You can't put a date stamp on what we have and shove it away on some shelf to rot! Do you realize what will happen to me without you? I can't live without you. You *won't* live without me."

"You're a crazy woman. Stop with the fatalistic bullshit and the distressed damsel routine. I can't take it anymore, damn it! You scare the life out of me!"

Suddenly, Chelsea's eyes, posture, and tone were dead serious, like that of a parent prepared to spank her child because she loves her child more than she hates what the child did wrong. She twitched with rage. "Any man would have eaten this up—a beautiful woman, throwing herself at his feet and declaring her undying love for him. But, no, Thaddeus Carmichael is too good, too self-righteous. He's scared. I'm *not* crazy. I'm just not committing the ultimate sin. I'm going after what I want most."

"Stop the goddamn sin references! Let go of those words I said. You're suffocating me, damn it!" Thad shook his head in defiance, pushed back from the table, and jumped up. "I know what you're doing—trying to make me feel doomed! Like it's you or no one, right? Well, guess what, Chelsea? I'm a step ahead of you, because I don't want you! You hear me? I don't want you, you psycho bitch!"

There was a delay between the transmissions of Thad's mouth and those of his mind. It took a few beats for him to realize he had said what he did; the piercing words played back in his mind. He had indeed done it. He had uttered the words he truly did not mean, and the moment hung in the air, stunning both of them.

Thad heard the imaginary ticking clock. Time moved at funeral pace. Chelsea stood in slow motion, her shock manifested in her heaving bosom. Thad returned her scathing hot gaze, wishing he hadn't spoken recklessly. But, it was out. He had to stand by his damning words or risk appearing at an impasse, out of control, stupid. He felt all of those things anyway.

Thad walked across the room and hid behind a plant near the stage, as Saadiq introduced Momo's Mo Down Revue. Thad was on pause as Momo and his men made the mature women in the audience melt at their rendition of a classic ballad. Emotionally removed from the uproarious environment that swirled around him, Thad's mind was stuck on how Chelsea's wait-and-see tone had seemingly sealed his fate. Tears trickled down his face to the tune of the tick-tock sound in his ears.

Vanquished, Chelsea staggered to the ladies' room. She sat on a stool and cried. As she wiped away tear after wasted tear, she contemplated why the new and improved Chelsea Fuller had failed to impress Thad. She wondered what he wanted from her, until she realized that he had made it clear he didn't want her at all. But the tears continued to flow, despite their meaninglessness to everyone else in the world.

Suddenly, Chelsea heard the restroom door open and footsteps walk toward the sink. She hushed her whimpering when she detected familiar voices discussing Parisian dance schools and feminist versus womanist song lyrics. Then, internally, she heard Carolina's voice compete with Dr. Rubenstein's voice from his motivational tape. Chelsea got a second wind when her "inner self" escaped from the trunk under her bed, tracked her down at the supper club, and sat in the bathroom stall with her. Awards and pompoms and tiaras flashed before her damp eyes.

Life seemed shorter, more urgent.

Chelsea smoothed her French twist hairstyle with her hands and burst from the stall, emitting attitude like a pissed-off maharani. She exchanged dirty looks with Asha and Nenna, who stared at her approaching reflection in the mirror. Tension filled the room. Chelsea stood behind them until they turned to face her. Chelsea posed, but Nenna, the smallest of the three, threw her just as much shade.

"I have a bone to pick with you." Chelsea pointed her attaché case at Asha.

Nenna forced Chelsea's case out of Asha's face, stepping between the ladies. "Well, if it isn't Miss High and Mighty. I didn't know they served BAPs here."

"Look, I don't have the time or patience for this childish crap. I'll have you know that I'm leagues above you, baby, and so is Thaddeus!" Chelsea pointed again at Asha, who nervously batted her eyelashes. "If everybody around here wants to see a psycho bitch, that's exactly what I'll give you, Miss Bohemian Nature Girl!"

"Wait. Listen here, sweetheart! You're in Brooklyn now, so your damn gold card is no good around here!" Nenna protested. "Take that prima donna shit back to wherever you came from!"

"I'm not dealing with *you* right now!"

"Oh, you'll deal with me, princess! I've got a bone to pick with your snooty little friend. I saw her checking out Saadiq. Tell that tramp Kayla to stay away from my man! You Ivy League bitches are all alike, coming down to our side of the tracks to get all the sensitive brothers we've groomed. You make me sick!"

"So small, yet a mouth so big. Get the hell out of my face, little girl."

"And if I don't?" Nenna dared.

"You're on the nerve before my last one. It's flaring up something fierce."

"My blood's boiling, too, bitch! So, what are *you* gonna do about it?" Nenna's words rolled from her tongue tauntingly.

"Thaddeus already filled my chamber with enough ammunition. I'm prepared to blow a hole in the next target if need be. Find some business of your own and go tend to it!" Chelsea put a dismissive hand in Nenna's face, before addressing Asha. "And *you*! You weren't half as shy as you are now, when you were slinging your ashy ass around that 'sensitive' man you hardly even know!"

"Girl, you don't even know me, and I don't want to know you!" Asha finally spoke up for herself. "Get off your damn high horse!"

"What did you say, you little hippie bitch?"

Chelsea reached for Asha, but Nenna shoved Chelsea hard to the ground. Chelsea grabbed Nenna's ankle, and Nenna came tumbling down on top of her. They tussled ferociously like Olympic wrestlers while Asha watched in horror.

Chelsea smacked Nenna with her attaché case. Nenna screamed in agony, as an unsuspecting old woman walked into the ladies' room, saw the melee, and quickly shuffled back out. Chelsea grabbed Nenna and pushed her into a stall with furious force. She slammed the door, and the lock snapped shut.

Hot, Chelsea spun around, charged toward Asha, and shoved her quivering frame against a Nefertiti-shaped mirror, causing it to splinter.

"Playing with adult relationships? You have no idea what you've gotten into, bitch!" Chelsea hissed, spitting in Asha's face and slapping the timid creature like a misbehaving stepchild at a family function.

A single tear tiptoed down Asha's face.

Nenna broke from her cage, rocketing toward Chelsea as the old woman burst into the room again, followed by Rush and Thad. Rush scrambled to pry Nenna's hands from Chelsea's hair, and Thad grabbed Chelsea, pushing her away from Asha.

"Get that crazy bitch out of here!" Nenna jerked away from Rush and soothed Asha, who fell to the ground sobbing. "She's a lunatic, Thad!"

"You're insane." Thad held Chelsea, forcibly escorting her from the club, struggling against her amazing strength. "Damn, what have you been eating?"

"Thoughts of you," Chelsea snapped, trying to slap him.

"Get lost, Chelsea! I don't ever want to see you set foot on this property again. Next time, we press charges. You're not well. Get some help," Thad fumed outside the club. "And stop looking at me with those eyes," he screamed, as Chelsea leaned in extra close to him. "Stop it, damn it! I don't want you, so go to hell."

On cue, Chelsea grabbed the back of Thad's head with one hand and between his legs with the other. She kissed his mouth and bit Thad's tongue. "Sin no more, lest a worst thing come unto thee," Chelsea professed faintly, clutching his personals, squeezing tighter with each word. Leaving Thad howling from the pain on both ends, Chelsea ran into the night, laughing and licking her fingers.

8

STOLEN TRUST AND STOLEN SANITY

"Nenna would've demolished that girl last night," Saadiq boasted to Rush the next morning as they walked into Virgil and Rozalyn's living room from the kitchen.

"I doubt that." The sting from Chelsea's bite was still on Thad's tongue.

"Oh, please. That lipstick chick against my little firecracker?"

"Enough already! No more play-by-play on the catfight." Thad grabbed his glass of juice from Saadiq and sat on Virgil's suede couch.

Her noxious perfume arriving before she appeared, Rozalyn sashayed out from the bedroom in a loud orange outfit, popping watermelon bubble gum.

"Baby, I'm on my way to the salon." Rozalyn kissed Virgil's shaved head. "Tell your trifling brother Melvin to stop using my phone line to call long distance and to wash his damn crusty ravioli off my dishes. I'm tired of his nastiness." She walked to the door, leaving melon lipstick on Virgil's temple. "And you guys better not leave a mess in my house for me to clean later!" Rozalyn waved sweetly before walking out. "Bye, boys."

When the room got quiet, Rush sighed. "Now, it's time for serious business."

"The point of this meeting is to discuss an issue related to the club...with you in particular, Virgil." Thad's words came out slowly and deliberately.

Taken aback, Virgil lifted his head.

"Two nights ago, I saw Melvin take a cut of the bar's register." Rush attempted to sound more diplomatic, less accusatory. "Are you aware of any underhanded business practices going on, Virgil?"

Virgil's eyes shifted all around the room, taking inventory. He rubbed his bulbous biceps, contemplating his next words. Melvin suddenly appeared in the hallway behind the couch where Rush, Saadiq, and Thad sat. Out of their view, Melvin stood in his boxer shorts, peering menacingly at Virgil.

"We want to know if any dirty politics are being played in our business," Thad explained, sipping his juice. "The club's books haven't been balancing, and it's the bar that's coming up short."

"Are you accusin' my brother of rippin' us off? Is that what you're sayin', Thad?" Virgil squirmed, as a nervous sweat began to coat his body and all the eyes in the room focused on him.

"We need to figure out if we have an embezzler on our hands."

From the hallway, Melvin sent quick, angry signals for Virgil to extinguish his partners' suspicions immediately—silently punching a fist in his other palm and slashing a thumb back and forth across his throat.

"Hold on, Thad." Saadiq jumped to the edge of the couch. "I'm not digging this firing-squad approach directed at Virgil. What's the deal, Rush?"

"Okay, I'll cut to the chase," Rush replied. "I hoped you'd just offer up an explanation so you wouldn't feel like I was beating it out of you. Virgil, I saw Melvin give *you* the cash under the table."

"What?" Saadiq was on his feet.

Melvin ducked behind the wall. He popped his head back out and, sneering at Virgil, he mouthed: "Handle these boys, *quick!*"

Virgil stood up, using his physical size to defend himself. "I manage the bar's profits, so what's the big deal about him givin' me the cash?"

"You can tell us what the deal is without being guilty of a felony. There was a discrepancy in the final paperwork and no note explaining the missing funds. We discussed this at length in the beginning, and everyone's aware that we have a system in place— to avoid assuming the worst when money situations like this arise."

Saadiq interjected, "Virgil, we're blood brothers first and business partners second. What exactly does everyone else know that I don't?"

Virgil flopped back down onto the new leather recliner behind him and wrung his hands together. He breathed heavily, looking forlorn, thinking faster than a computer. "Okay, Melvin's clean. He was, uh…just following my lead."

"What?"

"I'm embarrassed as hell that I had to do what I did, but I'll come clean," Virgil said, watching Rush continuously eyeball the apartment's walls. "I planned to put the loot back before anyone noticed, but you know my grandma's been fightin' the cancer in her breast, right?"

"How's she doing?"

"Nothing's changed much." Virgil tried to form tears as he shook his head wearily. "The treatments are expensive as hell, and the insurance can't cover it all. Pamela and I help with the extra home-care costs. But between my baby sister's hotel job and my small cut, until NRK starts turning a larger profit, it's hard as hell taking care of things around here and looking out for Grandma Belle, too."

"That's heavy, man." Saadiq went over to comfort Virgil.

Rush remained tight-lipped. "Sorry for calling you out before getting the full story, Virgil. I saw the money exchange hands and jumped to my first conclusion."

"We're on your side. Why didn't you just come to us, Virgil?" Thad asked.

"I don't know, man." Virgil shrugged, noticing Melvin nod his head before disappearing completely behind the wall. "I didn't want to bring my family's financial problems into our brand-new business, but I ended up doing that anyway. If I had told you guys, I'd feel like dead weight early in the game."

"Never feel like that, Virgil. NRK is supposed to help our friends and families—in all kinds of ways."

Rush took his eyes off of the wall unit full of complex, shiny new electronics and looked straight into Virgil's eyes without a trace of sympathy.

"Virgil, the next time you're backed into a corner, please call on us," Saadiq pleaded, forming a huddle of forgiveness around Virgil with Thad.

"I will. Thanks." Virgil sniffled. "Hey, I need to make an important phone call. I'll meet you guys downstairs," he said, hustling his friends to the front door.

Rush stood slowly from the couch and strolled toward the door, taking one last look around. He glared into Virgil's eyes as he passed him on the way out.

In the stairwell, Saadiq put his arm around Rush's shoulder. "It's hard to see a grown man break down like that. Didn't realize Virgil's going through so much."

"I don't know." Rush pulled away, edging farther away from Virgil's front door. "I'm not feeling Virgil's tragedy so deeply," he whispered. "Amends aren't paid in full yet. Something smells fishier than a seafood platter to me."

"Rush, this whole time, you've begged me to keep my cool, and now *you* say something like *that*? The man's grandmother is sick as a dog, for godsake," Thad scolded through clenched teeth, pushing past Rush and stomping down the stairs.

Meanwhile, Melvin limped into Virgil's living room, yawning and scratching his posterior. "Mornin', baby bro."

"You see what you're gettin' me into, Mel?"

"Don't look at me like that." Melvin reached deep inside the couch's cushions and pulled out a stuffed tube sock. "You really handled those boys. That little sob story was cool. You deserve a fuckin' Oscar for that act."

"You got a kick out of tramplin' on Grandma Belle's grave?"

"The old bitch is dead, bless her soul. She can't feel it." Melvin laughed, shuffling the stack of bills he pulled from the sock.

"Damn it, Mel, I didn't even know those guys were comin' over this morning, and you've got these high-priced toys in here like we're running a pawn shop!"

"You're tellin' me how to spend your—I mean, *our* money?"

"I'm not doin' this anymore." Virgil smacked a chunk of cash out of Melvin's fingers, watching the bills fall to the floor like big green snowflakes.

"We're just startin', boy!" Melvin peeled off a few hundred-dollar bills from the remaining bushel in his hands and, as he stood up, pushed them into Virgil's fist. "Big Pete says stuff's poppin' in New O."

"What pisses me off is I know I could kill you right now. I could kick your puny ass and just be done with all of this." Virgil threw the gift back in Melvin's face.

"I love the smell of dirty money." Melvin sat back down. "By the way, you ain't kickin' shit around here. Now look, Big Pete used to do repo for the state, and he has access to some unclaimed wheels. Cedric and Jojo get sprung from the state pen on probation in a week. With my expertise in GTA, we're all gonna make real green. Virgil, let this pretty-boy shit go and be down with us!"

"Mel, I'm not a big-time hustler like you and your boys."

"Who used to be *your* boys."

"I don't get down like that—with crime rings and grand theft auto. Hell no!"

"Sorry. I forgot that you're a *serious* musician who only did time for bein' a prizefighter, beatin' up punks in nightclubs. Face it, your little supper club is chump change. Besides, your heart ain't really into it. You call yourselves soldiers? Your lame band doesn't even have a record deal, so why are you carryin' that damn flute in your back pocket like a pistol—it's not *real* protection. Ain't no use tryin' to forget where you came from, Virgil. Let's get your investment back on the quick and get with this foolproof gig in New O. that involves half the work and triple the return."

Virgil flexed, thinking aloud as he stared at the front door for a long time. He looked at the crisp currency in Melvin's hand until his eyes grew with awakening. "Now that I think about it, I've had this burnin' desire to separate church and state, you know, business and pleasure."

"Preach, bro!"

"Rush, Saadiq, Kahlil, and Benny are cool, but music was just my hobby."

"Say it!"

"They take it too seriously. Especially Rush. He's a damn slave driver, and it gets tough havin' them chase me around twenty-four-seven." Virgil's anger continued to rev up his engine. "Now Thad is lettin' ofays sing at the club that I put *my* money into. And if it's one thing I can't stand, it's white folks raiding *our* shit."

Melvin left the couch and reached up to put his hand on Virgil's shoulder. "Ditch these highfalutin' eggheads, drop this bitch Rozalyn, and let's go back to the Seventeenth Ward and get your street credibility back, baby bro."

"But I can't shaft my blood brothers. They've had my back for a long time."

"But I'm your big bro, your family. I raised you and Pamela. I wouldn't steer you wrong. Come on. We'll go back home, make some quick loot, get out of the game, and just chill with all those fine Southern women, remember—the good old stress-free times? Nobody down your back, no rules and regulations."

"I don't know." Virgil shook his head, walking away to get Melvin's sticky little hand off his back. "The guys are waitin' for me downstairs. I've got to split."

"Torn? Confused? There's a way we can do this and make it look like you were never involved. You said you talk to Thad's old girl, what's-her-name?"

"Chelsea. Why?"

"Yeah, Chelsea. Chelsea's sexy. You said she wants Thad back pretty bad, right?" Melvin smiled while Virgil nodded reluctantly. "We'll put her on the case."

"No way, Mel. Chelsea and I talk off and on since she and Thad went out with Roz and me one time. I barely know her. Plus, she's not mentally ready for a street game like this."

"Virgil, I saw Chelsea lose it at the bar on openin' night at the club when Thad was flirtin' with that new chick, Asha." Melvin rubbed his sticky hands together. "Oh yeah, this is gravy. Call Chelsea this afternoon and invite her to the club tonight, and I'll take it from there. Those peace-freak punks won't know what hit them."

Chelsea left another phone message at the club because the fourteen calls to Thad's apartment had no effect.

Beep. Message twenty-six: "Thaddeus? Chelsea. Listen, I don't know what came over me last night, but you weren't there when those girls accosted me, so it's not what you think. Thaddeus, don't shut me out, because I'm not crazy, just filled with angst. Please, call me so we can talk." *Click*.

Chelsea put down the phone and completed the "S" in the "THADDEUS" she had spelled out in raspberry-flakes cereal on the dining room table. She exhaled with force, releasing only a smidgen of her pent-up frustration.

"I was *so* close last night," she told herself. "Regret was in his eyes...he was almost there. If it wasn't for that bitch!" Chelsea spat. She revisited the brawl in her mind. She reveled in the perverse pleasure she felt when the mirror broke against Asha's back—the sheer terror in Asha's young eyes when her baby-soft face was slapped. Chelsea laughed out loud, until exasperation took over again. With a quick brush of her arms, she flung the raspberry flakes from the table onto the floor.

"I need him." The sensation of Thad's family jewels was in Chelsea's palm again. If physically possible, she would've been a jewelry thief the night before. She wanted him in her hands right then. "God, I can taste him!"

Chelsea went over to the sofa. She rested across from the frame that contained the photo of her with Thad. She stared at it. She stared long and deep into Thad's two-dimensional eyes until they sprang from the picture and became real, looking at her the way he used to do. Before long, Thad was in the room. His presence was surreal.

Chelsea closed her eyes and imagined Thad caressing her breasts. With the weightlessness of a sweet daydream, he mounted her and began seeking pleasure inside her...sexual tension gradually building up...driving...until the stroking motion turned into a violent travail of passion.

Chelsea's pleasure surged, swelled and spread until it overwhelmed the nerves that connected her fantasies to her softest spot.

"Take me, take me, take me!" Chelsea begged thirstily as her inner world rocked and rolled. "Hurts so good."

Though too much for one person to handle, she wanted the satisfaction all for herself, fearing a release would flood the apartment. Greed eventually cost her. Quakes rumbled through her, forcing out quiet screams and heavy huffing. The intense waves sent her brain and body into a tailspin.

Then the tremors began to diminish. Her moans trailed off and her breathing slowed. The room stopped whirling. She heard the quiet again.

Her eyes opened. With bitterness, she realized that Thad was still in the picture frame. Her left hand had caressed her breast. Her right had crept up her slip and fondled her damp depths. Suddenly, keys jangled in the front door. Chelsea jolted, yanking her hands away from her personal places.

Kayla walked in looking professional, gorgeous, employed. "Ugh," she muttered, giving Chelsea a dirty look. "Gingersnap, we need to discuss this Sloppy Jane thing you've got going here. It's not kosher, girl."

Chelsea covered her face with her hands, groaning helplessly.

"Look at you, lazy and untidy, sprawled out on the sofa like a—what the hell?" Kayla slammed her leather tote bag on the dining room table in disgust. "These are my damn raspberry flakes all over the floor! What is this?"

"Kay, don't start. My guts hurt so bad," Chelsea whined, rubbing her navel. "I barfed again, and I feel like a bowl of shit."

"Well, could you have at least used a bowl for the raspberry flakes? You look like shit, too. Your wretched regurgitating is the baby telling you to pull this mess you call a life together."

"I know," Chelsea mumbled. "I feel like such an ass, forever accusing Thaddeus's friends of being shiftless, and now they're taking care of business, and I'm the one looking like a pile of trifling, tacky poop."

Kayla shook her head solemnly, sitting on the loveseat beside Chelsea.

"I went to see Carolina this morning. I've been logging her outrageous stories in my journal along with the spooky parallels to my life. The stuff leading up to the day you visited Carolina's penthouse with Adolfo would blow your mind!"

"I don't want to hear about it. I can't believe you're going to write this murderer's memoirs or whatever. I don't get this thing, this so-called 'connection,' you have with her."

"You know the woman from the Soundview Projects finally admitted that it wasn't Carolina who attacked her, right?"

"So what?"

"The attacker was a woman who claimed to be Carolina's friend but secretly desired her husband, Michael."

"You whipped Asha last night at the club. You want her naming *you* on Channel Two tomorrow?"

"That's different. I had every right to jack up those girls, but this project mistress didn't name her real attacker at first because she wanted Carolina to suffer more before she admitted the truth."

"My God, Chelsea! This is such a soap opera. The world's gone mad." Kayla moved to the edge of her seat. "Every newscast, every paper, every magazine, everywhere—it's Carolina Smithey! Every-damn-where. At home, I wake up in cold sweats because of her; meanwhile, at work, I look for more leads, more factoids, more talking heads willing to say something about this cuckoo. I'm choking on Carolina Smithey and I'm choking myself!"

"There's a lesson in that, isn't there?"

"Wait. Miss Discombobulated is giving *me* lessons now?"

"Forget it."

"Gladly." Kayla lifted Chelsea's photo from the coffee table. "Let me guess. Reminiscing again?"

"Did I ever tell you the fun part of angering Thaddeus was the consequence?"

"He'd bang you like an animal? I heard you two through these walls some nights."

Chelsea made a face. "Well, yeah. I guess you could put it like that. I loved when he was angry and passionate. For me, it was steamy, turbulent thrashings of him against me, a stress-relieving spanking with our most tender parts." Her voice turned sappy, and Kayla rolled her eyes. "In a way, it was what I did for him. All he had to do was be a strong, successful man for me."

"And you'd allow him to pound out his frustrations from the rigors of that role on you."

"Don't get me wrong, sweetie. I liked it, too. A kinky fantasy."

"To have him rip you open?"

"Yes. To share extreme passion. We're soul mates."

"Chelsea, what the devil are you talking about?"

"A bittersweet passion strong enough to maim, hurt…even kill. I did what Carolina did." Tears streaked Chelsea's face. "I laid my soul bare for Thaddeus to stomp on. I made the ultimate sacrifice—even told him I'd change for him. I told him I accepted the things he wanted, that I was willing to forgive everything."

"Chelsea, it's official, honey. You've lost your fierce edge. Poof! Gone. Look at you! No man, no hair and makeup, no attitude, no work ethic, nothing! I hate to say it, Chelsea." Kayla stood over her. "But I'm shocked and disappointed. I mean, I actually admired you like a big sister once. That's the only reason why I've put up with your eccentricities for so long. I've endured stuff that's going to send me to a mental institution before *you* go."

"Don't do this, Kay."

"Growing up, you were always the prettier one, the smarter one, the sweeter one. I just did what I could to keep up. But, now, I've managed to leave my best friend, big twin sister, and role model in the dust."

"Kay—"

"It's a letdown, because you're not the mentally strong woman I used to know, with the power to outsmart everyone on her way to the top. Instead, you're this big bad brat that has resorted to beating up little girls in barroom brawls? Come off it! That's dangerous in your condition. You need to get it together, gingersnap. I think you should go see your shrink tomorrow."

"Why are you cutting me with your words?" Chelsea grabbed her head, grimacing in the grip of a migraine.

"You need your pills?"

Chelsea nodded in pain.

"They're on your dresser, right?" Kayla asked, approaching Chelsea's bedroom door and reaching to turn the knob.

"Wait! Don't go in there!" Chelsea sprang up as if the sofa was on fire.

Kayla jumped away from the door. "Why?"

"Uh, I just remembered that, um…" Chelsea quickly positioned herself between Kayla and whatever she was hiding in the bedroom. "Just don't go in there!"

"Chelsea, what the hell do you have in there?"

"Nothing."

"Let me see!" Kayla struggled with Chelsea, whose persistent denial only fueled Kayla's burning curiosity.

Panic was in Chelsea's eyes as she guarded her secret with everything she had. She gently pushed Kayla back to the living room. "It's just…really messy, and I know you'll berate me some more if you see it. So, please, don't go in there until I can clean it up. Okay?"

"Okay," Kayla groaned, giving up for the moment.

"So, anyway, did I tell you I overheard that Asha floozy talking about trying to go to some French dance school last night? *Hello?* I mean, how realistic is that? She wouldn't know what to do with Paris," Chelsea ranted incessantly. "She and Thaddeus are both such freaking dreamers. She can't do a thing for him."

"Wait. Why are you bringing up Asha and Paris all of a sudden? Look, Chelsea, I don't want to hear about it anymore," Kayla replied resolutely. "My psyche can't take much more of you tonight. Say no more, Chelsea! That's it."

"All right. I'm sorry." Chelsea sat next to Kayla, breathing a sigh of disappointment. "Well, Virgil called me this afternoon. There's a party tonight at the supper club. Want to go?"

"I thought Thad banished you from that place."

"It's Arianna's birthday party…hosted by *Saadiq*," Chelsea sang.

"What does that have to do with anything?" Kayla asked, fidgeting in her seat. "Since when are you such a big Saadiq fan?"

"Negative, honey. I figured that would convince you to go. You're the dingbat who thinks he's God's gift. Too bad Nenna has her claws in him. Actually it's good that she's stuck with him, because you really don't even need to go there with that toad. I swear, just the thought. Ugh! Anyway—"

"You hardly even know him, gingersnap." Kayla flipped her hair.

"I know enough to know he's bad news. Want to go or what?"

"Well, I guess," Kayla admitted. "If anything, I'll get a kick out of watching you try to walk on water like a fool to get your Mr. Perfect back."

"So you're sure Thad won't be countin' the entire safe tonight?" Melvin asked for the fourth time as he huddled with Virgil behind the bar at Nubian Rhythm Kitchen.

"Yes, damn it," Virgil whispered, glancing over his shoulder.

"Concentrate! Stop lookin' so fuckin' paranoid."

"It's Thursday. Thad just counts the till for each night on that night. He only counts the entire safe on Monday nights, after the weekend rush. Then he makes a deposit to the bank after that."

"Cool. I'm makin' sure the receipts total up tonight. I've got the bogus paper cut and stacked like bills in this backpack. I'll snatch the loot and refill the money bags in the safe with this stuff. Since Thad's the only one with access to the safe, there's nothin' anybody can prove. We'll be long gone by Monday and before anybody realizes the big switch was made, dig? You know how to crack a safe?"

"What?" Virgil shouted his whisper. "Hell, no."

"Just jokin', fool." Melvin snickered. "That's my job. You just make sure—"

"Virgil, I finally caught you!"

"Who's that?" Virgil spun around suddenly. "What's up, Rush?"

"Something's been weighing on my mind that I want to clear up."

"Arianna's party is about to start. Can this wait until later, Rush?"

"Actually, it can't," Rush replied, taking a barstool. "When we were at your pad this morning, I noticed that the place looked a little more cluttered with upscale big boy's toys than it was the last time I visited."

Melvin stared Rush down. "Sweatin' the personal business in *our* home?"

"Mel, chill." Virgil pulled Melvin back from the counter.

"Yeah, Melvin, *chill*." Rush glared at him. "Virgil, it's *our* business I'm concerned about. Suits from major companies are coming to check out the band this weekend, but you've been faking the funk at our jam sessions. Now, I just want an explanation for all the new expensive artwork and stereo equipment in your place."

"Whoa. Yellow light, poet laureate," Melvin chimed in. "You were at our place checkin' out the stuff *I* purchased with the money *my* granddaddy left *me*?"

"Oh, that's *your* stuff?"

"Damn right, it is. It's for the place I'm gettin' in Harlem next month," Melvin exclaimed, before his voice went low. "I bought it a few weeks before Grandma Belle's emergency surgery. I offered to return it, but my generous baby bro told me he'd cover the medical bill." Melvin put one hand over his heart and the other on Virgil. "So tell me, why are you ambushin' my baby bro, Rushon?"

Rush sighed out the last breath in his body, raising his hands in apologetic surrender. "I'm really sorry, guys. Virgil told us about your grandmother's illness, Melvin. I had something else on my mind, and I guess I just—"

Subconscious Soul's saxophonist, Benny, walked up to the bar and signaled to Melvin by pointing to his pocket and then to the kitchen.

Easing from behind the counter, Melvin winked at Benny. "Hey, no hard feelings, Rushon. We're all stressed. Join Benny and me for a little pre-party party. He's got what we need to mellow out." Melvin grabbed Rush's shoulders, led him to the kitchen, and set him in front of the storeroom next to the deep freezer.

Rush's eyes darted back and forth from Melvin to the puffy bags of white powder on the steel cart between Benny and two girls in cornrows and short, retro dresses with their brown, baby-oiled legs attached to sexy stilettos.

"Rush, you're hanging with us tonight? I didn't invite you because I didn't think you were ready for the major leagues. This stuff is *realer* than grass." Benny smiled. "Well?" He waited for a response. "This isn't a spectator sport! Either bring your tired asses in here or scram, just close the damn door," Benny spat, pulling a blade from his shirt pocket, while the girls fluttered their eyelashes at Rush.

"You guys get started. I'm going to set up the bar for Virgil to take over, and I'll be right back." Melvin shoved Rush into the storeroom and shut the door.

Virgil stared at Melvin as he returned to the bar. "What are you doing, Mel?"

"Takin' care of that freakin' fiend. That was perfect timing. You should've seen Rush's eyes pop out of his head when he saw the coke and the cute ass in that room." Melvin laughed, walking behind the bar and nudging Virgil out from behind it. "Still with me on this, baby bro?"

"No." Virgil almost pouted.

"It's too late to discover your damn conscience now, Virgil. You're in too deep. And if you try to get crafty and wimp out, I swear I'll rat you out to your boys—tell them the truth about Grandma Belle and that I had nothin' to do with the missin' loot, that I never saw it after I slipped it to you. I got nothin' to lose, remember?"

Fear made Virgil's biceps bounce. His brother's desperate voice made him shrink back to the scared thirteen-year-old kid who had appeared on Melvin's doorstep and begged his big brother to take care of him thirteen years before. "Mel, you've got to promise me that when we back to New Orleans, you'll—"

"Virgil, go wait for the rich chick outside. When she gets here, bring her over here to me, and I'll take over." Melvin shooed him away. "Go. Go."

Virgil mumbled cuss words as he waded through the maze of

people congregating for Arianna's soirée. Outside the club, he looked at his watch, cursing Nubian Rhythm Kitchen, Subconscious Soul, and the whole clean-cut vibe of it all under his breath. Virgil hadn't even recognized consciousness or souls or any such inner, softy stuff until he stumbled into the neo-soul movement. Anger overtook him, because he'd started to care about those things and about people and about the power in his actions. Virgil waited under the street lamp for fifteen minutes, thinking about how returning to his old life would make things easier.

"Hey, Chelsea, you're a little late," Virgil announced when he finally saw her approaching the supper club with her girlfriends.

"I thought the party starts at ten," Shola gasped, checking her watch.

"Ladies," Virgil greeted. "The party's just starting. I was just giving Chelsea a hard time. How are you holding up, girl?"

"You two go on in. I need to talk to Virgil," Chelsea said, handing her purse to Kayla and waving her friends into the club.

"Well, pardon me. She needs to catch up with her *new* best friend. Whatever!" Kayla rolled her, grabbing Shola's arm and stomping into the club.

"Why is she so salty?"

"I don't know, Virgil. Kayla's been throwing *much* attitude around lately. Anyway, my palms are sweating. I can't believe Thaddeus said he's willing to see me," Chelsea shrieked, wiping her hands on her slinky red dress. "Where is he?"

Chelsea's childlike excitement made guilt coat Virgil's bones like glue, but he fought it. Sequestering his soft side under a mask of macho apathy, Virgil knew Big Pete, Cedric, Jojo, and all of the Seventeenth Ward would've been proud. "Hold on, babe. Not so fast. Let me introduce you to my brother first," Virgil said, escorting Chelsea through the pack of neo-soulers inside the club.

The walk seemed endless for both of them. In the thick of bop, blowouts, and beatniks with connecting roots, Chelsea and Virgil—polar opposites on the roots continuum—felt the most displaced. They knew that despite the culture's claims of unity, in actuality, everyone didn't fit in. That night, the affluent princess and the poor convict unconsciously pierced the center of cultural consciousness to restore life's order, as he or she knew it.

"Chelsea, this is Melvin Davies. Melvin, Chelsea Fuller."

"Hi, Melvin. I remember your face. Whenever I come here, I order—"

"Red rum," Melvin interrupted, pulling a glass from under the counter. "I know it well, Chelsea, and I poured a *special* shot of your usual just for you. How could I forget a lovely lady who likes a dangerous drink?"

Chelsea took a stool as she took the glass. "Ooh, I don't know if I should. On top of the pregnancy and all my medications, I haven't been feeling well lately."

"Oh, come on, sweetheart." Melvin encouraged her with a smile. "One little sip before you go talk to Thad and have to put up with his dysfunction."

"You know about our messy breakup, too?"

"I was there when Virgil had to beg Thad to agree to see you tonight, and Thad was still being wishy-washy about it. He's in the office wrappin' up some paperwork. So, hurry, take a sip and go tell him to get his act together, baby doll."

"You're right. Maybe just one tiny little sip." Chelsea tilted the glass to her lips and drank the red potion.

Melvin moved to the front of the bar with his trusty backpack in hand. "Virgil, watch the bar while I walk Chelsea upstairs. Make sure you can see everyone, and *everyone can clearly see you behind the bar*." Melvin winked at his accomplice. He took Chelsea by the shoulders and stood her up. "Let's go, baby doll."

"Thank you," Chelsea said, walking to the stairs with Melvin.

"Whoa, careful, sweet thing," Melvin soothed, catching her as she tripped on the first step. "Chelsea, remember, Thad will probably be a little stubborn when he first sees you, but Virgil told me you always get what you want."

"Something like that."

"I can't stand to think about how he's been ignorin' your feelings. Go in there and show Thad that he can't mess with Chelsea Fuller."

"Well, okay." A confused Chelsea blinked fast as they climbed the stairs slowly. "I brought a surprise for Thaddeus that I had wanted to show him yesterday before things went haywire. It's downstairs with Kayla."

"Virgil told me you were bringin' it. You up to gettin' physical tonight?"

"Excuse me," Chelsea stammered, missing another step. "Damn, that drink. What did you put in that thing?"

"Easy now." Melvin held her. "Thad may try to use his work as an excuse. So loosen him up, get him downstairs quick, and then spring your surprise on him. Use those foxy legs and that pretty smile, and he can't help but get with the program."

"*Ooh*, you're right. Good idea, Marvin or Mel—I'm sorry, what's your name again?" Chelsea asked as they came upon the office.

Melvin shoved her through the door and hid in the darkness of the hallway.

Chelsea stumbled into the office. "Thaddeus."

Thad's pen fell from his fingers and looked up toward her voice. "Jesus! You scared me. Chelsea, what the hell are you doing here? Didn't I tell you never to come here again?"

"Thaddeus, you didn't mean that. I called you a hundred times today, but you never called me back." Chelsea slid over to the desk. Inching her way around it, she reached over the back of Thad's big leather chair. As her fingers made contact with his muscles, a shudder deep in Chelsea's womb shook the lower half of her body. Chelsea slowly massaged Thad's shoulders as the fragrances of his cologne and the gingerroot oil in his hair mingled into a masculine aphrodisiac that melted her.

"Chelsea, I told you…I would call…the cops, if you…" Thad fought the gratification of each deep roll Chelsea gave his shoulders. He wheezed as she spun the chair around until he faced her. His eyes traveled up the caramel leg that she raised on the armrest. "Chelsea, don't even *think* about it. I mean it. I won't tolerate your violent, psycho outbursts."

"Don't use that word around me." Chelsea's tone changed to grave instruction. "I despise that word—*psycho*." Her nerves turned to cunning as she dug her heel into the chair, tearing the leather. "Thaddeus, I heard about your big family weekend. Everyone's going to be a part of it except me and the baby."

"Chelsea, I'm warning you. Don't do this." Thad closed his eyes as he felt her gently take a seat in his lap.

"You don't miss me?" Chelsea cooed, rubbing herself against his response. "I can't believe I'm actually touching you again, Thaddeus. It feels like it's been a lifetime, and I've craved for every inch of your body," Chelsea whispered, spreading her legs further over the arms of the chair, clasping the back of Thad's neck and pushing her bosom into his face. His breath in her cleavage warmed her all over. "Fuck me, Thaddeus. Make angry love to me."

They exchanged arrestingly heavy breaths.

"Damn it!" Thad grabbed Chelsea's buttocks, his fingers feeling the wetness of her panties. He lifted Chelsea from his lap. "I want you to get out of here right now, and I sure as hell don't want you around here this weekend."

Frustrated, Chelsea dug her fingers in her hair with one hand and pulled her damp underwear from its hiding place with the other.

Meanwhile, peeking from behind the door, Melvin was turned on. He started to sweat, cursing quietly outside the office. "Come on, girl. You can do it. Move this seduction along and get him downstairs."

"Thaddeus, I have something to show you downstairs."

"Chelsea, I'm busy." Thad fumbled his papers. "Don't throw me off track by messing with my mind. You're the reason I stopped wearing a damn watch."

"What in the world does that mean?"

"You're toying with my kismet."

"Your *kismet*? Oh, now who's full of fatalistic bullshit?" Chelsea paused. She squinted, walking coolly toward him. "It's starting to get to you, huh?" She nodded slowly, reading him. "Those words you said, the ones you don't want me to repeat—they're making you want to confess your undying love for me. Thaddeus, the only thing messing with your kismet is your denial of what you truly want."

"Stop it." The ticking of the imaginary clock returned to torment Thad.

"What? Hitting a little too close to home? You're always pushing your family's values away, but I bet all the lessons you were taught growing up are making *you* crazy now. Your disobedience eating at you?" Chelsea got closer, seeing through him as if he were a sheet of glass. "Your parents taught you to do what you set your mind to, go after what you want, right? That's why you're so damn successful."

"Quit, Chelsea." Thad stood and faced the back wall. The ticking grew louder.

"It's so clear now that it's sad. Thaddeus Coleman Carmichael, Jr., wants to be a world-class creative maverick and ends up at Columbia with a virgin he can screw like a horse. Tells his family he's finally in control of his life, but can't get a grasp on his own kismet. Because he lives under the thumb of a father who resents himself and in the shadow of a brother who killed himself... because neither could do the very things they wanted most to do."

Truth had never struck with such might. An unseen force yanked Thad's body around. He raced to Chelsea and grabbed the nape of her neck. His eyes bulged with contempt as he whispered in a consuming hiss, "I swear, say one more word and—"

Chelsea gasped, feeling his hostile fingers pinch the rear of her skull. "You'll kill me? Fuck me?" Her options were dry, dooming. "The truth is too real. You're hiding your passion for me, losing your faith in you, committing the *ultimate* sin."

"Get out," Thad whispered, letting her go.

"Thaddeus—"

"Leave!"

"I have a sonogram of our baby." Chelsea's voice was a faint wind. "I would've shown it to you yesterday, but you said I wasn't good enough for you or something."

A lullaby's chimes interrupted the ticking clock. "A sonogram?"

"It's in my purse downstairs with Kayla. Do you care to see it?"

"Call me a sinner or a heathen or whatever, but I truly do love this child."

Chelsea sighed. "I can see it in your eyes." She grabbed Thad's hand and led him out of the office.

Behind the office door, Melvin stopped breathing as they passed him. He peered around the door and watched Chelsea pull Thad down the dark stairway. His own countdown beginning, Melvin dashed into the office and went to work on the safe under the desk.

Downstairs, Chelsea and Thad approached a table. "Shola, where's Kayla?"

"In the ladies' room. I think she's hiding from Saadiq."

Thad noticed Chelsea holding on to the table for support.

"Chelsea, I warned you. You best not be drinking that red rum crap with my child growing in you!"

Chelsea forced Thad into a chair.

"Girl, you won't believe this. Look over there. Look who's on Tyler's arm," Shola said through stiff lips, pretending to sip on a fuzzy navel. "Oh, no she didn't."

"Gretchen Hausbruck?" Chelsea gasped. "Thaddeus, are they together?!"

"Chelsea, I didn't come down here for a gossip fest. If Asha and Nenna see you, Nenna will kill us both. They'll never forgive me for allowing you in here." Thad looked around nervously for the twosome. "For your information, Gretchen's singing here on Saturday. Now, where the hell is Kayla?"

"You despise Dr. Hausbruck! You know they're related, right?"

"So! What's it to you?"

"Chelsea can't let bygones be by and gone. She's not over Gretchen beating her for Homecoming Queen our senior year." Shola sucked her teeth.

"Zip it, Shola. I can't believe you're letting her perform here, Thaddeus. Damn, do you purposely *plan* to like everybody that I don't?"

"Believe it or not, my life goes on without you. Now, I'm losing my patience."

"Thaddeus, you may not believe it, but my life has also gone on without you. But I don't like where it will eventually go without you. If you only knew the changes I've been through. I've come to respect what you're doing with your life and—"

A voice cut Chelsea off. "Thad, what is *she* doing here?"

Thad sprang from his seat and spun around to see Asha's surprised face. He put an arm around her small waist, which caused her to wince.

"Careful, babe. My back is still sore from the attack by this monster."

"Sorry, baby." Thad pecked Asha's cheek. "It's all right. Chelsea was just leaving."

"Suddenly you're Mr. Step-and-Fetch-It, Thaddeus?" Chelsea traded spiteful stares with Asha. "You jump to her commands like a lapdog?"

"I told her I'd protect her from you," Thad replied.

Sensing the storm, Shola put her face in her hands as Chelsea stood up.

"Sweetie, I have an issue to take up with my baby's father, so if you stay out of my face, I'll stay out of yours."

Suddenly, Thad flinched. "Damn! I forgot to lock the office door. I've got to lock it. I'll be right back. Asha, do you want to come with me or will you be okay?"

Asha's eyes were aimed at her opponent like poisoned arrows. "I'm a big girl."

"Chelsea, we'll finish up, and then you can leave." He disappeared.

"Let's get out of here." Chelsea pulled Shola out of her seat. "Go get Kay. I'll be outside."

"You're demented, you know that?" Asha taunted, following Chelsea to the door. "But I've already made Thad completely forget about your crazy ass! Hey, I know what it's like, girl. My ex-man trampled on my feelings, because I was caring and understanding and blind too. Always the damned softy! But I'm tired of playing second fiddle in relationships. Since I was dogged, I just wanted a little lapdog of my own. Payback is a bitch, ain't it?"

"No, *you* are, Asha!" Chelsea turned on her heels. "Now, I swear, if you don't eliminate yourself…" Chelsea warned, while Shola dragged Kayla outside.

"What the heck is going on, Chelsea? Why are we leaving?" Kayla shouted.

"Let's go, Kay." Chelsea began walking off.

"You killed the good girl in me, Chelsea," Asha yelled to the backs of Chelsea and her friends. "And I want to thank you, rich bitch, because now I've done a lot of growing up. Hopefully, your brainless little shadow, Kayla, will wise up to your game, grow up, and get a life of her own. I don't even love him, you psycho! I was only in the fight for the kicks, to see if I could get the prize, and I won, bitch! *I won!*"

Asha's words echoed throughout every alley in Brooklyn, down Seventh Avenue, and straight into Chelsea's skin. An electric shock jumpstarted Chelsea's instincts as her blood turned to grade-A, octane gasoline. Anger's fuel turned Chelsea into a speedy torpedo propelled by red rum rage, but Kayla and Shola called on all of their might to hold her back from further confrontation.

Thad appeared at the club's entrance. "Where's she going?"

"I don't know," Asha cooed innocently and turned to hug Thad. "She stormed out like a wildebeest. She just can't seem to control the animal in her."

"Using my unborn baby to get to me again."

"That is so low."

Thad shook his head. "Anyway, let's celebrate with Arianna for a little bit. Then, we'll slip out early, so we can have the brownstone to ourselves."

Despite a forecast that called for a partly sunny Friday, the sky refused to give anything more than an overcast morning. The night before had not been quiet, and the world's stillness came on eerily the next day, requiring all guilty noisemakers to reflect on the virtue of silence.

"Sonia Sanchez, Nikki Giovanni, Toni Morrison, Michelle Wallace. Wow, you've got some great reads up here." Thad admired the enormous bookshelf in Arianna's living room. "Self-help addict Chelsea Fuller could use a recommended reading list from you. But you still need Michael Eric Dyson, Nathan McCall, Eldridge Cleaver, and Amiri Baraka, and then you'll be set."

"Thanks, Mr. Testosterone," Arianna replied from the sofa, swathing her braids in a white headwrap. "But I keep those delightful reads on the bottom."

Thad knelt and found his grocery list of authors on the bottom shelf.

"Yep. Right where you and your kind belong." Arianna laughed, grabbing her silver arm cuff from the table and sliding it on. "Ready to go?"

"Ms. Feminist Queen." An overtly chivalrous Thad opened the door for her.

"Doing the interview at the club will give the article more context," Arianna explained as she grabbed her backpack and headed down the stairs.

"Listen," Thad said in the stairwell, referring to the funky sounds coming from his apartment. "Subconscious Soul will be rehearsing all day, so maybe it's good that we do it at the club."

"Proper." Arianna stopped as she opened the door of the brownstone. "Wow! Who licked this front stoop clean?"

"I couldn't sleep last night," Thad said, walking down the stairs past her. "I'm a little nervous about this weekend."

"I remember when I was the only one who'd sweep this stoop. I gave up after a while." Arianna continued to look back after she left the stairs. "Anyway, I don't mind Subconscious Soul's jam sessions. The rhythm helps me write sometimes. That was the one condition I gave them when they moved in and told me they were in a band—that I dig their music. And I do. They're prepping to cut a demo, right?"

"Yes, ma'am, and they're showcasing for the bigwigs from Mystic Music tomorrow at the club," Thad told Arianna as they walked down the street.

Arianna flipped through a copy of *VIBE* magazine. "Don't call me *ma'am*."

"You're damn near thirty."

"I just turned twenty-eight, thank you. Watch that mouth." She laughed, folding back a page in her magazine. "Speaking of the band, listen to this review. 'Subconscious Soul is an ingenious ensemble. The band's sensuous, breezy brand of syncopated razzmatazz and African rhythms, with a bluesy poetry-scat icing, is almost revolutionary. Each band member is a virtuoso in his own right. But audiences who have yet to hear of this Brooklyn-based quintet will have to wait for a daring record exec with some sense to take a chance and recognize their talent, which needs to be shared with a public hungry for soulful satisfaction.'"

"That's what I like to hear. With press like that, music biz people should be beating down their door. Arianna, I pray just as hard for Rush, Saadiq, Virgil, Kahlil, and Benny as I do for Birdie. Tomorrow's showcase is going to be colossal."

"Is Virgil still acting up?" Arianna inquired as they crossed the intersection. "The other guys said he's been a little out of it."

"They all are. I think Rush is moving on to harder stuff. I found a dime bag of rocks in the little box he keeps on the windowsill. He says the drugs are Benny's, but I just can't talk to him about it." Thad shook his head. "Damn, I wish the sun would come out already!"

"Why? You get nervous when it rains?"

"Yes," Thad replied as if his response was a revelation to himself as well. Thad still looked up at the sky as they came upon a corner bodega, and Arianna yanked his sleeve to signal a necessary stop.

Storefront wooden crates held peaches and mangos covered with dewdrops, and a barrel brimmed with cuddling tangerines. Plantains and various exotic vegetables lined a linen-covered table, and, to bless the produce and the passersby, the strains of reggae music drifted out from the adjoining store.

Thad watched Arianna lean over the rainbow harvest and inhale the sweet fragrance with her eyes closed. She dipped into the array of greens, golds, and reds, testing for ripeness with her fingers. As he watched her caress the fullness and roundness of random fruits, Thad realized how regular and beautiful Arianna Killborne was. She had Chelsea's every-woman drive wrapped in Asha's earth-mother loveliness, and Thad wished he could be as gentle as she was with the kiwi in her hand.

"I'll be right back," Arianna whispered.

Thad watched her long, tan skirt sway into the store. While Arianna chatted with the handsome Rasta clerk, Thad felt a strange jealousy bite the lining of his stomach. There was something painful in watching Arianna just be happy, just be her independent, aware self. He had never communicated this to her, but he felt such bitterness whenever he lusted after the Chelseas or exoticized the Ashas of the world. All the while, regular, beautiful, independent, self-aware Arianna asked nothing of anyone. With a sense of cowardice breezing past him on the street corner, Thad didn't like the part of himself that overlooked her ilk. He watched Arianna reach into her small backpack to pay for the kiwi she'd so carefully selected.

She shouldn't have to pay for anything in this life, he thought.

Suddenly, Thad turned off the voice in his mind, ran into the bodega, and gently guided Arianna's fist full of change away from the clerk's outstretched palm. "I've got this," Thad said, snatching a green bill from his pocket and pushing it into the clerk's hand.

"No, Thad, I've got it right here."

"No, it's okay. Really. Did you want anything else?" he asked, not realizing how desperate he looked, how guilt-ridden he sounded.

"No." Arianna smiled, palming the kiwi like the key to an ancient mystery that had boggled the sexes since Adam and Eve. "Thanks, Thad."

"No worry." Thad led her out of the store and back out to the mean street.

"Thad, that was sweet, the way you just ran in and insisted like that." Arianna laughed a little as they walked again.

"It would cost me more if I hadn't done it. Arianna, you're the kind of woman all men should work to keep content."

"Now, *that's* sweet. And to a damn near thirty-year-old?"

Thad tried to do the shy-boy thing but didn't feel man enough to show any more blatant vulnerability. He shrugged off Arianna's tender appreciation and looked at his shoes strolling leisurely.

"Do you think it's sick that people are attracted to qualities in their mates that remind them of their parents?"

Arianna thought for a moment. "Potentially. It depends on the qualities. But it's also a part of human nature. We want what's familiar to us."

"My mom is filled with tales about radical college days, painting posters for the Black Panther Movement. She used to be such a cool lady. She'll never admit it, but I think she lost a lot of her soul power activism when she married my father. Granddad was always a stuffy man; yet, my mom married a man just like him."

"Some women allow their risk-taking spirit to fade into the hazy romanticism of their marriage vows, and others let a man juice up their gambling habits when it comes to matters of the heart. From where I stand, either extreme can spell real trouble."

"Then again, there are women like you who…well, sometimes I wonder if you and I had ever…"

"Thad, please don't say anything that'll embarrass both of us."

"Nah." He laughed. "It's just that, like *you*, my mom was always instilling in people never to forget the struggles of folks who paved the way for our slices of opportunity. She always encouraged my sister and me to do what we must, to follow our hearts no matter what."

"You're doing that, Thad. Don't sweat the petty detours. It all works out like it's supposed to. The band will get everything together, and your baby sister will get her chance to be onstage again. She's the sweetest thing."

"Yeah, I know. It's funny. Cynthia said when she looks at Chelsea she sees a cut-and-paste image of what my father wants *her* to be in a few years—a perfectly pathetic, well-groomed princess with a detached air and all the education, but no empathic awareness, no real substance."

"Cynthia's too sharp for that. And, hey, at least Nubian Rhythm Kitchen is measuring up to the vision of its creators, right?" Arianna tried to lighten the mood as they came upon the supper club.

"Or maybe some of us are just trying to convince ourselves that it is," Thad replied, reaching to unlock the door. "Damn it!"

"What's that?"

"It's another scarlet letter from Chelsea," Thad huffed, ripping down the red paper taped to the door and unfolding it. "She leaves me these crazy letters. She scribbles a lot of desperate mumbo-jumbo about how she's doomed without me and me without her. Listen, she ends this one: 'Anyone who knows the good he ought to do and doesn't do it, SINS.' I hate that shit!"

"That's deep, Thad, in a kooky kind of way. A jilted lover quoting Biblical passages? What is that supposed to mean?"

"It's a long story." Thad balled up the note, entering the club. "Normally, I would at least consider Chelsea's safety, but there's no way in hell it would do a bit of good to forgive her! So, I don't know what she's getting at with this one."

"I guess you saw Chelsea's true colors when she attacked Asha and Nenna," Arianna said, with a shiver crawling down her spine.

"That wasn't a first. She's gotten violent other times, too. It's scary, because you'd never expect it from her, but Chelsea is by no means the helpless victim she proclaims to be."

"Thad, you can't allow her jive melodrama to cloud your bright days ahead. Even if Chelsea has lost her God-given mind, you have lots to look forward to."

"You're right. Carmichael Family Night is tomorrow and I have a child on the way, hopefully a son," Thad boasted.

They climbed the dimly lit stairs to the club's office. The note was still in Thad's hand. The confusion about its meaning and his reaction was still in Arianna's head. The rest of their ascent was made in silence. Thoughts of manipulation and mindplay steered their bodies, as they walked into the swallowing darkness of the top of the staircase.

Suddenly, Arianna screamed. Thrown by fear, Arianna fell back against Thad, who caught her before they both tumbled down the stairs. "Oh my God!" She clamored to hide behind him. "What is *that*?"

Thad felt her shaking from shock, and his pulse raced. He hesitated, gripped by surprise. "What the…?"

"What the hell is going on around here?" Arianna demanded, peering over Thad's shoulder and shaking him.

The cracked head and torso of the Nefertiti mirror protruded from the darkness. "Somebody dragged this from the Dumpster out back and put it here." Thad strained to make out the message written in what looked like bloody red lipstick on the mirror. "'He who conceals his SIN does not prosper, whoever confesses and renounces them finds mercy.' This is beyond lunacy. She's stark-raving mad! How did she get in here to do this brain-sick shit?!"

"You think Chelsea did that?"

"Damn straight! All of this *sin* crap is her sick little game."

"Thad, this is starting to freak me out. Do you want to call the police or something? I mean, what should we do?"

"I don't want to touch the damn thing. She might have put a hex on it." With trembling hands, Thad opened the office door and guided Arianna inside. "I'm not a sinner. You are!" Thad declared, approaching the mirror with baby steps. "You're the damn sinner, you schizo!" He kicked his reflection, shattering the mirror with a thunderous crash. Outside, the heavens followed his lead, shattering the sky, crashing with thunder, and shedding rain.

Arianna gasped as Thad charged into the office, slammed the door, and punched the wall to get the last word.

He raised a fist. "I'll be damned if Chelsea pawns off her guilt until I bear the cross alone! She's the cause of this Hell, not me!"

Arianna nodded, holding her hand over her heart.

"Look at that!" Thad pointed to the phone, and Arianna stood to examine it as instructed. "See? The message light's flashing like a bomb timer, and I know who set this bomb. Saadiq's obsession bit is starting to make a lot of sense now. But that crazed stalker can forget about getting a second chance from me."

"Second chance, my foot," Arianna snapped, smoothing her skirt. "Thad, these are not the actions of a right mind."

"I know," he replied, staring at the answering machine. "That maniac is fighting a losing battle with no one but herself." Thad forced himself to listen to the messages, most of them left in Chelsea's gratingly helpless voice proclaiming her innocence, her loss, her needs. "Damn her!"

"She deserves no sympathy," Arianna said, as the final message played.

Beep. Message Twenty-seven: "Junior, we're in New York City at the Waldorf Astoria, room 417. Everyone's here, and we're all ecstatic. We'll be at the club tonight to have dinner and to touch base about tomorrow. Your mother brought all her art pieces, Birdie's been practicing her songs, and I have my menu all lined up. I hope you were able to get all of the ingredients I requested. Son, I know the pressure is mounting, but so is the pride. I'm proud of you, Junior. I love you. 'Bye."

"You hear that?" The angry fear in Thad's stomach melted.

"Thad, that's what you need to concentrate on. Not the madness."

"Chelsea can't compete with *that*." His eyes glassy, Thad paused and drew strength from the tone of his father's message. "I'll deal with Chelsea, *after* tomorrow. I'll get a restraining order or whatever it takes to keep her at a world's distance from me, Asha, and the supper club." He scrambled to clean up the broken glass in the hallway outside the office. "Arianna, keep this between us. Tomorrow has to go off without a hitch. I want everything to be perfect for my family."

"Your secret's safe with me. If I told anyone, they'd think *I* was the crazy one." Arianna shuddered, helping Thad shovel broken glass bits from the floor. Finally, she whispered, "Thad, you can put Chelsea on the backburner but don't discount her. Never underestimate the fury of a scorned woman. Trust me."

"Right now, I don't give a damn. I just need to survive the next thirty hours or so." Suddenly, Thad's imaginary clock was accompanied by sand in an hourglass counting down the days of his life.

Arianna shook her head. "I hope Chelsea's insanity isn't rubbing off on you. From the looks of it, only one of you will survive this riot you called a relationship."

"She's the crazy one, not me."

"I'll be in the ladies' room centering myself." Arianna walked away slowly.

Thad dumped the last of the broken glass and went downstairs where he found Asha waiting at a table with four little girls eating orange slices. "Hey, Asha. How are you, cutie?" Thad kissed her cheek, while the girls giggled at his public display of affection. "And who are *these* cuties?"

"Kenya, Stephanie, CeCe, and Mona. They're in the junior class at the Kuumba Dance Studios. They're part of the big program tomorrow. Say hi to Thad, girls," Asha said, showing him off.

"Hi," they greeted shyly, snickering and licking their fingers.

"Is that your *boyfriend*?" Kenya asked with a hint of disgust.

Thad frowned, wanting to be more than somebody's "boyfriend"—a term that, to him, had gained a flimsy quality.

Meanwhile, Asha stared at Thad, trapped in a moment when a child's innocent question catches adults off guard. The answer is none of a small person's business, but the thought of lying to the kid hurts more than just telling him or her off. Neither Asha nor Thad responded to the four tykes, because it would've meant letting the kids win and forcing the adults to be honest with themselves.

Asha was quick on her feet. "Nubian Rhythm Kitchen proudly

presents Footprints: A Tribute to the History of Dance, featuring Kuumba's Youth Troupe!" Asha announced, waving her arms over the little girls in a splendiferous manner. "You'll be our little starlets tomorrow. Now, hurry on back and get your things, ladies. Your parents are waiting for you." While the girls cheered and trotted to the backstage area, Asha fell back into her seat breathing a sigh of relief.

"They're adorable." Thad sat across from Asha. "It's good to see your smile."

"Well, they're so excited. Nenna and I have been working all week to put this tribute together with Nick. He's bringing moves from his glory days with the Alvin Ailey Dance Theater."

"I love your enthusiasm."

"We've planned such a moving program." Asha reached for Thad's hand and slowly stroked it. "First, we revisit African tribal and war dance and move to tap and jazz, and then we travel through hop, disco, and street. We've got the Kuumba African Troupe, some former Ailey dancers, some college fraternities and sororities will be stepping—all kinds of stuff. You're going to be amazed."

"I am already. I can't wait to see you dance again, baby," Thad whispered, watching Asha's hands roll over his own.

"Thad…" Asha's voice trailed off and did not come back for a while. "Last night…when we went back to your place…you were very rough with me."

"I'm sorry. I didn't realize you weren't happy until it was over. I climbed off you and you just rolled over. I felt horrible, like I'd violated you. I couldn't sleep after that, so I went out and cleaned the stoop at four in the morning."

"What came over you? It's like something else was controlling you. You didn't seem like yourself."

"Crazy thing is I probably *was* just being myself, or maybe it was the frustrations of just trying to *be*—be black and be bold and be successful and be honest and be real and be free of old habits...I don't know what I'm saying. Asha, listen, don't run away from me because Chelsea's so damn irrational."

"Thad, please. I have no use for Chelsea and the estranged basket-case syndrome. The girl is a wicked mess, and, frankly, it's weak coming from someone supposedly with so much class. So she can keep on trying, but we're doing this now. I've got you right where I want you."

"You're so understanding, but I'm going to make it up to you. Tomorrow is my Nubian queen's birthday, and I have something very special for you." Thad leaned in and gave her a sweet peck, thanking God for cocoa butter and apples.

"What is it? No, forget it. Don't tell me. I love surprises."

"Between your birthday and my family getting a shot at their championships right here, tomorrow will be out of this world. You can meet them tonight."

"Uh...I can't stay...not tonight. I have to go through my steps again and, um, help Nenna with the narration. Tomorrow, okay?" Asha proposed, watching the light flicker from Thad's eyes. "Tomorrow is a big day for you, isn't it? You really want to make your family proud?"

"Girl, if you only knew."

"I think I do."

Outside, the rain stopped.

When Asha disappeared backstage, Thad became a newborn discovering his surroundings for the first time. It dawned on him—why Asha completed the circle he'd created to protect his world.

"Even through her wide-eyed innocence, she saw what Chelsea

couldn't see," he whispered. "I must make her forget this Zeké fellow, *for good*."

The day's on-again, off-again sprinkles let up just as Kayla came home from work. She placed her open umbrella by the door, kicked off her heels, and nestled herself in the cushions of the sofa.

"Chelsea?"

The apartment seemed quieter than usual.

"Chelsea?"

Kayla let her hair down from its bun and massaged out the waves with her fingers as her eyes researched the room.

"Hmm, she left the station this afternoon. Surely she beat me home," Kayla whispered, rubbing her feet.

She looked toward the hallway, starting to feel the quiet swarm like smog. She kept her eyes there for a few minutes, until nothing moved or could be heard but the sound of her heartbeat. Kayla rose slowly from the couch and tiptoed toward the hallway. She stopped at her bedroom door and shot a look over her shoulder at the front door.

All was quiet.

Kayla started again. Each footstep on the wood floor produced a creak that strained to break the concrete silence. Kayla edged closer and closer to Chelsea's closed bedroom door, until she noticed a yellow note tacked near the knob. With deliberate motion, Kayla removed the note. Slowly, she reached for the knob and tried to turn it and abruptly looked at the motionless front door that stared back at her. Kayla held her breath and tried to turn the knob again. She fought against a stronger lock, wildly turning and shaking and pushing.

She gave up, running back to the living room to find her breath again. Panting, Kayla jumped back in her space on the couch and unfolded the note noisily to kill more of the quiet. She read:

Kay,
Thanks for being there for me last night. My womb's upsetting me. I went to see the doctor. I don't think it's anything serious.
P.S. I put the chicken out for dinner. Stay out of the dungeon, because I haven't cleaned it yet.
Love Ya,
Chelsea

9

STOLEN WIND

She walked along a lush green, holding the hands of a little girl and a little boy. All three of them were dressed in gleaming white. The kids were oh so cute. The girl looked like a baby Chelsea, the little boy a baby Thaddeus. Too cute! They strolled along the serene surroundings, coming upon a colossal wooden cross next to a white picket fence. The children looked up, shielding their eyes from the beaming sun, and waved.

"Hi, Daddy."

Thad hung crucified on the cross. Gaunt and sullen, he was stripped down to a white loin cloth and a shimmering dog leash around his neck.

The chain of the leash extended all the way to the ground below, where Chelsea yanked it whenever she wished to hear from him. The sun was shining, so Chelsea fancied to hear his voice on this day. She yanked it, and Thaddeus uttered his only words: "Forgive me, darling, for I have sinned."

Chelsea blew him a kiss and turned to walk the children back to the big white house on the hill. She signaled that she would need a few more minutes to the driver of the shiny, white Perennial private car waiting to take her to the TV station. She had to be on air in thirty minutes. Saadiq, in an uncomfortably tight chauffeur's uniform, tipped his hat, climbed into the car, and proceeded to wait.

Meanwhile, Chelsea skipped to the backyard and was greeted by the family dog barking ferociously at her. She hated that ugly dog. The *mean thing had Asha's face attached to a scrawny canine body. She had kept it for the kids, but no more, damn it. Chelsea kicked the dog in the head. Again. Harder. Chelsea kicked the mutt once more, splattering bloody dog juice all over her pretty white gown.*

"Drat!"

She was at her wit's end. Chelsea pulled an AK-47 assault rifle from her bodice, almost breaking a nail. Staring squarely at the bone in Asha's nose, Chelsea cocked her piece and blew a hole in the blustering beast...

Chelsea awoke with an earthquake's jolt. She looked at the clock. It was 4:15 on Saturday morning. She looked around her dark bedroom. It was still and quiet, except for her rapid breathing.

"Chelsea, I'm so very sorry..." Her physician's voice returned, disembodied, loud and hurtful, to Chelsea's ears. She sprang from the bed and hurriedly rearranged the bethel on her bedspread. From a nearby Victorian chair in the corner, she grabbed the red sweater set and black skirt she'd worn to work and to her doctor's appointment the day before, when she'd first heard the echoing words that had just roused her. She scrambled to get into her clothes as she requested a taxi from the Upper West Side to The Bronx Women's Correctional Facility on her cell phone. Crying all the way to Oz, Chelsea was continuously taunted by her doctor's voice: *"I'm sorry. I'm so sorry."*

"I'm sorry, ma'am," the big-busted female guard told Chelsea for the third time. "Inmates cannot receive visitors at this hour."

"Please, officer. Please, this is an emergency. It's imperative that I speak to Mrs. Smithey. Please," Chelsea insisted, banging on the guards' desk, longing to see the only dazzling wizard who could help her have her greatest wish granted and deal with her tragic loss.

"No, ma'am," the guard said, with diminishing patience. "You've been here before. You know the rules. You've got to wait until ten."

"Shola, I promise you. Someone or *something* was looking out for that nineteen-year-old girl two nights ago, because she was spared in a big way," Kayla said into the phone tucked between her ear and her shoulder. "Asha's lucky we subdued Chelsea. But I swear I was close to taking care of that hussy myself."

"What is that chick's deal anyway? Did you hear what she said—that she just stole Thad from Chelsea for kicks?"

"The nerve of that twit, calling me Chelsea's 'brainless shadow'! Shola, you know that makes me violent. I've had to fight that image all my damn life." Kayla left her bedroom and entered the kitchen.

"Girl, the look in your eyes scared *me!* But *still*, romanticizing about Thad's macho mating practices as beautiful brutality in bed? That baffles me," Shola insisted. "Honey, Chelsea is the most royal and hottest of all messes."

"As the more experienced one, I warned Chelsea about the tragic flaw of the male psyche. I told her: 'Prepare to deal with like-father, like-son baggage. When you deal with a man, you're not only dealing with him, but also his father and his father's father. They take what they see and interact with women accordingly.' But in this case, Thad's father doesn't approve of what Thad's doing. Besides, Chelsea's forever telling me that's exactly what she wants—her daddy and Thad's daddy rolled into one fine piece of man." Kayla reached for the box of raspberry flakes on top of the refrigerator. "Oh!"

"What?"

"The dinner plate I left out for Chelsea last night is still sitting plastic-wrapped and untouched on the counter."

"Did she come home last night?"

"I hope so. She went to see her doctor yesterday," Kayla replied, pouring a big bowl full of cereal. "I hope everything's okay."

"How do you keep up with her? Living with all that madness?"

"I have nightmares. That's how I deal with it, remember? Shola, it's seriously starting to get to me, though." Kayla entered the living room, sat on the couch before the TV, and flipped on the music video channel. "Anyway, girl, Kendall's officially on the ex list. Saadiq is sexier than Kendall, no? Ooh, did you see how Saadiq ignored me at the club the other night? That's why I was hiding in the restroom—"

"Oh, darn. I've got to go."

"Shola, don't do that! I'm stuck listening to Chelsea's man drama all the time, so you should be stuck listening to mine."

"No, really, I've got to go. Walé's at the door. I saw a disgustingly cute puppy at the pet store a few days ago, and I think he's going to surprise me with it. 'Bye."

Kayla reluctantly dropped the phone. She turned the volume up on the television, but her mind couldn't focus on the singing box in front of her. Kayla looked at Chelsea's closed bedroom door. Unable to tolerate the enigmatic taste in every spoonful of her breakfast, Kayla quickly went to the telephone and checked the answering machine.

The computerized voice inside the phone replied, "*You have no messages at this time.*"

Kayla walked to the bathroom and stood on Chelsea's side of the counter. She felt the bristles of Chelsea's pink toothbrush. Dry. She sighed, thinking.

Kayla approached Chelsea's bedroom and pressed her ear to the door. She squinted, as if that would help her hear any sign of Chelsea inside. "Chelsea?" She knocked and looked pensively toward the living room. "Chelsea," Kayla said again, turning the knob. The door was locked, so Kayla went back to the sofa and tried to eat her soggy cereal.

Rush and Thad waited by the front doors of the supper club until a small black van pulled up to the curb. Nearly knocking Rush over, Thad hastened out to the van and hugged Cynthia and his parents. "I'm so amped to see you guys."

Mrs. Carmichael surveyed her son from head to toe. "Honey, I was just telling your father and sister on the way over here how proud I am of what you're doing for us and in general. It says mountains, son."

Thad took her hand. "I'm doing what I have to do."

"I'm glad. You seem to be the happiest you've ever been." Mrs. Carmichael patted Thad's back. "Meanwhile, I'm nervous and overjoyed all at the same time," she said, opening the van's sliding door to reveal her artwork inside.

"So let's start unloading this work," Rush said eagerly.

Thad reached inside the van. "Mom, this urban landscape is striking! Check this out, Rush." Thad handed the painting to Rush through the back door. "I've never seen a lot of these pieces before."

"Behold the one against the seat." Mrs. Carmichael pointed inside the van.

Uncovering a large painting, Thad stopped moving. He stared at the piece like a long-lost friend.

Cynthia saw wetness coat his eyes. "Isn't it great, Thad?"

"Mom, when did you do this?"

"I did it while you were away at grad school," she whispered, wrapping an arm around her son. "Dad and Cynthia never go down to the basement, so I haven't shown it to anyone. I had planned to surprise the family with it when you came home after graduation, but your plans changed. So it's just been covered up. Painting this one transformed me emotionally; it helped me to grieve, I suppose. As much as it still hurts, the time has come to unveil it and validate it. Do you like it?"

"Mom, this is unbelievable." Thad wiped his eyes and embraced her. "It completes this day."

"We'd never seen it until she loaded it in the van back home. Isn't it pretty, Thad?" Cynthia asked, approaching them. "Look at us."

"I used the family portrait we took right before you went away to business school, and I painted it," Mrs. Carmichael explained, admiring her work along with her children. "I used Brandon's old sports team photo to add him to it. I wanted to reunite all of us again."

"It's such a realistic rendering," Rush observed. "Remarkable."

"The Carmichaels back together again. It's beautiful," Thaddeus Senior said, dripping with pride.

"I'm going to start arranging the display. Do you want to come and advise, Mrs. Carmichael?"

"Sure, Rushon. Thank you."

"Junior, I'm going to inspect your kitchen and make sure I can work in the space. I want to show my menu to the culinary staff and make sure they understand the game plan." Thaddeus Senior went inside, flipping through his little notebook.

"There he goes again with the Mussolini routine." Thad laughed, clutching the family painting like a million-dollar check.

"Yeah, but it's kind of cute this time." Cynthia chuckled.

In the prison's waiting area, Chelsea nibbled her fingernails like chewing gum as she sat on a steel bench, watching the clock. She had gotten up once during her tension-filled five-hour wait, using the water fountain to wash down two migraine pills and a "pick-you-up." Meanwhile, the busty prison guard watched the desperate Chelsea, occasionally stopping her work to roll her eyes or shake her head disapprovingly. At 9:58, Chelsea rushed the guards' desk.

The guard raised a hand in the air to halt Chelsea. "Page Smithey," the large lady said to her skinny partner, while Chelsea beat on the desk and watched the clock's minute hand move again.

"Smithey wasn't expecting anybody and doesn't want to see anybody."

"She doesn't want to see you, honey," the big guard said with satisfied regret, swiveling in her chair to face Chelsea.

"No! Tell her Chelsea Fuller's here!" Chelsea insisted, smacking the counter.

The skinny guard whispered into the phone. She put the receiver down and walked over to the counter. "I'll buzz you into the visitors' booths," she told Chelsea.

Exchanging pissy glares with the big guard, Chelsea stumbled away from the desk. She was buzzed through the door into the visiting area just as the clock struck ten. She yanked up the phone before sitting down. "Carolina, I waited *five* hours."

"I thought you were my crooked lawyer coming back to badger me. He wants me to cop a plea bargain. He can forget it, because the jury selection process has begun, and I want to stand up for what you and I believe in," Carolina ranted into the receiver, as Chelsea fell lifelessly into the green vinyl chair across from her.

"Help me!"

"Chelsea, darling, you look a mess. What in heaven's name is troubling you? Is it that boyfriend of yours?"

Chelsea nodded, starting to cry.

"What did he do to you?" Carolina demanded.

Chelsea shook her head, bawling.

"That other girl? What, Chelsea?"

"He's a sinner. She's a sinner. They're all the damn sinners!" Chelsea sobbed.

"Lower your voice. Chelsea, what have you been taking? You look strung out, and I don't understand what you're saying."

"I got very bad news yesterday, and Thaddeus will kill me when he finds out," Chelsea whimpered through the glass. "But Asha doesn't love him. She doesn't want him most. Thaddeus needs to be saved from himself and realize that redemption is in *my* arms."

"News. What news, Chelsea?"

"Thaddeus is my everything. I'm utterly, stupidly, blindly in love with him. Carolina, I know I have exactly what you had in Michael, if not more, and I want to hold on to him—"

"Oh no. Wait one minute. Chelsea, slow down."

"—but I must hurry and act in the name of passion, before my dazzle fades or I get my platinum diva card revoked, right? I just need to get your blessing, please, oh Ice Queen," Chelsea begged, mascara streaking her face.

"Chelsea, wait. Don't move. Listen to me very carefully."

"I'm so lonely," Chelsea lamented, looking at the clock on the wall. "Oh, I need a new outfit. I can't express my love looking like Shitsville! I'll make you proud, Carolina. You'll see…"

Suddenly, the green vinyl chair was vacant. The phone receiver slammed against the counter, slid out of view and dangled from the wall of the carrel.

"Chelsea, no! Wait! You're going about this the wrong way. You're going the wrong way…"

"Well, Walé didn't show up with the puppy, so I sent him back to get it. Girl, wait until you see this adorable, chocolate thing.

I want to take it with me to Africa when Walé and I visit our families in Nigeria this holiday season."

"Oh Shola, take *me* with you instead." Kayla switched the phone from ear to ear, trying to button up her blouse simultaneously. "I need to escape this place. I've stared at Chelsea's damn bedroom door long enough. I'm worried, because I still haven't heard from her, but I'm dying to fling open that door to her dungeon."

"Dungeon?"

"Chelsea told me not to go in her room. She said it's a disaster area."

"Ms. Neat Freak barred you from her 'messy' room? Sounds a little suspect."

"Indeed. She's actually started locking her door lately. We've never locked doors since we've known each other. She's hiding something. I swear it's driving me insane, and there's only one way to ease my mind."

"Why are words like *trust* and *privacy* flashing like neon signs in my mind?"

"I'm sick of grappling with hefty issues like that! Where the hell is *my* privacy? All of Thad's and Asha's and Chelsea's crap have become a part of my life. I have every right to know what's making me lose sleep at night!"

"Kayla, don't do it. You have to respect—"

"'Bye." Kayla went to her cosmetics case and grabbed a hairpin. Bending the hairpin into a lock-pick, she crept over to Chelsea's bedroom door. She knelt down and slowly inserted the pin into the hole in the knob. Kayla poked and dug inside the small hole, frustrating herself. She began to sweat as she jiggled the lock. A strong force crept into her fingers, trying to pull Kayla away from the door, but was overpowered by a desire for answers. Her heart pounded with each twist and turn, until the door flung open and Kayla fell face forward into the room.

Astonishment strangled her.

"Oh my God!"

The space was dimly lit by an antique lamp. Kayla choked on the overbearing odor of Captivity, the cologne Chelsea had given Thad for Christmas. An album stuffed with Thad's pictures spilled his face in varying sizes all over the floor. Every card and note he had written was arranged on the dresser. All of the stuffed animals he had given as gifts were set up as an audience, facing the bed. The sheets were turned down. Thad's designer briefs, in the center of the bed, had a home pregnancy test on the crotch. His picture on the pillow smiled at Kayla. Fear gripped her.

Kayla read the words scrawled on the mirror in the reddest lipstick: "It is a SIN not to go after that which you want most."

Chelsea's journal lay open on the vanity. Pinching her nose, Kayla approached the confidential writings. She couldn't resist her hunger for explanations, but the red diary also begged enticingly to tell secrets even a best friend shouldn't have known. Kayla scanned Chelsea's personal musings that turned into her private moments and eventually became her most powerful mysteries.

With each new page, a profound secret was revealed. Secrets about Thaddeus Carmichael (*the selfish, judgmentally dense, but oh so delicious boyfriend*). Secrets about Kayla Harmon (*the slutty, slightly envious, but forever faithful best friend*). Secrets about Carolina Smithey (*the strong, equally wise, and wicked convict-confidante*). And Carolina's ungodly secrets about the grisly and grotesquely detailed blueprints on how to murder a mate.

Kayla dropped the journal like feces on fire, remembering where she was. Chelsea's bedroom appeared and felt and smelled and tasted all the more chilling. High from the intoxicating stench of

Captivity, Kayla's eyes burned. One million faces of Thaddeus, grinning, laughing, smiling and smirking, repulsed Kayla. The longer she stood in the room, she felt more invisible, cold, slimy hands crawling all over her body, under her blouse and up through her panties, ripping and tearing away at her flesh.

The Carmichaels, Saadiq and his stepmother, and Rush and his parents joined Virgil and Rozalyn, Arianna and Kahlil, and Benny and his three older sisters at a row of tables at Nubian Rhythm Kitchen. The congregation conversed and laughed in a big communal party after dining on a dream feast—curried rooster meat in crispy, sun-baked pitas and spicy, steamed vegetables followed by cinnamon-topped papaya pudding and nutmeg tea.

"Do you have everything you need for the dinner shift tonight, Dad?" Thad asked, following Thaddeus Senior to the kitchen after lunch.

"Yes. All I have to do is work my Creole magic." Thaddeus Senior tied an apron over his designer pants. "Junior, looks like you guys are running a tight ship here. I'm proud. Is all of the paperwork taken care of, the insurance and all that?"

"Uh, well, most of it," Thad lied. "Saadiq is supposed to deliver all of that insurance stuff um, next week."

"Son, don't let that stuff slip and slide," Thaddeus Senior warned, washing his hands. "It's critical. You never know what can happen."

"I understand."

"Now, leave me alone to create. Don't let anybody in this kitchen who doesn't absolutely need to be in here."

Thad laughed to himself, walking over to the club's gallery where his mother and Rush talked art with Ms. Biddle. Deciding not to interrupt, Thad stood in front of his family's portrait. "I still can't believe you're actually in Nubian Rhythm Kitchen, looking at me. What do you think, Brandon?" he whispered. "This is glory for me, big bro. One big championship game."

A tear balanced on the rim of Thad's eyelid, before falling from the force of a second tear pushing behind it. Swallowed by the intensity of Brandon's painted eyes, Thad saw pictures flash in his mind: *He and Brandon in their matching cartoon underwear, he and Brandon wrestling, he and Brandon and Dad at a Cavaliers game, Brandon running on clouds with a football in hand and fire in his eyes...*

Taps on his shoulder brought Thad back to Ms. Biddle's nasal voice, the smell of shrimp, and drumbeats creeping from a speaker. He looked down, his vision focusing on beads of tears on his shoes.

Cynthia whispered, "I cried the first time I saw it, too. It's eerie."

"Life's too short to be a race." Thad draped an arm over his sister's shoulder.

"Huh?" Cynthia's eyes smiled.

"No more running. I'll take my time to enjoy life, until I join Brandon where he is."

Kayla fled from the bedroom, to the living room, and straight to the front door. Grabbing the knob, Kayla was bumped as the door flung open. Chelsea stood in the doorway with a giant red shopping bag. Kayla screamed, backing away.

"Sorry, Kay. Did I scare you?" a disheveled Chelsea asked, closing the door and setting her bag down next to the coat rack.

"Chelsea, where have you been?" Kayla leaned against the dining table and gripped it with her fingers.

Chelsea removed her little red sweater. "I got in late last night, and then I left early this morning. I had to take care of a few things. What's wrong with you? Wait. Did you go in my room?"

Kayla bit her lip. She was speechless, memories of her nightmares interfering with her vision. The Bronx was back. The guilt, the blood, and the heavy air were back.

"Kayla, I told you specifically not to go in there! Damn, I can't even trust *you* anymore!"

Kayla slowly released the table and edged toward the front door. Chelsea chased after her, grabbed Kayla's hand, and blocked her from leaving. Outrage painted on her face, Kayla retreated, saying a thousand prayers. Carolina was back.

"Kay, don't leave," Chelsea begged, her voice hollow and lost. "Please, don't leave me alone. I've been alone too much lately. I need to talk to you."

"Chelsea, what's happening to you? Is it your migraines? Are you having episodes again? Do you want me to call your doctor?" Kayla backed away until she fell against the sofa, with tears of terror overflowing. "What's wrong with you?"

"I let you down, didn't I? Like a kid walking in on Santa in his fake padding, right before he puts on his red suit," Chelsea explained in a haze, sitting next to Kayla and securing her wrists. "Kay, don't run away with those Anderson Academy football boys. Don't look for love from those horny men on Columbia's fraternity row. Don't worry, though. I don't want any of them. I'm not as loose as you."

"What the hell are you talking about?" Kayla screamed, looking for a trace of sanity in Chelsea's eyes.

"Kayla, I've been filled with so much rage, but I finally know what I must do."

"This is about Thaddeus, isn't it? Your rage is for him?" Kayla whispered. She trembled, not knowing what was coming out of her own mouth. "What does all that stuff in your room mean? I don't understand."

"Kay, I have so much hate inside. I hate this girl Asha. I hate Thaddeus," Chelsea sobbed. "I hate what he does to me. I hate that I love him so much."

"Chelsea, this isn't right. You vegetate around here all day. You don't take calls from your parents. You pine for a man who doesn't want you," Kayla insisted. "I'm sorry I ever encouraged you to pursue Thad. I can't deal with this. I come home from work, and the apartment is a funky mess. I never know if you've been drinking or popping pills, or if I'm going to find you dead, or find some goddamn shrine in your room! You're scaring me!"

"I know. I'm sorry." Chelsea clutched Kayla's wrists. "Don't you get it? Kay, you're the only one who understands me. My room is ready and waiting for Thaddeus to repent."

Kayla winced. Her wrists began to burn. "All those days cooped up in here are playing tricks on you, Chelsea."

"I saw two doctors yesterday—my gyno and my shrink. My head doctor tried to tell me the same thing. He actually tried to *upgrade* my depression to some loony's disease. He said he's convinced I spend my days 'entertaining incendiary thoughts!' Whatever. I'm no one's loony!"

"Please let go of my wrists," Kayla begged, looking for an escape route.

"Kay, I haven't been myself lately. In fact, I've lost a lot of myself. But I need to know that you're still here for what's left of me," Chelsea pleaded.

"Yes, I am, okay? Now, let me go."

"I need to ask you something. Promise me you won't freak out on me."

"Let me go." Kayla was frantic.

"Listen!" Chelsea dug her nails into Kayla's wrists. "And don't get pissed off."

"Ouch. What is it?"

Chelsea's eyes became narrow slivers. Her voice turned bitterly quiet. "Kayla, would you—"

Kayla snapped, as Asha's insult and Alvarez's stern whisper came back to her mind. "No, I don't want to do it! I don't want to do this, damn you!" Kayla howled, wrenching her arms free from Chelsea's grip to slap her face. "Chelsea, I'm not your goddamn brainless shadow, you twisted bitch!"

The sting of disbelief exacerbated the pain in Chelsea's face, and she chased Kayla over to the window, screaming obscenities.

"Chelsea, I refuse to do this anymore. Leave me alone! I don't care what you have to say!" Kayla shuffled around Chelsea, striking out to keep her at a distance.

"You said you supported me! That goddamn doctor told me I've lost my mind. But I don't want to be a sinner, Kay. I know what I want. Everybody else is crazy, trying to tell me what I want! Kay, I need you to help me!"

"Damn it, Chelsea. Get away from me. I'm tired of being your goddamn lackey!" Kayla grabbed her tote bag from the table and swung it wildly. "And I'm tired of being your hostage. You're sick, Chelsea, and I don't want to see what you'll do next. I don't want my fingerprints, or my conscience, on any more of your psychopathic schemes! I'm going to Shola's place!" Skidding past Chelsea, Kayla reached for the coat rack, nervously snatching whatever garment was in her hands, and slammed the door on her way out.

Sobbing, Chelsea fell to her knees. She crawled to the front door and pressed herself against it, moaning and panting like a beaten dog. "Kayla! Kay! You're the only one who understands," Chelsea cried, curling up on the floor. Alone. Again.

Thad channeled his nervous energy by ordering another round of drinks for the record company executive from *Mystic Music*. Minutes later, the members of Subconscious Soul confidently strolled onto the Nubian Rhythm Kitchen stage.

"There were complaints about Virgil's attitude at his band rehearsal," Thad told Rozalyn, who sat beside him at the bar.

Rozalyn rolled her eyes. "He's been acting so weird lately."

"He's stressing over a lot of things, but he put on his game face. The guys in the band know they're good. This showcase is the opportunity they've waited for."

"Stressing over what?" Rozalyn made a face. "He's tripping because Melvin's going back to New Orleans tonight. Of course, I couldn't care less. Good riddance."

"Melvin's returning to Louisiana? That explains why he never showed up for work tonight. Luckily Benny's sister knows how to mix a drink and was able to fill in. Well, why is Virgil so worried about his brother when his grandmother—"

"Excuse me, Thad," Arianna interrupted him. "Let me introduce you to Bill Ward, renowned New York food critic. Mr. Ward, this is Thad Carmichael."

"Oh, hi." Thad stood up and shook the fat man's hand. "Thanks for dining at Nubian Rhythm Kitchen this evening, Mr. Ward. Tonight our kitchen features a menu of Creole cuisine. We have a table waiting for you adjacent to the aquarium. Arianna, would you first accompany Mr. Ward to meet our chef?"

"Sure. Right this way, Mr. Ward."

"Thank you, Arianna. Mr. Ward, enjoy your meal and tonight's entertainment. Excuse me, Rozalyn." When he saw who was at the club's entrance, Thad's eyes lit up like Christmas lights as he walked off. "Hi, Gretchen, Tyler, Dr. and Mrs. Hausbruck," Thad greeted them at the door.

"Hi, Thad." Gretchen smiled. "My parents couldn't come, and it took a lot, but I got Granddad here. I'm ready to do my thing. I need to run backstage and get ready. Take care of my grandparents for me, Thad. Thanks."

"Mr. Carmichael." Dr. Hausbruck smiled, clutching his wife, who was bigger than him. "I told my granddaughter there's no way the Thaddeus Carmichael that just left our beloved Columbia could already have his own establishment. What became of Perennial?"

"Perennial's performing strong. The New York expansion is still in the works. My father has a new partner in that endeavor." Thad escorted them to a table near the stage. "Nubian Rhythm Kitchen is the brainchild of myself and three partners."

"It's nice, don't you agree, Dr. Hausbruck?" Tyler asked, taking his seat across from the dean.

"It's quite nice," Dr. Hausbruck replied in a tone that lacked sincerity.

"It's wonderful to see you again, Dr. Hausbruck. Seems like only yesterday you were happily giving me my diploma."

"Yes, it does, doesn't it?" Hausbruck's eyes gave away nothing.

"Ah, yes, and tonight I'm giving you a chance to see your lovely granddaughter sing like Motown's Queen of Soul." They all laughed, as Tyler kicked Thad's leg under the table. Thad grinned. "Thanks for coming. I'll have a waitress come and take your orders in a moment."

"Thank you," Mrs. Hausbruck said, trying hard to look comfortable.

Thad hurried into the kitchen and stood next to his busy father, nodding.

"Junior, you're in my space. Why the devious smile?"

"Dr. Hausbruck's here."

"Ah, is he excited to see his granddaughter sing?" Thaddeus Senior closed the oven door. "I'm sure it's a treat for him to see what you've accomplished so soon after finishing at Columbia, but, then again, he always expects great things from us Carmichaels."

"Yeah right, Dad! He walked in, eyeballing the place like a KKK grand wizard at an NAACP convention. When I looked into Gretchen Hausbruck's crystal blues and told her she could perform here, I saw a crystal opportunity to prove I don't make idle threats. That pretty, young thing is the product of that wrinkly, old, racist bastard, and she's into rhythm-and-blues music."

"Junior, what are you saying?"

"The pleasure of his visit is *all mine*. He's on my turf now. Do you realize what kind of mammoth poetic justice it is for Thaddeus Carmichael, the bloody rabble-rouser with the BSC, to invite Dean Hausbruck, that backward-thinking bigot of the CU Establishment, to Nubian Rhythm Kitchen, a successful business built with the brains and brawn of 'those people in my group'?"

"Ouch, damn it!" Thaddeus Senior dropped a scalding hot spoon. "Hausbruck's no bigot for godsake, Junior."

"Dad, I recall *too* many battles to think otherwise—my visits to Hausbruck's office, on behalf of the Black Students' Coalition, defending proposals to include black speakers and businesses in Columbia's B-school seminars or lecture series. Hausbruck never budged. There was always a problem: the budget, the academic calendar, the random policy against such-and-such."

Thaddeus Senior rubbed his damaged fingers on a damp towel. "So, that makes the man a racist?"

"Hausbruck's here to see his precious grandbaby belt out some funky, soul-stirring tunes. Picture him sitting front row, downing soul food, and wiping his thin lips with a big kente-print napkin," Thad replied. "Tonight, good old Dr. H. will swallow his cavalier conceptions and patronizing principles, and wash it all down with a dose of good old humble punch."

"Junior, please. I'm cooking. There's no time for your rebel politics tonight."

Glowing outside, gloating inside, Thad returned to the club and joined his mother and Ms. Biddle for a good view of Cynthia's stage performance for the talent scout. Thad swayed to Cynthia's inflections, studying the appreciative reactions of the record label executive across the room. "I better go help Tyler out." Thad excused himself and headed for the Hausbrucks' table.

Out of nowhere, Shola burst into the supper club, her eyes flashing rapidly around the room until she saw Thad. She dashed over to him and grabbed him by the arm. "Thad, I need to talk you right now."

Thad's grits-and-gravy smile vanished. "Shola, what's with you?" He pulled himself from her tight grip. "If this is about Chelsea, save it. I don't care what it is."

"Thad, this is serious."

"Don't rob me of my good spirits tonight." Thad tried to walk away.

Shola grabbed Thad and spun him around. "Chelsea is in trouble."

Suddenly, Thad was hit with the terror in Shola's eyes. His adrenaline pumped. A starter's gun went off somewhere in the universe of his mind, signaling the start of a life-or-death race.

"NRK is proud to present this evening's feature presentation, 'Footsteps: A Tribute to the History of Dance,'" Saadiq announced to the room from the stage.

Thad was planted in place, oblivious to the show's pageantry—dancers in dazzling costumes moving in wild abandon to the music. The room whirled about, the drums beat, the crowd oohed and aahed, the clock ticked. Time ran, but he didn't. A voice within told Thad to run, but his shoes were stuck to the floor.

"Thad!" Shola shook him awake. "Did you hear me? Chelsea is in trouble."

Impulsively, Thad ran upstairs. Shola trailed him. He nervously opened the office door, while the shot still rang in his ears. The need to pick up the pace controlled him as he dug in the office closet.

Shola dropped into a chair and cried. "What are you doing?"

"Today's Asha's birthday. My special gift for her is in here. I want to surprise her with it when she meets my parents tonight. I know my mom will like her."

"You're thinking about a damn birthday present right now?" Shola screamed. "Kayla is locked up in my apartment, petrified. She kept trying to leave, but I told her to stay there until I got back. She said Chelsea has flipped out! It's all because of you, Thad. The girl needs help! They *both* do now!"

Downstairs, the first segment of the dance tribute ended, and parents scooped up their little steppers to carry them home. As the backstage area emptied, Asha stayed behind, packing her duffel bag.

The room became quiet when the back door shut tightly, sealing in the stillness. Asha was startled by a presence standing over her—an attractive woman with dark red lips and short red hair under a big black hat. The lady, wrapped in a black trench coat and black gloves, clutched a designer handbag and watched Asha as she packed.

Asha finally asked, "Hi, do I know you?"

"No, dahling," the woman's French accent drifted from under the brim of her fancy hat. "I juz witnezzed your performance, and I must say, *c'est manifique! Tu es une belle fille*."

"Thank you. I'm Asha Dare." She smiled. "I'm sorry. I didn't get your name."

Upstairs in the office, Thad emerged from the closet, faking control. "Shola, you see the message light on the phone blinking a mile a minute. I know it's her, but I refuse to let Chelsea rain on my party. I won't entertain any more of her silliness." He hit the answering machine's erase button. "See, I'm deleting the inflammatory bullshit she's filled my life with. I have the power to wipe her out with one finger."

"I'm begging you. This is serious," Shola pleaded, wiping away tears.

Thad sat next to her. "Is this a joke? Did Chelsea put you up to this?"

"Bastard! *You* are making the girl crazy. Chelsea built a shrine to you and she's *sleeping* with your *memories*. Kayla said Chelsea was talking crazy, and—"

"Slow down! What the hell do you want me to do about it?"

"I'm warning you, Thad. Oh, God! I don't know what that girl is going to do, but Kayla and I have seen this hysteria before." Shola stumbled over her words. "But now I'm the only sane one in the group. That's why I'm here!"

"How do you do? I am Chantal Théard. I am viziting New York from Paris, France," she said, extending a glove.

"Nice meeting you," Asha replied, zipping up her bag. She shook Chantal's hand, trying to peer through her glasses—shades too dark to be worn indoors, and at night, for that matter.

"Mizz Dare, I am wit zee world-renowned Champs Élysées Academie le Dance in Paris."

"Oh my God! Really?" Asha swallowed the peppermint in her mouth whole. Suddenly interested in what Ms. Théard had to say, Asha turned on the sugar shower. "I've heard so much about your dance academy. As you know, it's every dancer's dream to train at Champs Elysees and audition for its touring companies."

"Mizz Dare, I'm imprezzed with what I witnezzed here tonight, but your style of dance iz not quite the caliber of Champs Élysées, no?"

"Well, I realize your academy is a bit more Euro-traditional." Asha swung her bag over her shoulder. She straightened up, trying to look longer and more graceful. "And, between you and me, I know the girls at CEAD are *wrapped tight*—tall, strong, and usually white, but…well, you were really impressed?"

"*Ma chéri*, your agility is exquisite, beautiful form." Ms. Théard looked pensive for a moment. "Champs Élysées iz for zee crème de la crème, but you have supreme potential. Hmmm, I tell you what I shall do." She paused again, searching her pockets. "Lizzen, ma belle, it seems I have left my materialz in zee car right outside. Mizz Dare, be a love. Ztep outside wit me tout de suite. I will give you my biznezz card and a brochure to peruse."

"I'll take whatever I can get, Ms. Théard. Wannabes seek out CEAD; the academy never comes to the dancer. So, excuse me if I can't contain my excitement. By no means am I caught up in the glamour…" Asha rattled on, walking toward the club.

"No, no, dahling, right thiz way." Ms. Théard propped open the emergency exit door that led outside to the dark night.

"Excuse me?" Asha turned around.

"I'm parked right out here." Seeing Asha's hesitation, Ms. Théard snapped her fingers impatiently. "Tout de suite, dahling. A dancer must have quick feet."

"Someone's waiting for me...oh well, it shouldn't take long. Besides, my mother always said, 'Opportunity may knock, but it won't beg you to open the door.'" Asha scurried to the door that led to the opportunity of a lifetime.

"Thad, I'm here on Chelsea's behalf, but Kayla and I are also looking out for you. So, please don't be stupid and play what I say cheap. Help this girl."

"Shola, I wish I could help Chelsea, but I can't. I can't put out her fires every time she starts one and keep my cool at the same time." Thad rocked in his chair until the sound of the chair legs tapping against the floor turned into the ticking of his imaginary clock. Thad's eyes traveled from the clock on the wall to the closet containing Asha's present to the answering machine to Shola's wet face.

Shola looked away. Her voice was solemn and apologetic. "Thad, Kayla said Chelsea's been talking with the woman who murdered her hus—I gotta go. 'Bye."

"Wait! Hey! Come back here." Thad's heartbeat quickened, surpassing the pace of the ticking in his mind. The other runners in the imaginary race had taken off and he was still in the blocks; so Thad ran, too.

The backdoor slammed shut behind Asha as she stepped into the darkness of the alley. Asha's heart skipped a beat. She spun around. It happened so fast. Asha suddenly felt a stunning pain as a fist sharply whacked her temple. Aghast, she fell to the ground.

Panting vigorously, Asha stood to regain her balance, trying to register what had happened and trying even harder not to cry. But before she could do either, she was tackled and knocked against a row of trashcans. The crashing metal sent chicken bones and stray cats flying into the balmy night air. Asha's attacker had tremendous strength, yanking Asha up and slamming her against a brick wall. Asha tried to scream, but a satin glove was shoved in her mouth, forcing her to swallow her horror.

"You were warned!" The hair-raising whisper had lost its French accent.

Thad bolted from the office and bounded down the stairs and over to the tables near the stage. "Nenna, have you seen Asha?"

"Yeah, I left her backstage. She was getting her things together."

Thad raced to the backstage area. The abandoned room knocked the breath out of him, replacing it with thoughts of violent sin. At once, his head was ambushed with a riotous picture show: *Blinding white flashes between gruesome images of a shredded dress shirt, Asha against broken glass, a frothy-mouthed Chelsea, a scream-ing Shola, a shrieking Asha, and shattering blood-stained mirrors…*

Thad made a mad dash back into the club. Then he halted, overcome by queasiness when he saw Gretchen leave the stage. Thad watched Tyler applaud fanatically, while Dr. Hausbruck nearly broke his fragile back to give Gretchen a healthy embrace. From a distance, Thad saw a gleam in the old man's eye that he had wanted to see up close; instead, a greeting-card moment that Thad had created, and missed, trickled through his shaking fingers.

Powered by fright, Asha mustered the strength to reach up and smack her assailant. On impact, the woman's high-priced hat flew into a trash bin layered with fryer grease and food remnants, exposing the Fury incarnate.

"Get away! Leave me alone!" Asha flailed in a frenzy, attempting to flee.

She screamed with unholy dread, her blouse ripping as she was dragged to the ground with force. Suddenly straddled, Asha's throat was gripped by angry fingers.

"Please don't do this—" Asha gurgled huskily, convulsing under the pressure of the tightening clasp around her neck. "Please—"

"Shut your mouth, you little mousy bitch!" the French imposter seethed.

"Junior, what's wrong?" Mrs. Carmichael asked as Thad charged up to the table again, disrupting the good vibes.

"It's Asha. I can't find her. I don't know where she is."

"Why are you so damn paranoid, Junior? Calm down," his father boomed. "What happened? Who is Asha?"

"Thad, I'm sure she's around the club somewhere," Nenna said.

Thad fought the noise behind his eyes. "Help me find her. Rush, help me look around the club, inside and out. Saadiq, check the kitchen. Virgil...where's Virgil?"

"As usual, he disappeared right after our show without telling anybody."

"Whatever. Nenna, check the ladies' room. I have to make a phone call!"

"Thad, what's wrong?" Cynthia screamed, seeing the fear in his eyes while everyone scurried off in different directions to solve a nebulous mystery.

Thad was a blur, vaulting upstairs to the office, snatching up the phone, and dialing Chelsea and Kayla's apartment. Between rings, the ticking in his ears intensified. "Pick up the phone, Chelsea! Pick up!"

"Stop. Please—" Asha coughed, begging for freedom like a plantation slave. She received no mercy; her delicate neck was squeezed with an unforgiving clamp. The more Asha fought, the stronger the human noose became, until Asha could no longer struggle against fate. Asha's will to survive gave way to a waiting game...slipping, waning...panic in her bulging eyes, futile gasps for relief. She felt nothing but the pinching of her airway and the rough asphalt scraping the back of her head. Life slipped from her toes, from her lungs, from her throat...

Asha's last breath was stolen with a crowning twist of her neck.

"The soul who sins is the one who will die," the angry victor hissed, finishing off her victim with a vicious slap of her expressionless face. Grabbing the discarded pieces of her disguise, she disappeared into the darkness of the alley.

Like a door closing on a gusty winter's night, a sudden hush fell over the club's office. Thad instinctively dropped the telephone receiver, and the ticking halted with a resounding stroke-of-midnight gong. Time was up. The Earth stopped on its axis. An unabashed stillness enveloped Thad's immediate surroundings and the inner sanctum of his mind. He was a blank slate, naked, frightened.

10

SATAN'S STOVE

Having changed and cleaned herself up, Chelsea felt some-what better about approaching Thad with her bad news. Decked out in a red-hot cocktail dress, she mumbled to herself under the night's darkness. She turned the corner onto Seventh Avenue, teetering slowly down the sidewalk in her new stilettos. As she approached the supper club, Chelsea saw the ambulance. The flashing red lights of an EMT vehicle illuminated the alley and the stunned faces of passersby and NRK customers that had gathered to gawk at the gory scene.

Everyone was shaken, and Nenna was a crying mess. Chelsea pushed her way through the crowd, hearing murmurs and snippets of conversations about how Rush had discovered Asha's breath-less body. She ran over to where Thad stood cursing up a storm. "Thaddeus, what happened?"

"Chelsea! Did you do this? Did you?" Thad grabbed her by the shoulders, shaking her violently, messing up her hair. "Answer me, goddamn you!"

"Stop it, Junior! How dare you?" Thaddeus Senior pulled Thad off Chelsea. "How could you accuse her of such a thing?"

Chelsea stood motionless. Thad fell helplessly into his father's arms, whimpering, exhibiting a flood of emotion that reinforced just how much love he was capable of when pushed to the brink of his heart's capacity. His outpouring touched Chelsea, who knew he had once and would again feel that for her.

"Thaddeus, what I must tell you will only make you shed more tears. It's about—" Chelsea was shoved out of the way by Thad, who disappeared into the crowd. "Thaddeus!" Chelsea's howl was ice cold. Her muscles twitched as her veins, blood vessels, and nerves fought amongst themselves. Strangers' stares and whispers sharpened as Chelsea's mask of perfection was ripped off publicly.

Humiliated, Chelsea ran. She ran through the wall of people like a well-dressed bulldozer. She ran, breaking a heel, and she kept running down the street, until she fell into the alley between a barbershop and a bookstore. There, Chelsea cried. She cried in the alley like a tortured child. She cried, ruining her makeup, and she kept crying, until she saw the ambulance whiz by and heard all the voices eventually fade into a hush.

When order restored itself on Seventh Avenue, Chelsea peaked out from the alley, peering down the dead street at the supper club. All the lights except the one in the office flickered off, and Kahlil appeared at the entrance of the club. Chelsea ducked back into the darkness, peeking out again to watch Kahlil lock the club's front door. Her heartbeat thundered when Chelsea heard his footsteps approaching her hiding place. Every fiber of her being became paralyzed while she watched him walk past the alley within a few feet of where she pressed herself into the wall.

When all was clear and the hush resumed, Chelsea exhaled and quickly inhaled to feed her starving lungs with the night air. The nauseating pains shooting through her head threatened to overtake her as the drugs in her system mixed into a lethal cocktail. She was drunk—drunk with pain and guilt. Once more, she looked down toward Nubian Rhythm Kitchen. It looked back at her, resolute, unbowed, and with an air of supremacy. Offended,

Chelsea reached into her purse, digging for artillery, ballistics, something with which to slap its proud face.

Chelsea was already inebriated from remorse, but Thad had just forced her to drink her own conscience. She knew his sin could not, should not, would not go unanswered. She staggered across the empty street toward the club. After a quick check for witnesses, she ducked between the club and the adjacent boutique.

Chelsea limped over the recently desecrated spot in the alley, damning Kayla for not being there for her when she needed her most. With clumsy strain, she scaled a ledge on the side of the building, not caring that she broke a nail or that criminal thoughts came with her. She walked along the edge, feeling the surface of the building with her fingers until stone turned to glass. She slowly lifted the hem of her dress, focusing her eyes on a spot she couldn't really see. With an angry force, Chelsea used her last good stiletto to kick in a window to the supper club's kitchen.

The crash sounded like her heart breaking.

It was dark in the club. The only light came from the aquarium. Its underwater inhabitants ignored Chelsea as she walked slowly to the stage like a babe in a wonderland, taking in the accents of Nubian Rhythm Kitchen. It was nice. *Nice on the surface, pleasing to the eye*, she thought, *but laced with evil.*

At last, it was Chelsea Elizabeth Fuller against the world, against the Nubian world into which she had trespassed, that contradictory symbol of grassroots soul power, copious cultural arrogance and free-flowing sin. Alone. Again.

Determined to finish what she had started, Chelsea walked onto the club's stage. No audience was there to shower her with praise. She knew she had no right to that stage, one that had been graced by chocolate-smooth jazz players, honey-coated soul singers, spicy, feline-like dancers, and icy-cool hip-hop DJs. It was a world inhabited by the likes of those ultra-groovy, mega-mod subconscious souls who loved to hang out in candlelit, incense-filled rooms talking artistic revolution. And Thad had created it and banned Chelsea from it.

Loneliness wrapped itself around Chelsea's body in place of her expensive clothes, making her dilemma easier to resolve. Her plan to go out with glory, too, albeit cloaked in solitude, required a fabulous, Hollywood-style ending. She lit the slim cigarette dangling from her lips with the flourish of a finale. "Realize the power of your words. You broke your own law, Thaddeus. Good-bye, world!"

She puffed. Twice.

She dropped the match.

Chelsea exhaled the smoke slowly.

The match hit the ethnic-print rug under a wooden hutch and suddenly, in the fabric, the tiny orange droplet found food to grow. Chelsea's eyes grew big with wonder, watching the thing do its work. Crawling from the rug to the hutch, the flicker swelled into flames and, then, into a blazing trail of searing heat.

Though eyeless, toothless, and clawless, the fire was a destructive monster. A hot, reddish-orange swirl of angry determination, it was unwilling to take no for an answer. The fire's sheer power titillated the firestarter—lust at first sight. In that moment, in her final scene, the climax of her glory, Chelsea exploded from a freakish orgasm as the hot beast gave its victim rougher sex than her lover could ever give her. Deeply, she felt it, she loved it— the fire's temper gutting and ravishing the supper club's insides.

As seductive and amazing as the glowing inferno was, Chelsea lamented that she couldn't savor getting off on the fire any longer, lest she also be completely devoured by the monstrosity she had unleashed. She took a long drag off her cigarette. She smiled, strolling backstage and out through the emergency exit door, imagining her "shero" theme music soaring in the background, its melody accompanied by the fire's crackling lyrics.

Unbeknownst to the starlet, she was cooking the person who was on the phone in the office upstairs explaining that night's first tragedy to Asha's parents and sister in Atlanta.

The orange beast, meanwhile, did some explaining of its own. The sheets of fire spoke Chelsea's rage in a dialogue not meant for sensitive ears. The billowing flames screamed, ranted, and cursed, as they ate the floors and mahogany tables. The furious blaze communicated deep-felt pain, ravaging the cherrywood bar, the pine doors and the Carmichaels' family portrait. The fearless wooden warrior and the sphinx near the restrooms suffered silent deaths, as the shouting flames engorged them in a tirade of pandemonium.

He thought he had heard something going on downstairs, but he was absorbed in trying to console Naomi and convince Mr. and Mrs. Dare that the medical team was doing everything they could to revive Asha. "No, unfortunately, no one saw who did this to her," he told them.

Meanwhile, Eden had turned to purgatory. Heaven became Hades. Nubian Rhythm Kitchen was turned into Hell's Kitchen with a fiery ball of rage, jealousy and obsession-ridden lust.

Upstairs in the office, he smelled smoke. He felt heat bore through the floor. Then he heard the wall-sized aquarium come crashing in.

He jolted up.

He flung the office door open.

He was greeted by a surging wall of fire.

The fire begged to melt his face.

He screamed no.
He backed over the desk in a clumsy panic.
He turned to the window.
The window had iron bars on it.
The fiery wall surged in.
It was orange and hot.
He picked up the phone.
The hot wall would not take no for an answer.
The wall stopped begging.
He dialed.
He screamed.
He screamed in the swirling orange torridity.
He screamed.
He melted.

11

STAINED BELIEFS AND
BIRTHDAY SURPRISES

R ush was awakened by a call from the police department at 4:30 in the morning. The cops informed him that the fire department had been called to 1220 Seventh Avenue. Rush leaped out of bed and stumbled to Saadiq's bedroom, but Saadiq was nowhere to be found. Rush raced to Thad's bedroom. It was empty.

In a panic, Rush phoned the emergency room of New York Methodist Hospital and, after some cogent threats, he convinced Thad to stop pacing in the waiting room and meet him at the club.

When Thad finally arrived at the site that was once Nubian Rhythm Kitchen, he found Rush in the middle of the wreckage with his head bowed in utter defeat. Thad's eyes watered. His throat failed to produce any sounds. His lungs constricted.

Having roped off the club for arson investigators to rummage through later, the firefighters completed their job and eventually went back to their own lives, leaving Thad and Rush to do their job, to mourn the losses in their lives. Thad plodded through a hickory-smoked pile of bamboo and cherrywood and led Rush back to the sidewalk. They sat on the concrete and held each other up to keep from dropping to the ground in misery.

"Rush, what happened? Where's Saddiq?"

Rush spoke softly, looking at Thad with a tear-strewn face. "He's dead, man."

"Dead? How?"

"Saadiq died in the fire."

"What?"

Rush broke down. "He's dead! Our friend is *gone*!"

"Oh my God. Saadiq is…" Thad's chest caved in and he felt his tears drop like rain onto his hands.

"Damn it, Thad. When those detectives asked me to identify the body…" Rush shook his head in disbelief. "I swear…I can't get that image of Saadiq out of my mind. It's fucking unbearable, man!"

Thad tried to stand. "Man, I can't…I can't breathe."

"Why, Thad?" Rush cried. "Why?"

"I don't know, Rush," Thad whispered, trying to shake the shock from his weakening body. "Everything is not right with the world at this moment. Something's terribly off," he explained as Rush sobbed uncontrollably on Thad's shoulder. "I just had one of the best and worst days in my life all at the same time."

"The club is a fucking cemetery!" Rush screamed, jumping to his feet. "Damn, look at this! I can't believe it! This was my dream, man!" Rush grabbed a charred scrap and flung it against half of a blackened wall.

The crash jarred Thad. He swallowed his anger. "Maybe we should've known from the start this façade of a Promised Land was doomed, Rush."

"What the hell are you saying? Are you looking at the same thing I am?"

Thad slowly stood up and raised his arms over the one-time regal empire. "There was no way this place could thrive. It had to be destroyed, for the good of all our souls, right? Whoever did this either did the world a favor or did the world a disservice. Well, blame, like beauty, is in the eye of the beholder."

"Are you fucking insane? Save the speech, Thad. I'm standing on the curb in front of rubble, on the spot I bought with my blood, sweat, and tears." Rush got in Thad's face. "Excuse me, if I seem unwilling to give up that easily!"

"Wake up, Rush. There's no such thing as Utopia," Thad concluded with eerie calm. "Heck, even the real Eden had its share of sin. That's how it all started, remember Adam and Eve? And so, it was just proven again—people are fucked up and the world is doomed."

"Stop talking to me like you talk to that nutcase Chelsea!"

"The truth is the truth, no matter how you say it." Thad shrugged. "Can you handle the truth? The truth is I stopped by Virgil's apartment to bring him with me. Rozalyn was crying her eyes out. Rush, she told me Virgil's grandmother passed away over a month ago. He left Rozalyn and ran off to New Orleans with Melvin and $200,000 of our money. Virgil stabbed us in the back and twisted the fucking knives!"

"The bastard was a con man." Rush fell to his knees and struggled to form more words. "Every bit of the life we created is gone. Dreams, memories, friendships—burned."

Thad knelt beside his crumpled friend. "Rush, I realize that, in a way, you're the most innocent victim in all of this. All you ever wanted to do was share your soul music with the world. Now, you've lost Subconscious Soul, and a part of your own soul."

"My soul was killed in this fire. Saadiq was my soul. He was my blood brother!"

"Call me crazy." Thad sniffled. "But I'm not mad. It was a subtle decline. Gradually, this place became riddled with more sin and scandal that ate it from the inside out." His glassy eyes looked off into the distance as he placed a hand on Rush's shoulder. "Think about it—*NRK* sounds like *anarchy*, if you say it fast several times."

"What?" Rush pulled away from him. He stood and kicked the post of the street lamp with a force that vibrated under the pavement so that Thad, and perhaps the rest of New York City, could feel his anger. He walked away from Thad and went back to dwell on the embers and ashes.

Thad resumed muttering to himself. "I think about the sin philosophy I preached to Chelsea, and now I realize that in the club's short history *every* commandment was broken here in some form."

"Oh, God. I can't believe I'm hearing this."

"The place was built out of dishonor to my parents, because I lied and kept it a secret from them. The Sabbath became any Sunday that NRK had a good crowd and raked in a good take. Worshipping graven images? We held only the adoration of our families, friends, or fans as holy. Beyond that, green paper with dead presidents' pictures became the new Almighty deity. Some prayed for it, and others preyed upon it." Awareness spreading through him, Thad stopped to stare at his hands.

"Stop it, man."

"Nubian Rhythm Kitchen was the site of a tangled web of ruin. I coveted a girl I met here, a girl I tried to convince to put not only her body, but also her heart, into what we had together. Saadiq's adulterous affair was consummated in its darkest corners, and I kept it a secret. Virgil took more than the easy way out; he took our earnings with it. And the lies! Above all that, two lives were taken here last night."

"Who or what could have done this?" Rush looked hopelessly to the heavens for some clue as dawn began to open a new day upon them.

"I don't know," Thad lied, conducting his own search in the

salmon-pink and baby-blue vastness above them. He wiped his puffy eyes. "Someone somewhere is satisfied. If this is the aftermath of the Revolution, I wonder who won the war?"

"I can't stand to be here any longer. Damn, I don't how we'll break the news to Saadiq's family."

"Asha was twenty." Thad's voice was empty, barely there. "That's about how old we were when NRK was just a big dream. Now, Saadiq's gone and she's on life support."

Rush did not respond.

"Let's go home."

Chelsea sat on the sofa, eating a bowl of Kayla's raspberry-flakes cereal. She turned up the bowl and slurped the pink-tinted milk.

Full in her stomach but not full in her loins, she tiptoed to her candle-lit bedroom. She kissed the picture of Thad's face on her pillow and restarted Sade's CD on the tribal-toned "Cherish." The ambiance was just right for another round of gratifying relations, where Chelsea did all of the gratifying and relating to herself and by herself.

She slowly lit another candle and placed the matchbook, the initials *NRK* face-up, next to Thad's smiling face. Finally, she removed the red silk scarf from the bedpost and tied it over her eyes, prepared to enter Fantasy Land.

With his face still buried in the pillow, Thad reached over and snatched up the phone as soon as it rang. He looked at the time. It was three o'clock on Sunday afternoon, and he hadn't slept his troubles away as he had hoped.

"Hello," he grunted groggily.

"Hi, Thad Carmichael? It's Judy, the nurse from New York Methodist. You told me to call you as soon as we knew anything about Asha Dare's condition."

Thad wiped the slobber from his chin. "Judy, how's Asha?"

"Well, the doctors diagnosed her as suffering from asphyxiation from acute strangulation. They had her on a respirator, and then decided to operate on her trachea. They flushed her with oxygen—"

"Oh, God! They did everything they could, right?" Thad began to bawl. "Damn! They couldn't save—"

"Mr. Carmichael, calm down. Luckily, Asha was in excellent physical condition. The doctors were able to revive her. She survived."

"Oh, thank God. Thank you!" Thad dropped the phone as a tremor of exhilaration flew through his body. He wanted to scream his joy but didn't want to wake Rush. He ran out of the brownstone. Racing to the hospital, all he could think about was how much Asha didn't deserve to go out the way he thought she had.

Thad burst into the hospital, his face showing the stress of the past seventeen hours of his life. An excited mass of energy, he charged up to the desk of the nurses' station. "Hi, Judy. Can I see her?"

"Hi, Thad. Asha's family is over there." Judy pointed to a man and two women sitting in the waiting room. "Maybe you should talk to them first."

"Mr. and Mrs. Dare, I'm Thad Carmichael." Thad introduced himself to the sad, but relieved, family.

"Hi, Thad. I'm Asha's father, Jerome."

"Hello, I'm Laura and this is Asha's younger sister, Naomi. We want to thank you, Thad. The nurse told us how you rode over in the ambulance and looked after our daughter." The gushing woman hugged Thad tightly.

"Oh, your hug is just what I need. I feel terrible that all this happened while Asha was with me," Thad confessed.

"Asha's suffering from memory loss. She doesn't remember exactly what happened, but she's okay. Thank you, Thad."

"Asha's a wonderful girl. I knew she came from a great family."

"We flew in from Atlanta a few hours ago. We thought we had lost our daughter for good when we got the call from Saadiq." Mr. Dare shook his head in disbelief. "I warned her about this crazy place, but Asha just had to leave the South for the big city."

"Asha means a lot to me. I'm going in to see her now." Thad smiled, walking off in anxious haste, figuring he could always chat with the Dares later.

"Oh, Thad, you can't go back there yet." Judy stood, trying to catch Thad as he hurried past the nurses' station. "She has a visitor with her right now. Thad, we can't allow you to go back there."

But a force stronger than Judy pulled him to Asha's room, and Thad thought it was love, because all he wanted to do was get his hands on Asha, kiss her, hold her and tell her everything would be all right. Thad opened the door to Asha's room and found that someone had beaten him to it. He was shot with a bad-news bullet for the fourth time that weekend. Thad's heart sank like a lead weight. He saw the cascade of a man's dreadlocks hiding the face of the patient on the bed in what appeared to be a passionate kiss.

The chiseled man in a tank top and jeans removed his tongue from Asha's mouth, and they both looked up at the invader of their privacy.

In addition to the nauseating antiseptic odor of the hospital, the way Asha averted her eyes sharpened Thad's stomach pain. The poison in the emotional bullet that had been fired into his chest began to leak—her lack of an explanation the equivalent of laughing over his dead body. At that very instant, Thad wished he never had to be accountable to his emotions, or never met Asha, or never sinned.

"It's funny, Asha," Thad noted rather calmly. "It's your birthday, but I got the big surprise."

The man on the bed tried to stand, but Asha pulled him back down, using his muscles as armor to shield her from the castigation in Thad's eyes.

"Clearly you're captivated by the man who, according to you, treated you like shit, like you were less than human. Maybe there's something to that theory about women and their animal attraction to bad boys."

"Who iz dis guy?" the dark, oily man asked in an exotic African accent, attempting to rise from the bed again.

"It doesn't matter who I am. Because I already know all about you, and you're still the chosen one. But hey, I won't yell or scream or cry. I've done enough of that to last me a lifetime. Asha, I won't even ask you how or why, because, at this point, I don't give a damn. I just want to know one thing." Thad paused to get it right. "Are you going back to Atlanta with him…and is it because it's what you want most?"

"Asha, who de hell iz he?"

"I was the maker of her heaven on Earth," Thad said, as Judy appeared to escort him away. "But she'd rather return to hell with you."

"Asha, what iz he tawkin' about?"

Asha shushed her protective African adonis. Ashamedly but surely, she looked at Thad with her now twenty-year-old eyes, and nodded. "Thad, I'm less than. Less than all that you have going on in your life right now."

"So is he," Thad replied. "He's less than."

"You want and need more than I can give to you. I'm sorry, Thad."

Thad accepted what he could not change—the fact that he could not surprise Asha the way Zeké had done. Of course, there was his gift—the mini-statue of Asha hand-carved in ebony by an elderly Zimbabwean artist in Harlem who knew how to capture pure beauty. But it had gone up in the flames like everything else.

"Happy birthday. I'm glad you'll see the next one and the one after that. You'll need them to grow up," Thad said and walked out of Asha's life.

12

SELF-REDISCOVERY
AND STARTING OVER, AGAIN

Over the course of the last two weeks of that summer, Chelsea continued to wait for Thad to come around, to come crawling to her confessional and repent for his unseemly ways. She eventually ran out of Captivity cologne, cleaned her mirrors, and tucked away the album of Thad's photos. Still, things had not gotten any easier to bear since she'd received the news from Dr. Peters.

"How could I have been so stupid?" She would berate herself, recalling the physical detriment she had heaped upon her body.

During her visit from California, Chelsea's mother spoke with guarded speech, seemingly holding back words that needed to be aired.

"Chelsea, please listen to me. Transfer to Stanford for your master's degree or take a break from school and come back home to Calabasas," Mrs. Fuller begged as she sat next to Chelsea on the sofa. Under the cool glamour of her stylish ivory blouse and slacks, the slim mother tried to hide her pity for her damaged daughter. "Daddy's offer of a position at MicroTique Technologies still stands."

"Mother, a position at Channel Two in New York is my dream. Tell Daddy I'm not swayed by a guaranteed job at his company."

"Sweetheart, you've gone through a devastating experience. The news your gynecologist gave you piled on top of your migraines and this new psychological illness Dr. Castle diagnosed—"

"Dr. Castle is the nutcase! There's *nothing* wrong with me. Mother, I'm staying in New York."

"You shouldn't be here alone, especially now that Thad and Kayla have abandoned you."

"Don't even bring up her name." Chelsea shuddered with irritation. "Mother, why didn't you ever give me a *real* sister, so I didn't have to depend on that faux, knockoff Kayla?"

"Stop that, Chelsea Fuller. It's not that I *chose* not to have a second child to purposely torture you with the pains of only-child syndrome." Mrs. Fuller gently took her daughter's hand and stroked it. "Sweetie, listen. There's something I've wanted to tell you for a long time…about a condition…a condition that told my body that one was enough. Chelsea, it's a fear that I have for you now that—"

"Mother, I've heard enough about conditions lately. I don't want to hear anymore." Like a shy, embrrassed little girl, Chelsea pulled her hand away and aimed her eyes down to avoid contact with truth.

"You need to hear this. My life and your life…"

"Are two different lives. I realize that now, so I'm starting mine over. Forget Thaddeus and Kayla. I have a dear friend that needs my help to save her life. Coming back home would do nothing for me, except reverse all the progress I've made. I've let go of wearing our family's lavish lifestyle as a badge of honor. I want to reach out to the wronged and help them get things right in their lives."

"I never knew that our 'lifestyle' was such an issue," Mrs. Fuller professed, lovingly straightening strands of Chelsea's hair.

"I'm not complaining that we belong to high society, but now

I'm focusing on journalism and atoning for things I may have done to hurt people around me."

"That's quite noble, sweetheart," Mrs. Fuller whispered, looking at the wall. "Oh, you put that picture up? I haven't seen that in a while. Jesus, look at my hair."

"Yes, I love it. You and Daddy are so cute."

"That's, uh…nice, sweetheart."

"Mother, why do you look so sad?"

Mrs. Fuller suppressed unhappy memories under a smile. "No reason."

Thad walked alone along Broadway, feeling the same brand of disconnectedness he felt when he had taken the same walk after his graduation from Columbia. The disjointedness was not quite as strong the second time around. The towering empires, the faceless masses, the surreptitious activity, the quiet hysteria—they were too familiar. He had created his own microcosm of that world, complete with all of the above and a heaping helping of Nubian Rhythm.

Thad ended up on the same park bench where he'd had his first long talk with himself. The sun was out in force as were the kids. People-watching helped him pass the time. *That girl in the pink dress just broke a good man's heart*, Thad guessed. *The plump guy with the dog is heir to a fortune in Egypt. That kid in the shorts is a latent psychopath, and that…that's Reggie!*

"Reggie!" Thad called excitedly to the man's back. "Over here."

"Thad!" Reggie limped over to him. "How are you doin', son?"

Thad threw his arms around him. "Reggie, how have you been?"

The Exchange Building's security guard grinned. "It's been a long time."

"Have a seat." Thad made room on the bench for him. "I miss you, Reg."

"Ah, go on. You don't think about old Reggie."

"I'm serious. I always came to you for the straight scoop that I couldn't get from anyone else. Who else could I talk to at Freeman-Webber?"

"Too busy to pick up a phone or stop by and drop a word on me, Mr. Big-Time Entrepreneur?" Reggie smiled, rubbing his belly. "How's business? How are Chelsea and your blood brothers doin', especially that Saadiq?"

"Oh wow, Reg. It *has* been a while." Thad shook his head, going through a mental update. "Reggie, I'll be twenty-six tomorrow, and I feel like I've already lived eight of my nine lives over this summer."

"Share it with me, son."

"Living for, through, with, and by a dream, my blood brothers and I wanted to be renegades, modern-day Black Panthers. But our business degrees and djembe drums replaced their law books and guns. We thought culture could be our weapon."

"You always did go off about the black arts movement and things. You young cats wanted to relive the Sixties' renaissance with Seventies' spirit—"

"In this world of Two Thousands' chaos."

"But that was a different time. You kids have so much more now."

"Exactly." Thad drummed up a sad chuckle from somewhere in the darkness of his reflections. "We used to talk Revolution. Now I see that our touchstone code, about people being something other than what the world expects, is just garbage. Sure, Chelsea had her fantasies, but the touchstone theory was mine, and it's more unrealistic and farfetched than any fairytale in a book."

"I don't follow you."

"As fate would have it, each of us ended up right where we belonged. Tomorrow Rush returns to Howard to get his sociology degree and pursue a career in adolescent counseling, so he'll be lecturing—on drug prevention, no less. Virgil's nothing more than a thuggish thief among his element of Machiavellian opportunists in New Orleans, and Saadiq ended up playing dreamy music in the sky with the angels. Reg, he died…in a fire…a fire that destroyed our business."

"Oh my Lord! No way." Reggie leaned forward with his elbows on his knees. "Lord. That boy was smart. He had a ton of spunk. That's downright terrible. I can't believe it. Everything you kids worked for…I'm so very sorry, Thad."

"Just had a big funeral a couple days ago. All of Saadiq's friends turned out to see him off, and then they went on to wherever they were supposed to be, too." Thad sighed, looking off into space. "Nenna's moving to Atlanta and Asha miraculously found direction in her life. The two of them plan to start a dance and drama school for kids. Arianna finally published her anthology, *Excuse Me, Sir, Can I Have My Womanhood Back?* Kahlil and Benny started a new band called Soul Survivors. And I ended up enduring my father's endless I told you so's about failing to secure fire insurance."

Reggie patted Thad's back in consolation. "Everyone's got a path."

"Out of everyone, Brandon and Saadiq are in the best place."

"Aw, Thad."

"It's true, Reg. I mean, we tried to duplicate it, but now they're in the original heaven, the real Eden."

"What about Chelsea?"

"We're not together anymore. I passed a newsstand on my way

here and noticed that every publication had Carolina Smithey's picture plastered on it. Have you kept up with that circus?"

"Of course. The big trial starts today. The crazy thing is that no one can prove her old man tried to force himself on her. No witnesses, no nine-one-one call, or nothin' like that. But her lawyer said she's pleadin' not guilty on some real flippy defense."

"Well, I, for one, hope they fry the bitch. No mercy. When I think of the excessively exploitative coverage and the overbearing, telephoto lens scrutiny the media has used in this case, I think of Chelsea. I'd like to go up to all those news people, especially Chelsea, and check their hands for blood. Their guilt complexes must be grotesquely swollen."

"What?"

"Really, think about it; that bloodthirsty institution wrecks as many lives as it helps, if not more, and I think I've always associated Chelsea with that."

"Are you talkin' about the same Chelsea I know?"

"No, it's the Chelsea that you don't know. Only I know the real Chelsea inside and out."

"I still can't believe Saadiq has left us. That young blood had heart!" Reggie laughed sadly to himself, shaking his head. "The last time I saw him, he quoted H. Rapp Brown. He said, 'Reggie, we're buildin' NRK because a dream deferred leads to riots, and America needs a cultural riot.'"

"Well, H. Rapp also said, 'If this town don't come around, burn it down.' Nubian Rhythm Kitchen represented the opposition. Whoever picked up on that burned it down and killed the man who would've said it to their face. But we weren't millionaire business tycoons on the inside circle like Smithey. Our Revolution won't get in-depth coverage, because we didn't have sit-ins, we had *soul-ins*. We didn't beg to be let in to the culturally deprived

American Establishment. We were culturally lashing out." Thad's eyes blazed like a soldier recounting stories of a battle lost. "So Chelsea and the rest of her nosy news hounds won't take their cameras to Brooklyn to cover the aftermath of *our* lives. We lived in a brownstone, not the White House, and NRK didn't hold the same power as the FBI or the CIA."

Reggie stared at the sky. "That's heavy, Thad—you young bloods usin' different strategies to finish what older cats started. But you kids need to breathe. Don't get so heated that you burst blood vessels at your age."

"Stress knows no age, Reggie. I was never aggressive with women until I met Chelsea. I figured my rough-and-ready romantic style was a result of truly feeling linked to the Panthers my friends and I admired. An angry beast in an angry concrete jungle. But the original Panthers left work to be done, in a nation that insists such work is unnecessary. So, I prowled on black paws around an orb full of masked people who so lived for tomorrow, they forgot about today. These people let pastimes like art and music be replaced by email messages and Web sites as stimulus for the soul. This world has lost touch with its soul, the inside, the aching within that gives us art and social movements."

"But that's no excuse to release your rage with your love. When it comes to lovin' women, don't let pleasure be confused with happiness, or intensity with intimacy. Follow me, son?"

"I've never physically hurt a woman, but, with Chelsea, it was as if I was releasing the steam building within me in the most intimate moments. She allowed me access to softness I couldn't get anywhere else. I assumed women favored a healthy man who could deal with the world and could still be a strong Mandingo in bed. But Arianna, who's only a friend, made me own up to my twisted pincushion mentality. She represents the women who've paid for enough in life and teach you what it means to be a man."

"You lost sight of the bigger picture."

"I took fate head on. Challenged it, and paid for it in one night. After a three-alarm fire burned down the dreams in my mind, Asha put a bullet in my heart to go with the knife Virgil had put in my back and the hole Saadiq has left in my soul."

"You're a broken man. It's a wonder you're still standin'."

"Certain things are destined to happen to certain people. Some break down or get killed or go nuts or break rules. You are what you are; so why fight fate? Like you, Reggie. You wear your genuine spirit as proudly as you wear that powerless security guard's badge on your chest every day. You've fully accepted who you are and what you do, and I admire that."

Reggie was quiet, slightly confused and partially flattered.

Thad looked over his shoulder when he heard the laughter. The children in the park that day seemed to be skipping and running faster than normal. Watching the rows and rows of running kids, Thad almost fell off the bench. His breath caught in his throat. "Are you a religious man, Reggie?"

"Well, spiritual, yes. Why? Why are you so excited all of a sudden?"

"The answer just hit me like a stack of brick Bibles." Thad's eyes blazed. "I'll be twenty-six tomorrow. I've got a built-in security net back in Virginia. Perennial's a sure thing. Pull a few strings, and I'll have a business with ready-made success. Hell, I don't have to *earn* it. I'm of that fortunate ilk of trust-fund kids. I might as well own up to it—Gretchen Hausbruck did." Thad jumped from the bench, grabbed Reggie's shoulders and knelt before him. "I was running from the path that was already laid out for me. I've got it made, damn it!"

"What? Thad, what's come over you, son? That look in your eyes…"

"I'm ready to don my monkey suit and do the jig in the corporate cage again. I'm ready to take the easy route and be a rooted pacifist, exercising diligent caution in things other than those I dream about."

"Calm down. Sit on the bench and take a breather."

"I'm broken, and only one person would take me back in this beat-up condition!" Thad leapt into the sky, throwing his arms up in delighted defeat. "You win! I'm caving in to my mental castration at your hands, at last. You win!"

"You're losin' your mind, Thad!"

"I've got to get to Fifth Avenue!" Thad looked at his watch. He looked down at his track shoes, and, realizing he was wearing just the right shoes and had just the right amount of time to make up for the past, he ran off.

"Thad, wait! You're goin' the wrong way. That's the wrong way…"

Ignoring all else, Thad hurried over to the Primrose Café and ordered two chicken salads to go. "Not exactly the Last Supper, but it'll do." His soul could not rest. He raced uptown like his life depended on it, giving his soles no rest. "If I'm late for confession, I'll be crucified next."

As she dropped onto her sofa, Chelsea ripped opened the envelope in her hands. Having waited for any sign of communication for weeks, she pulled out the letter like a junkie discovering a long-awaited stash of meds in the mail. She began to read it slowly:

Dear Chelsea,
You are probably wondering why you have not heard from me in a while, but that is because I am writing to you from a place where I truly don't belong. In ways…

Booming knocks on the front door shook the room.

"Who in God's name is banging on my door like that?" Chelsea screamed, dropping the letter onto the floor.

"Chelsea, it's me, Thaddeus!"

The voice on the other side of the door sent an electric rush through Chelsea, as the planets of the universe suddenly realigned. The catalyst for rehabilitation had arrived, bearing gifts. She ran to the door, unlocked it, and swung it open. "Thaddeus!"

Thad smacked his lips, staring at her. "You look sexier than Satan in black garters and red pumps!" He threw his mouth on her neck and gnawed on her flesh.

"That's how you greet me? Thaddeus, you haven't taken my calls for weeks, and I have something very important to tell—"

"You don't smell like cocoa butter and apples, but I can see your nipples through that tight T-shirt." Thad tossed the gourmet lunch on the coffee table and grabbed Chelsea tightly against the expanding shame in his pants, pushing his pelvis harder against her. "You feel that, huh? That will vindicate me."

"Thaddeus, wait. Listen—"

"Shut up, Chelsea." Thad kissed her roughly. "Asha taught me this equation; see, it goes like this: woman gives heart to man, plus man treats woman like shit, equals eternal and everlasting love."

"No. Thaddeus, I want you to—"

"Oh yeah, I'll give you what you want," Thad whispered, breathing heavily. "No, better yet, I'm going to give you exactly what you deserve."

"Thaddeus—"

"Wait. I don't want to look at you while I do this. Where's that blindfold?" He darted to her bedroom and returned with the red silk scarf.

Thad clumsily tied the material over her eyes, while Chelsea tried to talk to the frenzied man manhandling her. Overwhelmed, Chelsea spoke in tongues, mumbling something about a miscarriage, but Thad shoved his tongue down her throat, just like Zeké had demonstrated with Asha. They fell onto the sofa.

"Screw honesty and trust. They don't pay the bills or satisfy the human urge. I learned that from Virgil and Saadiq, respectively," Thad grunted, between greedy kisses. "Besides, you're gorgeous. I'll be twenty-six tomorrow and, together, we'll be a well-off family with smart, perfect children."

"Thaddeus, I said I lost the baby," Chelsea whimpered, lifting the blindfold to her forehead and trying to push his face away from hers.

"Don't worry, we'll make a new one. No Immaculate Conception here. You're no Virgin Mary, thanks to me, Chelsea!" Thad boasted, looking at her like a raunchy demon. He tried to re-cover her eyes with the blindfold. "Now stop looking at me. Just go with the feeling blindly. I want you as blind as you tried to make me."

"Thaddues, stop this. Get off me."

"Since when does a sinner know how to stop himself?" He ripped her T-shirt, and she gasped as if punched in the stomach by her own fifty-pound fist of fantasies. "My sins are higher than my head, and my guilt has reached to the heavens," he hissed, reaching for more kisses.

"But, Thaddeus—"

"What? You wanted our reunion to be like the first time? Cuddle first, then work up to this rough stuff, huh? Forget it." Thad squeezed her so hard he could feel her ribs. "It can never be like that again. You can't re-create the past."

Chelsea kicked her legs wildly. "Thaddeus. Let go!"

"I can't. This is what you want!"

"What are you talking about?"

"Come on, Chelsea, you know." Thad yanked up her skirt and unzipped his jeans. "You've got all the answers…in your bedroom."

"No!" Chelsea screamed in agony.

Thad cupped a hand over her mouth to shut her up. He thought of nothing but sex when he looked at her. He didn't see all the pieces of her—her accomplishments, her experiences, her interests—in the chest under her bed, where the good sex happened. He had already kicked off his shoes. He didn't need them anymore.

"If you taught me anything," Thad huffed, forcing himself into her and thrusting maniacally. "It's that…in a race against time…I'll never have peace of mind…until I listen to my heart."

Chelsea bit his fingers. Thad yanked his hand away, granting her permission to scream obscenities. Thad paid Chelsea no attention as he pumped her full of him. All he heard was infectious drumming, answering machine beeps, ambulance sirens, breaking glass, and the ticking of an imaginary clock.

"Forgive me, Father, for I have sinned," Thad chanted over her noise, begging for the mercy of three fathers—hers, his, and the one they shared.

But Daddy couldn't help Chelsea. The book lover was getting the read of her life, the one she'd always wanted—a romantic tale written by the glorious Mr. and Mrs. Fuller, a hot bestseller being relived in all its twisted and perverted reality. Although she didn't know it, what was happening to her had happened before. It wasn't new. It was exactly how Terrence had forcefully convinced Paula to create a Chelsea Fuller in the first place.

"Shut up! Just shut up and enjoy my frustration like you used to," Thad instructed her. "You brought this on. I know you did it, Chelsea. I know you did *all* of it, and I want to thank you for destroying my other life." He held her face to stop the noise, then lowered his face to taste her lips and the bloody lipstick that had smeared his guilt on shattered mirrors. He continued to thrust and beg, confessing for his ultimate sin.

"Thad, stop it! *Thad!*"

Ignoring Chelsea, Thad was listening to his heart. The chaos was so loud, he never heard Chelsea finally call him what everyone else did—just "Thad." Chelsea was capable of being real, but Thad would never see that. He'd never see that she was a real person, and she wanted to be consulted, and especially at that moment.

As for making another baby, Chelsea knew such an encore was impossible, because she was like her mother in more ways than even she had originally thought—one chance at procreation was all she would get, and she had already blown it.

Nevertheless, Thad took Chelsea, begging for forgiveness, pounding away his primitive rage, trying like a disciple to wash away his sins in her holy waters—all under the watchful eyes of Terrence, in his Afro, and Paula, in her yellow bellbottoms, hanging on the wall.

New York woke to the sounds of clapping thunder the next day. Opening its bellows, the sky belched a wrathful boom. The world's roof, ashy and angry, spat wet needles against every New York borough. Inside, barely guarded from the rain's spikes by the walls of Chelsea's apartment, Thad wondered whether the news from the day before had brought it on, had caused the heavens to cry a descending wall of thorny tears onto Earth, had aggravated the impulse for the sad, sad Tuesday when he did what he had done.

Thad lifted himself off Chelsea, who lay motionless, emotionless, on the sofa with the blindfold over her eyes. The white paper Chelsea had dropped the previous day was dotted with red drops. Aching and cold, Thad picked up the letter from the floor and read it:

Dear Chelsea,

You are probably wondering why you have not heard from me in a while, but that is because I am writing to you from a place where I truly don't belong. I let myself down more than anyone else, because what I did still haunts me. But at the same time I am comfortable with my actions, so much as they relate to the intent.

Red rum spells murder backwards, a joke we often shared. Your affinity for the drink made me assume that if either one of us was capable of the act it would be you. That is what I thought you were trying to ask me to do the night I left you all alone, when you needed me most.

I thought I couldn't do it, but I got my chance, just as Adolfo Alverez had promised.

I'll have you know I didn't let my twin-sister-friend down in her greatest time of need. This letter is a confession of my commission of the ultimate sacrifice and the ultimate sin: I killed another human being to save someone else I love.

It's a sin not to go after that which you want most. Simple words that mean so much. When that bitch Asha said she didn't want Thad, had toyed with your love, and gone after something she didn't want to prove a fucking point, I felt all the more justified in snuffing out that sinner.

Asha Dare dared to play your "replacement game," but the girl didn't know the rules. She was pretty, but she could never have replaced you! Asha's admission was her death certificate, and I signed it with a twisted satisfaction and a tremendous sorrow.

Your anger and insanity began with the letters NRK, but I realize that no man has ever felt so strongly, so deeply for me, as Thad does for you. Thad needed to be saved from himself and convinced that forgive-ness waited in your arms, in your bedroom.

Carolina Smithey's jealous best friend may have tried to kill the woman from the Soundview Projects to frame Carolina, but, believe me, my cruelty against Asha was an act of love for you. So, please don't send Adolfo and company after me. I killed your worst enemy; yet, in the wake of her paltry death, I can't bask in the glory of my triumph. Horrified, I look at my hands, these murderous weapons. The reality is I killed that girl, and I continue to wonder if Thad was worth it.

Thad Carmichael may very well be the devil in disguise. I'm not sure, but, in mid-indiscretion, I told myself that Chelsea will get what she wants most, what she deserves. I'll get Saadiq, who you thought was your worst enemy, and the four of us will be happy together.

If the law of the land doesn't come down on me before the law of God does, I pray that someday I will be able to face you, after the things I said to you. More importantly, I hope I can face myself in the mirror after what I've done in the name of surrogate sisterhood.

Sorry as sorry can be,
Kayla Marie Harmon

PS. I never told you that Saadiq and I made love, probably more wildly intense than anything you and Thad ever had. So, tell Saadiq I love him and I miss him.

PPS. I left your black Byron Lars trench coat at Shola's. Au voire, ma amie.

In a manic fit, Thad ripped the letter to shreds until there was nothing left of it. Shaking, with the chills of a thousand wintry rages rattling the marrow in his bones, he looked around at the carnage in the living room. Sin had not gone unanswered. The bits of paper fell silently onto her. The rain fell outside.

Blood was everywhere.

ABOUT THE AUTHOR

Andrew Oyé is a novelist, journalist and screenwriter. He earned a bachelor's degree from Vanderbilt University and a master's in communications from Stanford University. A fitness enthusiast, Andrew resides in Hollywood, CA, where he is working on multiple book, TV and film writing projects and feeds his affinity for pop culture, music, media and critical thought. Andrew Oyé can be reached at andrewoyeink@gmail.com or www.myspace.com/drewoye

SIN IN SOUL'S KITCHEN
READER'S GUIDE

Use the following questions regarding "Sin in Soul's Kitchen" by Andrew Oye to aid in your own analysis of the novel's themes and characters or as an outline to guide your book club's dialogues and discussions.

• What role does the media play in the story? How do the characters view the media and their connection to it (e.g., Chelsea, Kayla, Thad, Roz and Arianna)? How are other forms of expression (music, dance, poetry) viewed?

• How are the issues of social status and classicism dealt with? How are the issues of prejudice and racism woven into the story? How are the issues of cultural identity and assimilation explored?

• Compare and contrast Thad's two worlds. How does Thad interface with (or react to) the characters and symbols of his first world (represented by the Upper West Side, Dean Hausbruck, the university, Chelsea, the brokerage firm, Thaddeus Sr. and the family business) and his second world (represented by Brooklyn, NRK, his running partners, Asha, the brownstone, music and poetry)?

• Define "soul." What role does identity and belonging play in the lives of "revolutionaries" versus "realists"? Why would complete opposites (e.g., Chelsea and Virgil; or Kayla and Saadiq) get along when thrown together in an environment that supposedly promotes inclusion and consciousness?

• Has "the struggle" changed, morphed or remained static? Rather than fight the old fight against police dogs and water hoses with fists and artillery, the characters claim the contemporary battle requires new tactics. Can a war be fought with art, culture and politics as the weapons?

• Examine the importance of symbols of image and vision as vehicles to review the past, understand the present or look into the future (e.g., photos, mirrors, glass, paintings, physical human resemblance).

• How do love, relationships and friendships affect the sanity of the characters (e.g., Carolina, Thad, Chelsea, Kayla)? Analyze Kayla's nightmares and Chelsea's dreams.

• How is the notion of revenge justified by the characters ever justifiable? Would you ever commit a "crime of passion" (for a friend)?

• Interpret the title "Sin in Soul's Kitchen." How are the notions of Heaven and Hell; sin and repentance; good and evil explored in the story? How is each of the Ten Commandments broken over time? Given the overriding theme, what do you want most in life and are willing to do almost anything to attain?

• Discuss the parallels between: Carolina's and Chelsea's sagas; the advice of the sage (Reggie) and sorceress (Carolina), and their respective impacts on the ending.

• Is the ultimate fate of the characters a product of destiny or their own design (e.g., Virgil, Thad, Chelsea, Kayla, Saadiq)?

• What actually occurred in the final scene?

• Author's Note: The novel was written using a technique called "circular storytelling." Do the characters end up exactly where they started, or have they actually evolved? What, if anything, have the characters learned? How does each character ultimately deal with his or her biggest threat/fear? Is it better/worse (easier/harder) to challenge or accept the forces outside of us? When, if ever, should one "go with the flow" or "go against the grain"?

• Are you interested in a sequel to this story?

SIN IN SOUL'S KITCHEN:
A NOTE FROM "THE CHEF"

The year was 1997. *Love Jones*—a film about the romantic trials of a struggling photographer and a struggling writer—was the flick du jour among the artsy set and middle-class moviegoers. Some proclaimed it was an "antidote" to a plague of sameness with regard to a recurring theme in films about, or directed at, African-Americans.

There was a lot of new or "neo" soul music spinning on the radio airwaves. Poetry slams were slamming in coffee houses, hip-hop clubs and college unions across the land. Folks were gettin' down and getting downright cultural. I was there, down with it all. I was also a fan of *Fatal Attraction*, a film that had been released ten years prior about an obsessed woman who terrorizes her lover.

Fresh off an internship at *VIBE* magazine in NYC, I had just graduated from Vanderbilt University. As a creative youngster with a love of music and the slamming of pen to paper, I decided to write a novel during the summer before my grad school stint at Stanford University.

Initially hand-written in a leather-bound folder while I worked at an executive gym in Atlanta, my first novel was born. The basic premise? To combine themes from the aforementioned films. To throw the characters from one story into the world of the others. To explore obsessive insanity in the world of peace-loving poetry and soul music.

Book reviews and discussions often include an assessment of what an author "attempted" to do in the eyes of others, versus the author's statement of what they actually did. Individual interpretation of literary works dictates this. It's the name of the game. Clearly understanding that each reader will taste something different, I'll touch upon how the chef prepared this printed meal without an attempt to sway you.

I wanted to play with literary concepts and techniques such as "circular storytelling," symbolism and parallelism. As with any author's work, the effectiveness of the execution is debatable.

I like the idea of "dropping in" on characters in the middle of living life; suddenly throwing life-altering events in their laps; and then circling back to where they started to check the result. By the way, it's not always a happy ending tied with a pretty bow…at least not in the worlds I live or write in anyway.

For me, certain objects, people and places symbolize certain ideas or concepts, which are tied to each character's fate. This notion also applies to which storylines and relationships mirror, parallel or influence each other. However, since an author should not dictate to readers what they are to deem symbolic, I will not offer extensive details. Readers will interpret the story as they choose. After all, for an author, there is a joy in stepping back and watching the varied responses your work will inevitably receive.

What does one do when he perceives himself to be unwelcome in a particular world despite an "open arms" policy? Is it fair for the insider to begrudge the outsider his angst? Does a revolutionary who goes against the grain to spite the "unwelcoming" world only bring trouble upon himself? Is a war waged with art and culture just as powerful or brutal as a fight with fists and weapons? Can you create your own Heaven on Earth, or is it impossible to escape the larger world? When, if ever, should the revolutionary acquiesce? Does it matter who teaches you life lessons—whether it's someone you love, despise, respect, detest, admire or fear? When pushed to the edge, is it ever justifiable for a sufferer (even a self-perceived one) to destroy the "threat" to his sense of self?

I probably raised more questions than I answered in this Author's Note, but these are the main character's struggles. These were the main ingredients thrown into the pot when I cooked up *Sin in Soul's Kitchen*. I mixed in the spice of family tragedy, health issues, love triangles, scandal, twists and a cliffhanger for dramatic flavoring. With limited references to dates, I added a few current cultural references in an attempt to bring the story forward to today. But let's face it. The world is a different place now. So I struggled with how to revive a "modern" tale that is re-released a decade after its conception.

Simply put, "Sin in Soul's Kitchen" is the portrayal of the most heinous acts (sin) in the most idyllic setting (soul's kitchen), while exploring this question: Should you do *anything* in your power to feel fulfilled, loved or validated? Whether or not readers are "entertained" by the book is determined by factors I cannot control. The rest is up to you, the reader. Humbly, I admit that I don't have all the answers where "literary superiority" is concerned and would never make such a claim. I am but one scribe who wrote an imperfect story. Thanks for the consideration of eating at my table.

—ANDREW OYÉ